A Citizen of the World

A CITIZEN
OF THE WORLD

———— ❧ ❧ ❧ ————

S H O R T
F I C T I O N

Maclin Bocock

𝒵

ZOLAND BOOKS

Cambridge, Massachusetts

First edition published in 1999 by
Zoland Books, Inc.
384 Huron Avenue
Cambridge, Massachusetts 02138

Copyright © 1999 by Maclin Bocock

FIRST EDITION

"Don't Save Your Kisses," "The Tree," "Play Me
'Stormy Weather,' Please," "Heaven Lies About," and
"The Funeral" previously appeared in *Heaven
Lies About*, published by John Daniel and Company.

The quote from "Don't Save Your Kisses," written
by Dick Manning, Sid Feffer, and Buddy
Kaye used with permission. (Budd Music Corp.,
Rancho Mirage, CA)

Book design by Boskydell Studio
Printed in the United States of America

05 04 03 02 01 00 99   8 7 6 5 4 3 2 1

This book is printed on acid-free paper, and its binding
materials have been chosen for strength and durability.

Library of Congress Cataloging-in-Publication Data
Bocock, Maclin, 1920–
A citizen of the world/Maclin Bocock. — 1st ed.
p.   cm.
ISBN 1-58195-000-4
1. Southern States — Social life and customs — Fiction.
2. Women — Foreign countries — Fiction. 3. Women —
Southern States — Fiction.
I. Title.
PS3552.O284C58   1999
813'.54 — dc21   98-54309 CIP

CONTENTS

INTRODUCTION

For more than fifty years, Maclin Bocock has been practicing the writers' craft with acumen and elegance. Whether writing about the intricacies of friendship and race in the South or dealing with the rules of love and loyalty in the far-flung corners of the earth, Maclin Bocock tells us stories in a unique and compelling voice. Her extraordinary vision, which John Hawkes calls "powerful" and Denise Levertov has applauded as being filled with "a grace of spirit," creates a universe of innocence both lost and found.

Born in Baton Rouge, Louisiana, raised in Virginia, a resident of Cambridge for many years and then of Stanford, California, a world traveler, Ms. Bocock has always been willing to voyage into uncharted territory, both in her life and in her fiction. She takes risks other writers might not have the courage to try. Just when you think you know the "sort" of writer she is, she astounds you by changing direction, which leads you into another fictional country, one you would have never visited without Maclin Bocock as your guide. Her heart-stopping stories of childhood trauma might bring to mind Eudora Welty. Her cool, reserved novella might be a cousin to one by Hemingway. Her impassioned stories of love and marriage may remind you of Colette. And yet, Ms. Bocock's voice is singularly and wonderfully her own.

This collection, the fruit of decades of work, is marked by compassion, intelligence, and a dark wisdom. Ms. Bocock has been not just around the block but around the globe, and she's not afraid to report back to us, to charm or startle or simply to tell a riveting tale. Many of these stories deal with the complexity of personal identity: a child's attachment to a family, a woman's attachment to a man, a citizen's attachment to the world in which he or she lives. Like a spy in the house of love, Ms. Bocock travels easily from culture to culture, heart to heart, exploring the pain, irony, and beauty of the human condition. Some of the stories in this collection, like the gorgeous southern stories, are traditional in their telling, others are mind-bending in their modernism, still others are shimmering fairy tales. Here you will read of a heartbroken girl's search for a perfect Christmas tree, a tragic interracial friendship, of a baker with extraordinary culinary powers, of women betrayed in the name of love, of searchers and seekers, and of those who have never left home.

A graduate of Radcliffe College and winner of a PEN Fiction Award, Maclin Bocock has long been admired by other writers, along with those who have read her stories in magazines such as *The Southern Review, Canto,* and the *Denver Quarterly.* Now, with this beautiful collection, the rest of the world can become acquainted with Ms. Bocock's fiction. It is a rich and satisfying journey. Travel well, reader, and enjoy. You have never been here before.

— Alice Hoffman

I

The Funeral

MOST OF US have had our special moment, and I have replayed mine more than once since that April afternoon long gone in time and far away in distance. Whenever that segment of the past floats by, I smile at the seriousness with which I, then seven, played my role. But it was after all, or so it seemed to me then, my moment. That triumphant exit! That retreat down the road to town!

Sometimes I re-create the whole scene, the run-down station in need of paint, the baggage cart with only two mail sacks and the crate of baby chickens all peeping without letup like crickets on a summer night, the distraught mourners huddled together, the engine slowing to a stop with steam curling upward from its shiny wheels. Or I zoom in on one person witnessing the scene. The undertaker's assistant, for instance, leaning against the hearse and chewing on a toothpick. Or Lou, Mrs. Gardner's cook, rocking her head from side to side, about to belt out a mournful wail. Or Mr. Magill standing in the doorway of the station the way he did three times a day when the trains pulled in. Or myself, holding tight to the jonquils, running, stumbling toward the coach for colored people.

Sometimes I start at the beginning of the saga, the afternoon when Aretha first mentioned the secret. And sometimes, for fun,

I change a fact or two. I go down Main Street, reveal myself to
some questioning adult like Miss Lucy, instead of slipping as I
really did along the edge of town. Or I push my way into the
group of mourners and wail as loud as they.

Aretha, our cook, was tall and black and she had a large mole
near her right eye. "My beauty spot, honey." She had a habit of
throwing her head back and laughing. In all my long life I have
never heard any that could match that laugh. It started somewhere deep inside her, then worked its way up and burst forth
in ripples of sound.

"Honey, I was born on Sunday, and Mama said I was born
laughing. I ain't never stopped and I don't have no mind not to
keep on." Aretha managed to draw pleasure from whatever life
tossed in her path. But if she felt her days getting dull she did
something about it.

When I was five my mother died, and while I loved my father,
it was Aretha who came closest to taking my mother's place.
Nothing was too good for me. No matter what time of day, if I
asked, she'd throw extra wood in the stove to heat up the oven
and bake me a gingerbread boy. Some afternoons, she would tie
one end of a rope to the pecan tree and turn it, and I would
jump until I was so tired I could hardly stand up.

> Sticks and stones
> Can break my bones,
> But names will never hurt me.

For a long time after I gave up jumping rope there was a
bare spot on our lawn, testament to my energy and Aretha's patience. And, as if that weren't enough, Aretha always knew
when I felt sad.

"Come on, honey. Let's you and me go to the five-and-dime and buy us something nice."

I still have, in the bottom drawer of my desk, a miniature monkey carved from a peach seed, bought on one of our expeditions to Kress's ten-cent store.

I would not have guessed it, but Aretha was a witch. "A good witch, honey. Mostly." After midnight, several times a week, she raised her bedroom window and flew about the town doing nice things for people.

"Don't you ever go out the front door?"

Aretha thought for a moment. "Nor. I got to have the elevation."

If Mrs. Reynolds left her front door light on, Aretha would turn it off. The same for Mr. Fowler if his garden hose was running. She was always having to lift Tim Epes's tricycle out of Lee's Alley, where it might get run over, putting it down nice and easy by the Epeses' garden gate.

Sometimes Aretha's reports were more dramatic.

"Last night it was raining so hard, I couldn't see my hand before me. Mr. Wilson done left all four of his car windows down, and if I hadn't run them up the inside of that car would have been a big mess."

One time Aretha got mad at Mr. Campbell. I don't know why because she hardly ever got angry. "You should have seen what I have done for him. Garbage from one end of his yard to another!"

Aretha had sworn me to secrecy. She and I were the only people in the world who knew she was a witch.

"Can I see you fly?"

"Nor, honey. If you sees me, or anybody does, I wouldn't have no magic power no more."

So I never did put down a blanket and pillow by my bedroom window, or try to stay awake, hoping to see Aretha, her arms like wings, flapping by our house.

From time to time we had other secrets too.

If I happened to be in the kitchen when Aretha was making applesauce, she was careful to cut the peelings in one long strip, and hang them around my neck and over my head and I became a gypsy girl. One afternoon, when she had just finished draping me with apple peelings, she suddenly said, "Listen, honey. I'm going to tell you a secret, but you mustn't let on to your daddy nor nobody."

I raised my hand and said I hope to die if I did.

"I know you won't." Aretha paused. "I'm going to take myself a little trip."

"Why?"

"Cause I needs a change."

"Can I come?"

"Not this time. Don't worry, I won't be gone no time. And I'll bring you a surprise."

"What?"

"Won't be no surprise if I tells."

"You going tomorrow?"

"Nor. I'll wait for the Lord to give me a sign."

"Suppose He doesn't?"

"I just might go on no matter."

The next morning when Aretha served my father and me breakfast, she didn't seem any different, so I decided she must not have gotten a sign. She was the same on Wednesday and Thursday and Friday. Then I felt guilty because when I said my prayers I asked God not to let Aretha go. I left out that particular prayer Friday night, and the next morning I was sorry.

I woke up and heard my father talking to someone in the backyard. I dressed and ran down the stairs to the kitchen. There was no sign of breakfast. I looked out and saw it was Jim, Aretha's husband. He was clutching his face and pushing his head up and down.

"Gone. She done gone."

Jim was a short, stocky man and several of his front teeth were missing. He worked in a feed store in town. Occasionally he went on a drunken binge and my father would bail him out of jail. I didn't like Jim because I knew he had some vague claim on Aretha, but that morning I felt sorry for him and wished I could say that Aretha would soon be home.

A few minutes later, when I heard my father telling Jim good-bye, I ran down the hallway, up the back stairs, and then started down slowly. I reached the bottom step just as my father came into the kitchen.

My father was of middle stature, but he held himself so well that he appeared taller. He was a reserved person and it was only toward the end of his life, when I was divorced and he came to live with me and my two children, that I finally felt at ease with him.

"Where's Aretha?" I tried to sound surprised.

"I don't know, and neither does Jim. He was just here. She's done this before. Disappeared for a few days without saying she was going or where."

I had a vague memory of a morning when Aretha had failed to turn up. Mother told me she was off helping a sick friend.

"Don't worry," my father said. "She'll come back in her own good time. We'll make out the best we can."

It was arranged that until Aretha returned I would go to Annie Lee Nelson's house after school, and my father would pick me up on the way home from his office. Each afternoon when I reached the Nelsons' I telephoned home, hoping Aretha would be there. Thursday, when Annie Lee and I came in sight of her house, she nudged me. "Hey, look! There's your daddy."

My father was standing by our old Chevrolet, holding his Panama hat and talking to Mrs. Nelson. Annie Lee and I knew what this might mean, and we both broke into a run.

My father sometimes took us with him when he went around the county talking to farmers. The high point was the stop at Walker's country store, with its odor of stale tobacco smoke and pickle brine. Annie Lee and I would stand in the dim interior and try to decide whether to have an Orange Crush or a grape soda. We could also have a package of gum — we almost always chose teaberry — and a dime's worth of hard candy.

By the time we reached Annie Lee's we were out of breath, but Mrs. Nelson didn't seem to notice. She was a pretty woman except for her front teeth: so bucked she could hardly close her mouth. She gave me a hug without saying anything, then hurried Annie Lee up the walk to their house. When my father and I were in the car, he reached over and put his arm around my shoulders.

"You know, sweetheart, life is at times happy, at times sad. We have to try to take it the way it comes. Aretha's dead."

During the time it took my father to close the door on me and go around to the driver's seat, I had been staring at a dogwood tree in the Nelsons' yard and wondering why he had come for me so early. When he told me about Aretha I started crying, and the dogwood blossoms began to swirl around and around until they were one massive blur of white. For years afterward, no matter what time of day or evening I walked or drove by the Nelsons' yard, even after that tree had died and been replaced by another,

I saw myself and my father, together on the front seat of our old car, him saying the words that were as hard for him to speak as they were for me to hear: "Aretha's dead."

Someone in Atlanta, someone Jim didn't know, had written him that Aretha had died suddenly. There were no details, only that her body would be arriving the next day on the two o'clock train.

I spent the rest of the afternoon in my room, crying until there were no more tears to come. My father sensed that I wanted to be by myself and let me alone. I kept seeing my mother, her blond hair hanging loose the way I liked it best, putting out her arms, welcoming Aretha to heaven. And then Aretha would throw back her head and laugh. "Yes, Lord Jesus. I'm here! Lord Jesus, I'm home at last!"

I wondered what I would do now the two people I loved most in the world were dead. I decided there was no point in living, and I began to make plans to join them in heaven. I quickly gave up my first idea of setting the house on fire. I didn't like the idea of my father losing both daughter and house at the same time. I wondered about getting into the pasture with the bull, but I was afraid of the electrified fence. There was the iodine bottle in the medicine cabinet with its skull and crossbones label. But Aretha had made so vivid the image of your stomach slowly being eaten away if you swallowed even one drop that I decided against that too.

At last I reached a decision. I would jump from the barn loft, from the opening through which each summer the hay was lifted and dropped for storing. I saw myself standing in the huge opening, looking heavenward, then a second later my crumpled body on the ground. As I gazed at my lifeless form, Aretha, now an angel with huge wings, swooped down laughing and gathered me up and we disappeared into the cluster of white clouds beyond the sycamore grove.

Toward evening my father called me down to supper. I rushed into his arms, thankful to have them around me, even though they weren't soft like Aretha's. And when it was time for bed I was grateful that he made up the camp cot and put it in his room.

During the night something woke me. I felt chilled, and for a moment I didn't know where I was. Finally I recognized my mother's bureau. Somehow I managed the terrifying journey across the room to my father's bed. I closed my eyes and sank back against the warmth of his body.

The next morning I decided to put off my dying until after Aretha's funeral. At breakfast, when I asked if we could meet the train, my father shook his head. That might be intruding. We would go to the funeral. But I felt I had as much right to be at the station as anybody else. I was sure Aretha would want me there. A few late jonquils were still blooming in the side yard. I picked them all and put them in a mayonnaise jar and hid the jar under my sweater in the cloakroom at school. The morning seemed to drag on forever. I didn't feel like eating lunch and gave away my sandwich and cookies.

Finally the clock on the classroom wall reached one-thirty and I raised my hand and Miss Gwaltney, my arithmetic teacher, gave one quick bob of her head the way she always did when you asked to be excused. I started out in the direction of the bathroom, but once in the hall I circled back to the cloakroom and grabbed the jonquils. I didn't dare look around until I was out of sight of school, afraid I might see some teacher's face in a window. I went around the edge of town. If I went up Main

Street, I would be sure to meet some grown-up like Miss Lucy Hancock, a kind but boring woman who wanted to know everybody's business. She would certainly ask why I wasn't in school. Miss Lucy always wore a hat and gloves, and some people said she kept them on at home too so she would be ready in case someone invited her out.

By the time I got to Reed's Mule Exchange my side ached from running and I stopped to rest a minute. A few mules were standing placidly in the open shed, splotches of dried mud on their legs and early spring flies buzzing around their ears.

When I reached the station the undertaker's assistant was leaning against the shiny hearse. The baggage man was pulling a cart toward the tracks. Nearby a group of black mourners huddled together. The light-skinned and slightly stooped Baptist preacher stood a little apart. Suddenly one of the mourners gave a loud wail and all the others joined in.

I can see myself so clearly, standing there hesitating, my legs about to give way under me and the sap from the jonquil stems dripping down my arm, making it sticky. I wished I was back in school. God was punishing me for disobeying my father. I knew that I would never have the courage to go and drop the jonquils on Aretha's casket. Just then the train whistle sounded, the engine pulled into the station and screeched to a stop, hissing steam.

The baggage car door slammed shut and all that was on the cart were two sacks of mail and a crate of baby chickens. No casket.

Then I heard it, louder than I ever had before. The laugh! And so did Mr. Magill and the baggage man and the mourners and the undertaker and his assistant. We all turned our heads toward the end of the train, to the coach for colored people, where a conductor was helping down an old man with a battered suitcase held together by string.

And then there she was! Aretha! She was wearing a pink floppy hat and a purple dress with ruffles and pink pumps, and carrying a bundle wrapped in brown paper. She waved away the conductor's hand and moved down the steps like a queen.

"Aretha! Aretha!" I began running and finally stumbled into her outstretched arms. She pressed me to her and I smelled the scent of violets.

"Honey, is you all right?"

I nodded my head.

Aretha gave the bundle a little shake. "It's in here, honey. The surprise. A Kewpie doll!"

The next think I knew, Aretha and I were walking hand in hand toward the mourners, who were still standing in a tight little group. We stopped in front of them, and for a few seconds no one moved, no one spoke, not even Jim. One of the women continued to sob, only she sounded more like she had the hiccups. Tom Mason, who drove Mahone's delivery truck, managed to say something.

"We done heard you dead."

"Well, I ain't."

Aretha threw back her head and laughed and laughed while the mourners continued to stare at her. When she finally caught her breath, she waved in the direction of the hearse. "Good-bye! No funeralizing of me today! Maybe someday. A long time from now."

What I was to remember on the faces of the mourners, and the undertaker and his assistant, was not outrage so much as disbelief.

"Don't look at me like I was some kind of haunt." Aretha laughed again. "It's me, back from a little trip."

The Baptist preacher cleared his throat. "Sister, you have deceived us!"

"Deceived you? Ah now, Rev'rend, can't you take no joke?"

Still the mourners stood staring. Aretha stared back. Then she took my hand. "Come on, honey. You and me, we got better ways to pass our time."

After all these years I carry the image, unclouded, of Aretha and me walking away from the station toward town, she holding fast to my hand. With my other I still clutch the jonquils intended for a corpse. I glance back once more. The mourners, their huddle unbroken, have turned half around like mechanical figures and continue to stare, the expression on Jim's face the most incredulous of all.

Our exit, I feel, demands silence, at least until we are beyond hearing. Then my questions pour out. Is she going away again? Can I come? Where did she get the new dress and floppy hat? Who wrote to Jim and said she was dead? What color hair does the Kewpie doll have?

Aretha gives my hand a squeeze, as if to say we will always be together.

"Kewpie?" She raises the bundle and looks at it. "Red. Yeah, honey, Kewpie got red hair."

I look up at Aretha and she smiles down at me, and I notice on her beautiful black face flecks of pink powder.

Don't Save Your Kisses

IN 1933 WHEN the salaries at the college were cut my father
began teasing Mother, saying maybe it was time to sell the
silver tray. The tray had been brought from England to
Virginia in 1745 by one of her forebears. Mother always gave the
same answer. We'd go to the poorhouse first. What we'd done instead was to take in a boarder, Lane Williams, or "paying guest"
as Nornie, my grandmother, liked to put it, and we were about
to take in another, Blair Reid, coming from Kentucky to work in
the college library.

My life improved greatly after Lane came to live with us. He
was a candy salesman and covered town and country stores in
several adjacent counties and he was always slipping me a Baby
Ruth or a Peter Paul Mounds. He kept a small boat on the river
and occasionally on Saturday or Sunday, if he wasn't playing
golf, he'd take me sailing. And there were evenings when he
might say, "Come on, Bits and Pieces," a nickname he gave me,
"let's see what's brewing uptown," and we'd jump into his Ford
roadster and drive to Brown's or the College Pharmacy for ice
cream.

Nornie was right. Even without the mustache Lane would
have resembled Clark Gable. In her eyes Lane could do no
wrong. He was always kidding her in a gentle way and hardly a

week went by that he didn't bring her whatever fruit happened to be in season, raspberries or peaches or winter apples fresh from some farm. I think Nornie imagined him the son she never had and perhaps when he left it was she who missed him the most.

The afternoon of the evening Miss Reid was to arrive, Lane came back earlier than usual. He was taking a bath, my turn came next, and he was singing a song I found out later was from a new movie playing in Richmond.

Don't save your kisses
Just pass them around,
You'll find my reasoning
Is logically sound,
Who's going to know
You passed them around
A hundred years from today?

I was in my room and for a moment I had a vision of Lane uptown standing in front of the post office where the people selling paper poppies on Armistice Day always stood. He was holding out Mother's silver tray piled high with Hershey's chocolate Kisses and telling everybody to help themselves. And then I realized it wasn't that kind of kisses he was singing about and I shivered.

When Lane knocked I was looking in the mirror wondering if Miss Reid would like me.

"All yours, Bitsy."

I opened the door. Lane was in his bathrobe, a towel slung over his shoulder and a celluloid soap dish in his hand.

"Remember. People from Kentucky think they're just as good as Virginians, so scrub well. Above all, don't forget the ears." I stuck out my tongue.

I liked taking a bath after Lane. For one thing he did a good job of cleaning the tub, and I loved the scent of his hair tonic strong in the steamy room.

That evening we were sitting on the side porch waiting for Mattie to call us in to supper. The September heat still held and it was cooler there. A few fireflies drifted around the yard. Our new boarder was arriving on the 8:21 and would be wearing a white eyelet suit and a leghorn hat. My father allowed it was a waste of time Miss Reid writing what she'd have on as though more than a handful of people ever got off the evening train. After all we weren't Louisville. Nornie claimed she'd yet to meet anyone from Kentucky she hadn't liked, and after Mother said she didn't think it very sensible traveling in white, Lane made the remark about Kentucky being famous for its beautiful horses and fast women. It was the first time I had heard the saying.

At supper Lane suggested we all go to the station. Father said that might overwhelm Miss Reid. We'd put our best foot forward and send Lane alone. I could see that Nornie was disappointed, but she always leaned over backward not to go against anything my father said. The world was ruled by men and that was the way it should be. She reared my mother accordingly.

I was disappointed, too, but then Lane looked at me. "At least you must come, Bitsy, and help carry the bags. She's bound to have a dozen."

As it turned out she had only two. In her white eyelet suit and leghorn hat Blair Reid looked as though she had just stepped out on a veranda to greet guests, not taken a long journey with a change and a two-hour stopover. She thanked the conductor who helped her down and turned to greet me. Then she leaned slightly forward toward Lane and again put out her hand.

Blair Reid's appearance, she was beautiful, had the same effect on me as it did on Lane. I managed to get out only one sentence voluntarily, "I hope you had a nice trip." She had and she was happy to be in Virginia again. Again? It was a perfect opening but neither Lane nor I picked up on it. But no matter, for Blair smoothed our silences with a flow of words. She asked questions and made appropriate comments after our replies. Did I have a favorite subject in school? English had been hers, too. She looked forward to living in a small town. She never had before. How wonderful that Lane's job took him to country stores. When she was a child she went with her father on forays looking for antiques in counties around Louisville and they always stopped at some backwoods store to buy pickles. Part of the fun was lifting the top off the barrel and using the long-handled fork to spear the shriveled cucumbers.

That night if anyone had told me Blair's life had been anything but untroubled, I would not have believed it. By the time we had pulled in our driveway, my father halfway down the walk, Mother and Nornie standing on the porch, I knew it was not Miss Craig, my Latin teacher, I wanted to be like, but the stranger sitting beside me.

From then on until she left less than three months later, we all danced around Blair, Lane and I swirling the closest. She was twenty-three, two years younger than Lane, and I had just turned fourteen. But she made me feel older talking about things Mother or Father or Nornie would never have mentioned in my presence. Only a few days after she arrived I found myself trying to toss my head the way she sometimes did. I began taking smaller portions of food but lifting my fork without, I knew, the same graceful curve of arm. And I started saving my small allowance to buy Shalimar. As it happened the money was spent on something else because when Blair went back to Kentucky she left her bottle on my bureau with a note saying the perfume was for me.

And Lane? Every other week before Blair arrived he would spend the night in Richmond, he had a cousin there, or get back late, but after Blair came he was always home for supper. And there was breakfast. My mother and father were early risers. Nornie wasn't. Sometimes Lane and I had ours together but more often than not he had gone by the time I was up. But that changed, too. I began listening for the sound of Blair's heels on the steps before I went down and Lane was obviously doing the same.

Blair worked crossword puzzles with Nornie and she astounded my father with her knowledge of sports. She fit exactly Mother's idea of a lady. At the end Mother even lied, unheard of for her, trying to protect Blair. As for Mattie, she kept fresh flowers in Blair's room, something she never did for Lane or any of our subsequent boarders. But that was the effect Blair had on everyone she met.

The weeks Blair worked on Saturday she had Wednesday off. On those days I rushed home from school hoping to find her, and often she was there waiting for me. Sometimes we would go to the matinee, sometimes walk in what was known as Tyler's Woods, where paths circled a lake. It was during these walks that Blair told me things about herself that I never revealed, not only because I felt they were given in trust, though that may not have been what she intended, but also because they seemed to set us apart.

Blair had been in Virginia earlier as a student at Miss Madeira's. From the first day she hated the school. Once a year St. Albans choir came to give a concert, and once a year the boys at Episcopal High were invited to a tea dance. "Imagine, Bitsy! That was it as far as male company went." Toward the end of the second year she managed to sneak out and meet a young man who had come down from George School. "We didn't do anything wrong." They simply had fun driving around on some of the back roads of northern Virginia.

Blair's dismissal from Miss Madeira's was immediate and final, just what she wanted. But even if they had begged her to return she would not have been able to. Her father would shortly lose everything in the Crash and die of a heart attack. He left some insurance, enough to see her brother through the final year in law school, and able to take care of her. But she didn't want that. They had never gotten on. And so she took what seemed to her the best way out. She married. Her husband was from Chicago. But the marriage didn't last. He was jealous beyond belief and would go into a rage if she much as said good morning to their sixty-year-old deaf and half-blind postman. After two years she returned to Louisville with a divorce and her maiden name back and a settlement, but no more than was necessary to get a library science degree. She could have come away with a small fortune. Actually she didn't want to accept anything but neither did she want to be dependent on her brother. "Sometimes, Bitsy, you have to swallow your pride."

When Blair told me about her husband we were walking around the lake. The path had narrowed and she was a few steps ahead of me. I was glad because I felt blood rushing to my face. Not only had Blair been married, she was a divorced woman! I was sure my parents didn't know this. There was only one divorced person in town, a man, and he was from out of state.

Then Blair murmured, "The worst thing, Bitsy, he abused me physically. He beat me!"

Blair's husband, a white man, did that to her? I knew that negro men when they got drunk sometimes beat their wives. It had happened to Mattie, but that a white man would do such a thing! How naive I was. That afternoon when I learned there could be reasons for women to be divorced I felt all the more bound to Blair because I wanted to make up in some way for the suffering that husband had caused her.

Almost from the day Lane came to live with us, I had a crush on him but it was different from the crushes I had on boys my own age. I would flirt openly with them and write without embarrassment their initials on the front of my notebook, but my feelings toward Lane were secret and involved a life apart. Often before falling asleep I pretended he was holding me in his arms the way they did in the movies but I never imagined him my husband. What at the time seemed a vast age difference must have prohibited that fantasy. That fact and my worshiping of Blair made impossible any jealousy I might have felt when it became apparent that Lane was in love with her and she in turn was attracted to him. At breakfast if she glanced down to butter a biscuit and I saw Lane looking at her out of the corner of his eye, it was as though he were surreptitiously looking at me. And each time Blair accepted with such grace and pleasure Lane's offer to drop her off at the library, I felt as if I were Lane receiving her favors. So I was not only witness to this drama, I was from time to time playing both roles. I was exhilarated by this secret life, an existence I found far more interesting than my real one.

And so the days slipped by until that Saturday night, or early Sunday morning rather, when I suddenly awoke. Moonlight was spilling through the windows. A few seconds later Blair in a white negligee floated past my room. I thought I was dreaming. But then I heard Lane's door open and close softly. I don't know how long it was before I fell asleep again. I kept seeing them over and over, as though I were there too, their bodies coming together.

Mother awoke me and I had to hurry to get to Sunday School. Both Blair's and Lane's door were still closed when I left.

It was my turn to stay after Sunday School and help put things away and by the time I walked past St Mark's the main service had already begun. There was no one in sight. When I turned onto Spotswood Street I saw it coming, a long black car headed like a bullet toward Richmond. It was one of those moments you never forget, the automobile skimming the street as though about to take to the air, its occupants, the older man sitting up stiffly in the backseat, the younger a white chauffeur in uniform, both staring straight ahead and seeming to hold their breath. Maybe they thought they had to until they cleared the town because if they didn't they might be trapped forever in our backwater community. When they were opposite me . . . of course it wasn't true but receding time has made it so, the car froze and I saw the older man's jowls hanging, his lips set, the gray felt hat covering what must have been an almost bald head. And perhaps I saw a lap robe across his short, fat legs.

It was not unheard of to see a chauffeured car in town, especially during the autumn or spring when wealthy Northerners were on their way to Florida or on their way home. They would leave the main highway and come the few miles to the college library, where there were portraits of several Virginia patriots and a collection of books from the colonial period. The courthouse too was a place of pilgrimage. It had been built after a design of Sir Christopher Wren and because Federal troops had bypassed the town the county records were more or less complete. But when I saw the Georgia license I was sure the man sitting up so straight in the speeding car wasn't an ordinary tourist. In fact I was sure I knew who he was. Friday evening when Blair got in from work I happened to be coming down the stairs and I saw her pick up her mail from the hall table. She ripped open one of the letters. "Mr. Cottingham I wish he'd leave me alone!" Mr. Cottingham was a wealthy man from Atlanta, old enough to be her father.

I ran a good part of the way home. Mother and Nornie were in church and my father left early that morning to go fishing. I found Mattie upstairs in Nornie's room changing the sheets. If I happened to be around when Mattie was making the beds, I would help.

After their breakfast but before Lane and Blair had driven off together, Blair gave Mattie a sealed envelope with "Mr. Cottingham" written on it and asked her to please give it to the chauffeur when he came to the door. Mattie didn't have to say anything. But knowing Mattie, I am sure she must have at least greeted the man with "Good morning."

After we finished Nornie's bed, we went into Blair's room, then Lane's. When we pulled back his covers, in the middle of the bed was a lace handkerchief with the initials B.R. in blue. Mattie picked it up as though it were the most natural thing in the world to have found there, a piece of lint or a feather escaped from one of the pillows, and without so much as glancing down put it into her apron pocket. She didn't say anything, but she looked straight at me and I knew from her eyes she counted on me to keep quiet. That I was now not the only one in the house who knew about Blair and Lane brought me a certain relief but also a certain regret that the knowledge was no longer exclusively mine.

Sunday nights Mattie was off. That evening Mother, Nornie, and I were cleaning up the kitchen when Blair and Lane got back. Blair came in to see if she could help and reported a wonderful day for sailing, the wind just right. They had a late lunch across the river at a restaurant famous for its seafood. For once she had had enough shrimp. I felt uneasy in Blair's presence and

I pleaded homework rather than hang around downstairs. I set my alarm for seven the next morning. I wanted to be out of the house before she and Lane came down.

That day at school my mind wandered more than usual. I kept seeing Blair float past my room or I imagined her in the back of the sailboat, the tiller fastened, her legs stretched out, her head resting in Lane's lap and he looking down at her.

One night some days later I was in my room studying. A few minutes before Blair and Lane left for the nine o'clock movie she knocked on my door. She was planning to sleep late the next morning, her day *off*, but what about an afternoon journey around the lake? She needed it, librarian stoop and all. I was pleased. I was ready to be alone with her. I knew I would feel better if I told her I had seen Mr. Cottingham. But we never took the walk and what seemed like an appropriate time to bring up Mr. Cottingham never came.

When I got home from school Mother said Blair had decided to go to Richmond to do some shopping. Mother had driven her to the bus station and arranged to pick her up at five. Around four the phone rang. Blair's voice sounded strange but I assumed it was a poor connection. She would be home later, after supper. Had I forgiven her for skipping out? She had something for me and hoped I would like it.

Later Mother and Nornie and Father and Lane were in the living room playing bridge and when I was on my way downstairs to tell them good night the front doorknob began to rattle. By the time I opened the door Lane had come into the hall. Blair was leaning against the jamb.

"God damn door!" Her tongue seemed to fill her mouth. "Thanks, Bitsy."

She glanced up at Lane. Her eyes had a glassy look.

"Hi, sweetie. Did you miss me?"

Blair leaned forward and left a smudge of lipstick on Lane's chin. I don't think he could have been more embarrassed had she slapped him. She gave a beautiful smile and handed me a box from Miller and Rhodes, the elegant store in Richmond. Lane and I watched her move toward the stairs and sink to the steps.

"Oh, God, I'm tired!"

And then she began to cry.

The rest of us thought Blair was drunk but Nornie knew as soon as she saw her eyes that it was drugs. When Nornie was first married she lived in Roanoke next to a doctor whose wife was a "dopefiend." Later Mother asked and my father said there were taxi drivers in Richmond who could have given Blair the information and driven her to get what she wanted.

Mother and I helped Blair to her room. She kept apologizing for being such a bother and saying she could get herself to bed, so we left her. Later Mother went back. She slipped off the shoes and covered her with a quilt Blair had brought from Kentucky.

The present Blair gave me from Miller and Rhodes was a cashmere sweater with pearl buttons. I had the cardigan all during college and was still wearing it when my second son was born, though by then the elbows had been patched several times.

The next morning I pleaded a sore throat, but Mother saw through me and said there was nothing I could do for Blair by skipping school and that she would probably sleep all day. Mother telephoned the library and reported our boarder ill with an upset stomach.

That afternoon when I got home from school I found Mattie in the kitchen. She had just taken some soup and tea to Blair. I put on the sweater and knocked on Blair's door.

"Bitsy, you look beautiful! I knew you would. And it fits perfectly."

Blair was in bed, the tray pushed aside. She had hardly touched the soup. Her eyes had lost the glassy look but she was extremely pale.

"I should have sense enough to stay away from alcohol. Mama had problems with it, too."

And then she wondered if Lane had said anything.

When Lane got in I told him what Blair had asked. He looked embarrassed but after supper he wanted me to find out if she felt like seeing him for a few minutes.

Did Blair confess the drugs? Describe the depressions when she could not stop crying? The blackness, the longing to escape, even to die? There was a moment of silence before Lane left her room and went down the stairs and out the front door. I wondered if he had kissed her or if they had simply stared helplessly at each other.

Friday morning Blair said she felt fine though she still looked pale and I noticed her hand shake when she lifted the coffee cup. Lane had left early to get to Richmond for a salesmen's meeting. When Mother offered to drive her to the library, Blair declined graciously, saying she needed the exercise. We walked together as far as the courthouse, where I took the cutoff for school. Later I tried to remember if there was anything she said, any gesture that might have given a hint of what she must have been feeling. In front of the Gardners' house she reached up and pulled down a yellow maple leaf, one of the last on the tree. "Isn't that beautiful, Bitsy?" and then she began to twirl it between her fingers. She must have felt the blackness coming on again and known that before the day was out she would take the bus to Richmond to get what she was desperate to have.

It ended with the brother, unsmiling and tight-lipped, coming from Louisville to take Blair home. The morning they left, Mother let me skip the first three periods of school. At the station when Blair embraced me, she whispered, "Oh, Bitsy," and I thought I heard a faint sob, but when she stood back she was smiling like she was sure nothing but happiness lay ahead, and that's the way she looked when my mother snapped the picture of us just as the train pulled in.

That afternoon I slipped into the house by the back door. I wanted to be alone with Mattie for a little while before facing Mother and Nornie and Blair's empty room. When I put my head down on the kitchen table and began to cry, Mattie reached out and touched my shoulder. "Don't you worry. When she get home she be all right."

During the first weeks after Blair left I wrote her several times before I heard from her. It was a short note. She was in a sanitarium outside Louisville and it was almost as confining as Miss Madeira's! She missed us all terribly, including of course Mattie and her wonderful food. She hoped Lane and I were getting in some good sailing. Sometime later in a postcard she told us about her job in a Memphis library. And then for months we heard nothing. Finally Mother wrote the brother, who sent a two-line letter on business stationery signed by a secretary. Blair was back in the sanitarium. In spring of my senior year in high school a large ivory envelope addressed in Blair's hand arrived. The brother had the honor of announcing the marriage of his sister to Mr. Edward Cottingham. An enclosed card gave their address on Peachtree Street in Atlanta.

As for sailing, I went only once with Lane after Blair left. That gray November afternoon neither of us spoke of her but her absence enveloped us like the raw wind blowing up from the bay.

In early December Lane put the boat up for the winter and then one evening a few days before Christmas he said he would be leaving in January. He had been transferred to the area just south of Washington. He planned to live in Alexandria and keep his boat on the Potomac. We wondered, but we never found out if he, himself, had asked for the transfer.

It was a sad Christmas with Blair gone and Lane about to leave. But shortly the edge of that sadness would be dulled somewhat by a new boarder, a Mrs. Shaw from Boston, who clomped into our lives. She wore corrective shoes and that is exactly what she did: she clomped. After being advised by her doctor to move to a climate where winters were less long and less severe, Mrs. Shaw decided to try a small college town not too far south and after looking at several she chose our community. She inquired at the post office about private homes where one might board, and when Mother showed her the two rooms she said she would take them both. She had a son at Harvard who would be coming for spring vacation. Mother protested she could not take money for a bed so little slept in. "Of course you can." Mother protested no further. One did not argue with Mrs. Shaw. She was a plain woman who made no effort to improve her appearance. She never wore jewelry or makeup. How different from Mother, who loved beads and earrings, and Nornie, who said she was going to use rouge as long as she could see to put it on. And Mrs. Shaw had a minimum of clothes, two outfits for spring, two for fall. In winter she added a sweater, in summer she removed a jacket. "Why be burdened with more?" I was dazzled by this woman's independence, by the control she seemed to have over her life. She was an active alumna of Radcliffe and she told me at length about the college.

But the arrival of Mrs. Shaw and the windows she opened did not banish Blair and Lane from my mind. I often thought of them. Occasionally Lane sent Nornie some teasing two-line sentence on a postcard and several times a year he telephoned to see how we were. Just before my high school graduation in 1940 a package arrived from a jewelry store in Toronto. It was a silver pin, delicately wrought, a boat, its mast carrying full sail. The card read: "For Bits and Pieces. Congratulations and love, Lane. P.S. I'm now a brilliant member and about the oldest new flier in the R.C.A.F."

When I wrote a thank-you note I told him I had won a scholarship and would be going to Radcliffe in the fall. He answered quickly but with the usual briefness: "So you're headed for the greatest of oceans. Congratulations, but watch those waves!"

Then one night in early November when I was studying for an hour exam, Lane telephone me from somewhere in Canada. He sounded far away. He had a few days' leave and he was thinking of spending them two weekends hence in Boston. Would I be free to show him the sights? He hoped I wasn't becoming so learned we'd have nothing to say to each other. I started to tell him the truth, that he had been right about the waves, but I didn't.

I was elated at the thought of seeing Lane, not because I still had strong feelings for him. I didn't. At that time I was trying to get the attention of my History I section man, the person who would be my first husband. But Lane was a link with Virginia. I'm sure he wanted to come not to see Boston but because he too was homesick and with the uncertain future wished to reconnect however briefly with some part of his past.

But on the Thursday afternoon of the weekend he was to arrive I found a telegram in my dormitory box: "Complications. Can't come. Please keep the home sails sailing. Love." This could mean only one thing: Lane was being shipped overseas. I spent a sad weekend feeling sorry for him and for myself.

The card he sent at Christmas was addressed to all the family. He was somewhere in southeast England. He had survived two close calls. He'd be much obliged if Mattie would send him some of her fudge. Sweets were hard to come by. There was only one other communication from him, a thank-you note to Mattie, before the announcement in the *Richmond Times-Dispatch*. Mother sent me the clipping in the same letter telling about Blair. Blair's suicide in a hotel room in Atlanta had nothing to do, of course, with Lane's death, but in my mind it did because during those brief weeks when Blair was with us, almost from the first moment Lane and I met her at the station, I wanted them to be together and some remnant of that stubborn and impossible wish remained. If not in life, why not in death?

So it was a public war that brought Lane down from the sky into the English Channel, for Blair a private one she had long been destined to lose. The capitulation to Mr. Cottingham must have been a last desperate hope.

For a few days after I received Mother's letter, I kept seeing Blair in the white eyelet suit stretched out in a landlocked grave and Lane's body on the other side of the world drifting along the ocean's dark floor. But those images and the memory of Blair stumbling thick-lipped into the hall, the brother unsmiling come to take her home, have for the most part vanished. What comes back to me again and again is Blair in the white negligee floating down the hall. That and the way Lane looked at her the first time we all went sailing together and the way Blair smiled back. I had never before seen that kind of look between a man and a woman. And even now after all these years, whenever I hear the weather report, the words "from Chesapeake Bay to Cape Hatteras," I see for a moment Lane's boat, full sail, skimming the river's sapphire water. We are sitting Blair and I, facing

Lane, our backs to the bay and he is in complete control, his hand on the tiller and he looks at Blair that way and she smiles back. It is there in my mind, that moment, and safely sealed against the destiny that would encircle Blair and the fate that awaited Lane over other and distant waters.

Play Me "Stormy Weather," Please

THEY WERE both eleven, born only a month apart.
Sonnyman looked toward the uncle's automobile parked
under the mimosa tree. "Someday I'm goin' to Baltimore
and I'm gonna get me a car like that."

They were halfway up the back porch steps. She stopped,
turned around to face him.

"Why you want to go to Baltimore?"

"Wyatt's grandma say it the onliest place. She gonna have her
funeral there."

"Is she dead?"

"Naw. But when she do."

She pushed open the screen door, closed it gently. The
kitchen was in semidarkness, its shades drawn against the afternoon sun. A fly, trapped on a roll of uncoiled flypaper hanging
from the ceiling, buzzed insistently. She tiptoed through the
dining room, past the chest in the hall where a mirror reflected
tulips in a brown pitcher. Sonnyman followed, barefooted. Her
mother and father and her uncle Irby were upstairs resting. In
the parlor she pointed, whispering, "See. There it is."

The radio was on a table by the end of the settee.

He walked across the room slowly, looked first at one side,

then the other, and then reached out. But he let his hand fall before he touched the knobs.

She ran her fingers over the varnished top. "It's pretty, isn't it?" she whispered.

"Yeah," he whispered back. He looked at her. His eyes drooped slightly.

"Play me 'Stormy Weather,' please."

"I can't."

"How cum?"

"Because you have to listen to what the man in Lynchburg wants. Or the one in Richmond."

"Don't they never want 'Stormy Weather'?"

"I guess so. But you don't know when. You might have to sit all day listening. Anyway, I can't turn it on now, but the first time Mama and Daddy go 'way, I promise I'll come get you."

And they had gone the very next afternoon. They had gone with Uncle Irby in his new Cadillac over to the adjoining county to see about a heifer her father thought he might want to buy. She ran as fast as she could through the grove and along the creek path Sonnyman was hoeing in the small garden plot. She looked at him and he knew.

She found Ethel behind the house standing on ground packed hard and bare, except for a few patches of plantain, using an old broom handle to poke the sheets boiling in a tub. She asked Ethel if she could spare Sonnyman because her mother needed him to pull some weeds. Ethel said sure but he better wash his hands first. So he pumped water into a rusty basin, splashed his face and hands, and then slowly smiled as he tossed the water high in the air and chickens flew in all directions, and Ethel raised her voice, which she didn't do very often, wondering in the Lord's name who he thought he was making them chickens stir up dust, dirtying her clothes. And they raced back, Sonnyman ahead, but he kept stopping for her to catch up, and they went in the front and sat on the floor by the radio Uncle Irby had brought all the way from Atlanta. First it was she who switched from station to station. Then she asked him if he would like to do it. He held back and she told him there was nothing to be afraid of. She took his hand and put his fingers on the knob and he smiled. And they sat there side by side listening through the afternoon until they heard the car and then Sonnyman leapt up and ran through the house like black lightning and her mother walked in and said she thought she heard the screen door on the back porch slam, had anyone been with her? She said no, maybe it was Ethel coming to start supper and her mother allowed it was a little early for that and anyway Ethel never slammed doors; she quickly changed the subject, asked if her father had bought the heifer, standing there facing her mother and praying all the while, and God must have heard because her mother didn't say any more about the slamming and Ethel never asked Sonnyman what he'd done with the money he got for weeding.

She had just taken out the key her son-in-law had given her because she might get back before they did when someone emerged from behind the japonica bush and said he would blow her brains out if she made any noise and she handed over the purse and in that instant saw his face, the light from the street bright enough for her to see the features, young, no more than seventeen or eighteen, the same drooping eyes, and she couldn't believe it and without thinking she asked him where his father was. It was only later, when she was in the house, she realized it might have been his grandfather she should have wondered about. He had rushed down the walk and dis-appeared around the corner, but not before he mumbled, "What's it to, you old bitch."

It don't matta.

And she felt like she was in a dream, floating, and that she should have been carrying her grandmother's black beaded purse somehow seemed appropriate because her grandmother had liked him, the father, or maybe it *was* the grandfather, and whenever she came to visit always gave him extra money for bringing in wood to the library where she slept, because by then the grandmother couldn't walk upstairs. And it was only after she was in the house and had closed the front door that she be-gan to shake, her whole body shaking, and she turned off the two living room lights and collapsed in the wing chair, finally sat on her hands in hopes of controlling the body which seemed to have nothing to do with her now, because she was following him, the son or the grandson, running after him down Eighth Street on Capitol Hill in the District of Columbia, he tugging at the braided drawstring, his hand plunging into the purse, his head turning right, left, then back and all the while as he loped along his fingers digging, and she was sorry she had not taken more than ten dollars with her and some of that gone for the taxi, and suddenly she caught up with him, said she didn't want the purse back or the money or the glasses but wouldn't he please tell her where his father was or maybe it was his grandfa-ther she wanted to know about and he turned around, looked at her with the same eyes, the slow smile, and was about to say something when she heard the telephone ringing.

She knew it would be impossible for Uncle Irby to win the bet because her father always found things when they were lost or hidden. Never she. Never her mother. He could look at a patch of grass and if there was a four-leaf clover, he'd find it. No, she knew when she and her father and Uncle Irby went out to the kitchen, Sonnyman there, sitting on the stool, finishing his supper, Ethel cleaning up, and Uncle Irby made the proposal, she knew he couldn't win that bet in a thousand years.

"Yeah," Uncle Irby said, rolling the egg around in his hand, looking straight at Sonnyman. "I bet I can hide this where he'll never find it." And her father said he'd take on the bet and he went to the living room and waited while Uncle Irby hid the egg.

She was still shaking slightly when she picked up the phone and yet her voice was steady. He had just seen the eleven o'clock news, was glad it had been such a warm day in Washington, miserable still in Cambridge and more snow promised, how were the children and he hoped she was coming home Thursday. He missed her.

"Elliot, I was just held up."

"My God! Are you all right?"

"Yes."

"Carlton and Peter?"

"They went to the Kennedy Center for *Così*. I had dinner with Ann."

"Are the police there?"

"It just happened. In the front yard. I haven't called them yet."

And he said, *Damn it*, he had told Carlton at least two years ago she and Peter should leave the Hill, move out to Chevy Chase. She promised him she would call the police immediately and she was about to tell him, then changed her mind, told him instead that it had happened so suddenly, so unexpectedly she hadn't had time to be frightened. A drama involving someone else. And he asked if he was black and she hesitated and then said yes.

He was standing in the middle of the kitchen facing her father, his straw hat not back the way he usually wore it but pulled forward, and Uncle Irby, his hands in his pockets, was leaning against the window nearest the cedar tree looking like he wasn't the least bit worried about losing the bet and Ethel in the dining room pulling out the sideboard drawer, putting the mats away. Her mother wasn't there. She'd gone to a supper the Women's Guild was having at the parish house. And her father said he would have to give up. He had looked in all of Sonnyman's pockets, felt up and down the front and back of his overalls, even made him open his mouth. Yeah, he guessed he'd have to admit defeat much as he hated to let his good-for-nothing-no-count brother get the best of him. And Sonnyman standing up straight like he might have been having his picture taken, smiling, and then all of a sudden her father's hand had come down hard.

After she put the phone down she turned on a light in the kitchen, then went back, sat in the dark living room and for the first time in many years prayed. And again, for some reason, God must have been on her side because her daughter and her son-in-law did not get back until after midnight and they never told her husband that it was they who called the police, not she, or found out that when she left her friend Ann's house it was only a little past ten-thirty. She heard them coming down the front walk and met them at the door.

"You're still up." Her daughter looked surprised. "We were

sure you'd be in bed asleep and so decided to stop by the Millers' for a nightcap. I'm sorry."

"I just got in myself," she said. "Listen," she went on, "don't be upset, I'm fine. But a few minutes ago I was held up in your front yard."

Her daughter rushed over and threw her arms around her.

Her son-in-law looked at her as if he expected to see blood. "A black?"

She nodded.

"Have you called the police?" he asked.

"Not yet."

He walked to the phone. "What did he look like? Young?"

"I don't know," she broke in. "I didn't get a good look at him."

And Uncle Irby had said, "Boy, now you can buy yourself several hats and then some," as he tossed the five-dollar bill onto the kitchen table, "but watch your mama don't get her hands on it," and he had winked at Ethel and laughed. Then he and her father left but she stayed on, Ethel finishing up and Sonnyman sitting in the corner on the stool with a rag wiping the inside of his hat. Bits of raw egg clung to his hair.

"I gonna do it to Wyatt."

"No you don't neither. Wastin' a egg and makin' a mess. Go on home now, honey. Wash your head real good. I'll be 'long soon. We'll soak that hat in cold water and when it dry it be just as good."

She picked up the five-dollar bill.

"Mind you don't lose it now."

And Sonnyman had taken the money and she had followed him as far as the gate and the day slowly dying and she felt tears at the edge of her eyes and she reached out and touched his shoulder and said she was sorry and he had answered, It don't matta, and just at that moment a whippoorwill gave one short call and from then on as long as she would live Sonnyman and his three words and the bird would be laced together in her mind. But it was not only whenever she heard a whippoorwill, which wasn't often after she left home for a university in a city where she would spend the rest of her life, it was not only those few times early in her marriage when her child was young and her parents still alive and she was home for a visit and heard on summer evenings those small brown birds echoing each other's lilting calls, it was not only then that particular moment from her childhood would intrude but at odd times during her waking hours. She never dreamed about it. The image would thrust itself onto her mind's eye, she and Sonnyman at the gate, he about to lift up the wooden latch, about to walk toward the grove, about to leave her, she reaching out to touch his shoulder, *It don't matta*, and then the sadness would spin back, though the anger she felt toward her father, whom she considered almost as guilty as her uncle Irby, was to soften with the years.

It was a long time before she fell asleep. Twice she got up and looked down from the third-floor guest room at the japonica bush, its blossoms paled by a moon risen late. There was little space between the thick branches and the house. He would have had to squeeze himself in carefully to avoid the thorns. How long had he been there crouching, waiting? And had his father, or was it his grandfather, finally reached Baltimore but then been forced by circumstance to retreat to the District, or had he been from the beginning trapped in Washington, never even crossing the border into Maryland, never even seeing much less living in the paradisiacal city of his early dreams? And was it so impossible that he, whichever it was, now lay awake too and in all likelihood near her in this part of the District where blacks had retreated from Georgetown and other reclaimed areas, he too unable to sleep, worried about him, the son, or maybe it was the grandson, the police having come five times in the last six months questioning and the boy still out and almost dawn, the sun about to come up, first striking the goddess of freedom, then moving down the peristyle, then falling on the dome? And when he, whichever it was, crossed the Potomac River and saw for the first time that building at the top of the slow rise of ground, did he remember the gift, where he was when she gave it to him, how black his hands looked against the white paper when he took the present, smiling the slow smile?

She knew there was no way to avoid it. There was no way to beg off. In the morning her daughter, her son-in-law would make her go. They would remind her that next time he might kill someone, that maybe the police were right. She might re-member his face better than she thought she did. And she would be forced to dissemble again.

And she and her father one on each side led her mother with eyes closed down the steps of the Lincoln Memorial because her mother had walked up, completely forgetting about her fear of heights, and then they had gone directly to the restau-rant famous for its oysters and she had them for the first time in her life and her father smiled, allowed it looked like to him she was putting up with the oysters just to get the ketchup and if he had known that before he could have saved some money and they went from there straight to the ten-cent store as promised and she bought with allowances saved over weeks for the pur-pose a wooden plaque with a picture of cherry trees in bloom and the Washington Monument in the background and below the picture a thermometer and Ethel had kept it in her kitchen and then had taken it to Hopewell when she had to move and for him she chose a metal replica of the Capitol with the statue of the goddess of freedom on top and she was short ten cents and her father said he would advance her the amount against the next week's allowance.

She was in and out sooner than she had hoped, even though she must have looked at close to a hundred pictures and made a special point of not rushing from one to another, all photos of blacks, of course, because once she had admitted that to her husband, once the *yes* crossed her lips, it was already too late not to say the same thing to her son-in-law and to each of the four officers, three white and one black, who arrived the night before, or rather in the first hour after midnight, and over a period of twenty minutes and all to question her except the black one, who said nothing but good evening and good night and who sat up straight, not touching the back of the wing chair, his hands unmoving in his lap. So she had at least been truthful about that. And one of the white ones asked if he had been dark- or light-skinned and the black one sat expressionless, in plainclothes, his fellow officer volunteered because he, the black one, worked three blocks north, the ghetto, had informants, knew pretty much what was going on among the residents, mostly youngsters causing the trouble, and they had some ideas which ones they were and if she could try to help them, for instance, did he seem frightened or experienced, and there was a possibility her purse might be found. He brought it up, the one who did most of the talking, not she, because it was money they were after and they often just threw the empty pocketbooks into the gutter and as soon as they finished questioning her they would have a look around the adjoining streets and would she be willing to stop by the station in the morning or the afternoon if it suited her better because the victim is often so frightened they think they don't remember but actually they do and when confronted under calm circumstances with the picture and there was one last possibility, did she think she would recognize his voice and she heard herself saying she did not think she would because she had been taken by such surprise she had not paid any attention to the sound of the words, just the meaning and anyway all he said was *I'll blow your brains out if you make any noise.*

She cried herself to sleep the night she heard Ethel and Sonnyman had to move to Hopewell because Ethel's sister Rose had "high blood" and no one to look after her. But it was Rose who survived Ethel. A little more than two years later Ethel wrote a short letter in pencil on lined paper saying she was doing poorly and would they please come to see her. They had gone the next Sunday, driven the ninety miles and found her in bed, her thin arms laid out on the faded quilt, her eyes dull and sunk deep. The wooden plaque with the thermometer and the picture of the cherry trees and the Monument was hanging on a nail above her bed.

Several times Sonnyman glanced at her and she was conscious of her breasts and how much taller he was now than she. They had not stayed long. It was hard for Ethel to talk. They left the box of food and said they would see her again soon. Just before they turned the corner she looked back and he was standing in the doorway, his overalls a size too large, his bare feet flanked by peonies in full bloom like pink ruffles against the unpainted boards of the stoop. She thought she saw him raise his hand as though to wave but she wasn't sure.

It was the last time she saw Sonnyman. Ethel died in less than

a month. Later they learned that the day after her funeral, Sonnyman disappeared. No one knew where he went. One Saturday morning she found in the secretary drawer a map of Virginia
and Maryland and part of Pennsylvania and she took it up to her
room and with her thumb, which just fit the scale for twenty-five
miles, she figured out how far it was from Hopewell to Baltimore
and she wondered how long it had taken him to get there.

And there were two of them, one white, one black, and they
showed her into a small room, plain like a cell, and the white
one offered her a chair and the black one put a stack of photos
in front of her on a bare table and the white one said she must
remember she was in no way to assume the persons whose pictures she was about to see were criminals but if she recognized
him they would give her a Xeroxed copy of the sheet and she
would sign her name on the back of the picture. And she
wanted to say, *I am wasting your time,* as they stood watching
her, waiting silently, and she did recognize him with the
slightly drooping eyes, staring out at her on the third sheet, the
first one on the second row, fourth in the six unidentified faces,
and she hoped they had not noticed her eyes pause and she
wanted to say, *May I keep this,* but she put it on top of the other
two sheets and continued through the stack and she wondered
if the white one left the room for a moment would she turn
back to the third sheet, point to the photo, plead, say, *Look, if
you never do anything else for a white person will you please tell
me where this young man lives because I want, I need to see his
father or it might be his grandfather because . . . You do understand, don't you?*

She and Sonnyman sat side by side leaning back against the
trunk of the willow tree and she only thought once or twice

about the lying to Annie Ray's mother claiming she had a headache and wanted to go home, and that Ethel was there to take care of her. Both she and Sonnyman were holding bamboo poles. He cut them by the smokehouse, where the clump was so thick her father would never notice two were missing. Together they dug in the corner of the garden but it was Sonnyman who picked the worms up and dropped them in the tin can and it was he who put them wriggling on the hooks made from straight pins. They sat on the creek bank watching their lines, sunlight falling on them through the leaves, their shoulders almost touching and just across, near the opposite side, was a bar of sand which slowed the current. It might have been quicksand, Sonnyman told her, because Wyatt's grandma said a milk cow went down in the creek one time and nobody couldn't do nothing to help her. The cow just sank right on down till all you could see was the tips of her horns and then they went down too. The grandmother said sometimes you could hear lowing up and down the creek when there wasn't no moon and if you was walking along there, and it didn't even have to be at night cause it happened to a man she knew one rainy winter afternoon, and you felt something kinda brush your face or your hand and you weren't near no bush nor nothing you could be sure it was that cow's tail swishing, haunting the creek bottom. She looked behind her and saw a white butterfly dipping up and down in the clearing and heard a rain crow moaning somewhere off in the distance and she was glad Sonnyman was with her. He just said maybe they should move cause it didn't look like nothing was gonna bite here, when she saw it. She leaned forward, slipped, screamed, felt the water and looked up and watched it slide down the branch and then sail toward her like it was a bird. She knew it was coiling around her leg, knew that water moccasin would drag her into the quicksand. She gripped the bank, her arms spread out like a scarecrow's, and her pole floated downstream. Sonnyman leapt up and grabbed her shoulders and his pole fell into the water too, and drifted away. He pulled her up the bank, almost slipping himself, and when she reached the clearing she was still crying, shaking, wet from her waist down and the front of her dress covered with mud. Sonnyman took off his shirt and went back to the creek and holding on to a branch of the willow tree leaned over and let the shirt down in the water and then ran to her. He kept going back and forth, rinsing his shirt, until he'd gotten all the mud off her arms and legs. By then she had stopped crying and she told him if they left right away they would have time to wash her dress and his shirt and iron them dry before her mother and father got home from Richmond. Sonnyman ran to the creek once more and turned the tin can upside down so the worms wouldn't die, and they walked along the edge of the cornfield and through the grove, he naked from the waist up, his wet shirt in his hand, and she in her mud-stained dress. In sight of the house she couldn't believe what she saw but it was too late to run. Her mother was looking out of the kitchen window, and in no time Sonnyman had been ordered to put his shirt on and sent home and she was upstairs drawing a bath and crying and her mother telling her what a terrible thing it was to lie. She must stay in her room until morning and without any supper and think about the awful thing she had done. But toward dark her mother relented and brought her some milk and hot biscuits. Her mother had made the biscuits, not Ethel because Ethel had been given the evening off because she was supposed to have been at Annie Ray's house and her parents have supper somewhere on the way back from Richmond. But they hadn't gone as far as Richmond because her father found what he wanted at a new feed store in Petersburg. Later that night when she should have been asleep but wasn't she heard her parents arguing and she crept out of her room and listened at the top of the stairs. Her father said they could not afford to send her away to school and he would not under any circumstances ask Irby for help. He would speak to Ethel. She would certainly understand. But her parents did not have to worry long about her and Sonnyman because it was the very next morning when Ethel came to cook breakfast that Ethel said on account of her sister Rose being ill, she and Sonnyman would have to move to Hopewell.

play me stormy weather please
I can't
how cum
because

The Tree

IHAD BEEN standing for what seemed like hours by the window next to the nail where Rachel had hung the new 1933 calendar with President Roosevelt's picture. I was looking across the field to the dirt road that led to town. Rachel was behind me peeling potatoes at the kitchen table.

"Why doesn't he come?" I asked.

"Don't worry, honey. He'll be along. You won't want for no time to go." I started to remind Rachel that it got dark early, tell her that it was a long way. But didn't bother. I looked toward the dining room. The box of Christmas decorations lay unopened on a chair. The year before I had helped my mother put them away. When I pressed on the crossed string and she tied the knot, my fingertip was pinched a little.

The road was still empty. I heard sparrows in the cedar tree. Two of them darted among the dark boughs.

"What time is it, Rachel?" I asked.

"Listen. Don't you know no watch pot never boiled? Mr. Walker ain't no man for to waste time. He'll be coming when he can. Why don't you go on and do something else?"

I turned around and looked at Rachel. She was tall and thin and one of her front teeth was gold. I watched her pick up a small pine log from the wood box with the corner of her flour-sack apron and open the stove door.

"Git on in there." She gave the wood a push with her fingers.

"Mama said you'd burn yourself someday doing that. Why don't you use the poker?"

Rachel pointed her long, thin finger. "I done told you a hundred times I ain't studying no poker. But, honey, let's don't fuss." She glanced over my head. "Look! There he come now."

I turned and saw the car, a square, black box moving slowly down the road. *Why can't you drive faster, Father! Why can't you?* The car crept past the fence posts like the slow-moving shadow I had seen on the edge of the same road the summer before. It was after the funeral was over, and the hawk, high in the August sky, had hardly seemed to move.

I screamed at Rachel. "Why did you have to see him first?"

"Can I help it if I was looking out the window?"

"Yes, you can! You're supposed to be cooking."

"What's the matter with you? You must got out the bed on the wrong side this morning."

I grabbed my coat from the kitchen hook and slammed the back door behind me.

As we started out that afternoon, my father reached down and gave my orange beret a pat. He had the ax over his shoulder, and I walked silently beside him. Every few minutes I fell behind and had to run to catch up. We skirted the chicken lot, went down the slope past the tobacco barn and cut across the cornfield toward the old building. The front door was missing. Tenant families had lived in the house once, but now my father used it for storing extra hay and grain. As we got closer, I reached for my father's hand. Rachel claimed someone had been murdered in one of the upstairs rooms and that his ghost came back at certain times and sat by the cold fireplace. I looked toward the doorway. Just then a sparrow disappeared into the shadowed interior.

A little later we came to the row of cedar trees where the old dirt road from Greensboro had been. A path still there made walking easier than in the cornfield. From time to time I smelled the oiled leather of my father's hunting boots and got whiffs of the strong tobacco he kept in a cloth bag, stuffed in his hip pocket.

A few drops of rain began to fall and I imagined if I ran fast enough I could catch them all before they reached the ground. Beyond the cedars, the branch moved silently toward the creek in the bottomland. It had been early summer the last time Mother had brought me to swing on the grapevine. We had seen a water moccasin slip from its sunny spot on the overhanging bank and drop into the water. Nearby, beneath the dead leaves and moss, he would be hiding, waiting for a warm March day. I was glad it was winter.

We left the path and the cedar trees and crossed the branch into a field of scrub pine. Near the middle of the field was a dense grove of taller trees. I had been there often with Mother to peer at the sunken mounds, ancient Indian graves, now covered with vines and underbrush. I knew from Rachel that the trees guarded spirits and that sometimes at night the Indians danced, weaving in and out among the holly and pine and gum trees. Again I reached for my father's hand.

The rain was thicker now and the woods beyond looked dark. I ran ahead toward a persimmon tree just on the edge of the field. It was here I had come with my mother, the autumn before, after the first heavy frost, to gather the orange fruit. I hoped if my father and I started from the persimmon I would be able to find the other tree. A few minutes later through the falling rain and out of the vanishing afternoon, I led my father into the silent woods.

I was vaguely aware of his following me as I moved among the trees. Occasionally I stopped to look around. The fourth or fifth time I hesitated, he called. Ten minutes had gone by and he wondered why I was taking so long to make up my mind. I did not answer. We circled and retreated and circled again. It had begun to rain harder and the gray squirrel collar on my coat felt cold and sticky.

By now I was in a panic. None of the trees looked familiar. I decided there was only one thing to do. We had to go back to the persimmon and start over.

"Nonsense." My father said he would give me two more minutes. I had a thousand trees to choose from and I should be able to make up my mind. I began running first in one direction, then in another. The ends of my hair flopped in my face and twice I slipped on damp pine needles.

"This is ridiculous!" my father shouted.

"I have to find it! I have to!" I screamed.

My father walked to the nearest spruce and began to chop at its trunk.

"Don't!" I yelled. "I won't have it! I won't, I tell you! I won't!"

My father straightened up. "What do you mean, you won't have it?"

"I won't! I don't care what you say."

Then I rushed at him and pushed him as hard as I could. He lost his balance. In trying to save himself he half-turned but failed to grab a branch of the tree he had begun to chop. He fell across a shallow gully, his left shoulder bearing the brunt of his weight. I watched him get up and come toward me. I do not think he heard. I could not speak above a whisper and my voice was shaking. I told him that last spring somewhere nearby

Mother had pointed to a beautiful spruce, and said it was special, that we *must* have it at Christmas.

My father grabbed me. I was sure my head would come off. When I wrenched free I fell backward and something sharp cut across my eyebrow. I looked up and my beret, snagged by a bough, hung over me like an orange moon. I touched my forehead, and when I saw the blood I began to cry.

My father carried me most of the way home. When we finally reached the house, it was long past dark. He lit the lantern on the back porch and went directly to the barn to milk the cow.

I cannot forget the sensation of being gently lowered from my father's shoulders, my feet numb, and of the warmth from the kitchen on my face when Rachel opened the door, for, in the intervening years, I have gone over the scene again and again. I am both audience and actress. As spectator I have watched the stage from different parts of the room, from the hearth a little to one side of the stove, from the passageway between the kitchen and the dining room. I have even imagined myself floating outside the window by the cedar tree, watching Rachel comfort me in her arms. The action never varies. She opens and closes the door behind me.

"How come you took so long?"

The light from the kerosene lamp shows my face red and swollen and the cut lies across my forehead like a crimson thread.

"Good Lord! What done happened to you?"

My eyes fill with tears.

Rachel bends down and puts her arms around me. "Don't worry, honey. You'll be mended 'fore you marries." It was a favorite saying of hers.

She takes off my wet beret and coat and spreads them on the

edge of the wood box and we sink into Rachel's ancient rocking chair. She unlaces my shoes and rubs my cold feet and then she wraps her long arms around me. As I draw in quick breaths between sobs I smell the faint odor of her hair pomade. The only sound in the room is the rocker creaking back and forth. In a little while my sobs come at longer intervals and I am able to tell Rachel about the lost tree, not revealing, or course, what I had done to my father or he to me.

She is silent for a moment and then I hear her soft voice. "Your mama wouldna wanted you to get wet and your face hurt and yourself all tired for some old tree." She pauses. "Anyway, honey, save your crying for them big troubles. Them little ones ain't worth the salt in your tears."

Her arms draw closer around me.

"Yeah. Save yourself for them big miseries cause they'll come, sure as the Lord."

In a little while as from a great distance I hear across the shadowed room the wood in the stove pop and settle. Before long I am asleep in Rachel's arms.

The next morning my father was in such pain he asked Joe, Rachel's son, to drive him to town to see Dr. Lewis. Then they had to go to Greensboro for an X ray, which showed a broken bone. I know his shoulder gave him trouble from time to time until the day he died, but he never alluded to that afternoon but once. It was a rainy day. I must have been around fourteen, and he smiled and rubbed the spot over the mended bone. He said the shoulder was complaining about a first-class ride it had once given me.

My father came back from Greensboro with a cast. He offered to go to the woods again, Joe coming along to do the chopping, to try to find the tree, but the guilt I felt about his shoulder overshadowed my desire to do what I thought my mother wanted. So Joe went alone, and even though Rachel kept saying the Christmas tree Joe chose was the most beautiful one we had ever had, I was frightened by the impostor. Its long green arms reached out proclaiming my betrayal, and I imagined my mother's spirit far across the fields, hovering sadly over the real tree waiting for me to come.

For a long time now I have known that Rachel, so wise about everything else, was wrong about one thing. Even after all these years, when I look into the mirror and happen to notice the almost invisible dot of scar above my eyebrow, the guilt and sense of loss rush back almost as fresh as if the December day were only months gone. The past circles back and for a minute images melt into each other without order. For that brief second I am everywhere, everywhere I was on that dark afternoon. Yes, Rachel, you were wrong that once. It is not the big troubles. We somehow manage them. It is the private, the small, those immeasurable early sorrows which feed on the heart and make us what we are.

Heaven Lies About

ON APRIL 14, 1933, Miss Ida Hampton, a tall woman in her early sixties, leaned against the bureau which had belonged to her great-grandmother and peered into its flecked mirror. The bedroom was in semidarkness, shades drawn against midday warmth. Miss Ida pulled her hat slightly forward. Her hair, never cut or subjected to permanents, had remained almost as thick as when she was a young girl. But more than her hair, Miss Ida was proud of her aristocratic nose. Unfortunately, the nose had been forced to reign over a face that was all but chinless.

"You're wellborn, precious," Miss Ida's mother had reminded her over and over. "No money now on either side, but good blood. Never forget it."

And Miss Ida hadn't.

Downstairs Miss Ida pushed open the screen door to the front porch. The child was slouched in an oversized rocking chair, a chair made to order for Miss Ida's father, a huge and querulous man, now long dead.

"I've told you not to sit like that, Carrington. You want to be old before your time?"

The child pulled herself up, wiggled on her tiny buttocks until she touched the back of the chair. Her thin legs stuck out, straight, taut, as though they were wooden. She began rocking.

"Jessie not here yet?"

"No'm."

"Wonder why? I asked Sara to send her early." Miss Ida glanced down at the gold pocket watch which had been her father's and which she always wore on a chain around her neck. "I guess I'll go on. You wait right here till she comes. Hear?"

The child said nothing. She began to rock faster.

Miss Ida reached out, grabbed the chair. "Didn't you hear, Carrington? Look at me."

The child tilted back her little head, the shape of a hickory nut, and stared past the eyes of her great-aunt at the small green caterpillar measuring itself along the brim of Miss Ida's hat.

"When you are spoken to it is rude not to answer. You know that."

"Yessum."

Miss Ida let go the chair. "And you should look directly at people when they're talking to you. You know that, too."

"Yessum."

Miss Ida was quick to forgive.

"I suppose, honey, I could take you to the service, but I was afraid you might get a little restless. Next year you'll certainly be old enough. Then you'll understand better what Easter means."

God was the hub around which Miss Ida's life had turned until, that is, the child had appeared "like a bolt from the blue," as Miss Ida was wont to say. It was not that the Lord had been displaced by the child but rather that now there was a terrestrial as well as a spiritual center which controlled Miss Ida's diurnal turning.

"You and Jessie eat the broken cookies I left on the table. They'll taste just as good. Don't touch the others."

"Yessum."

The child was rocking rapidly and the old chair was inching slowly across the creaking boards toward the steps.

"Watch out, honey. Mind you don't get too close to the edge." Miss Ida smiled. "I used to love to do that, too, when I was your age. I'd rock and rock. Pretend I was driving Papa in our buggy up to Atlanta."

The child stared straight ahead and in no way slowed the rocking. "I'm driving to New York and by *myself*."

Miss Ida ignored the remark. "You know, honey, the service lasts till three and after that I have to do a little shopping. I think your hat needs a new ribbon. Would you like yellow this year instead of white?"

The child did not hesitate. It was as though she had expected the question. "No'm. Red."

"Red? But red won't go with your dress. Anyway it isn't an Easter color. You didn't say 'please.'"

The child stopped rocking.

"I *want red, please*." She dragged the words out as though she were pulling each one on a string past her teeth, the size of popcorn kernels.

Miss Ida didn't say anything. It was one of those impasses. She went on down the steps around the house to the barn where the car was kept. Since her grandniece had come to live with her it had not been beyond Miss Ida's imagination to feel an affinity with Job, and almost from that time she had prayed each morning and each night for strength to endure the burden.

Four years before when the telegram arrived Miss Ida did two things she never expected to do. She put in a long-distance call to New York City and the next day she boarded a Southern Railway train that would take her across the Potomac. She had been listed as the only kin and the agency wanted to know what to do with the child. As the train carried Miss Ida into the North, she searched the dark cloud hovering over her until she found a possible bright lining. The child had been sent by God to comfort her in her declining years. But as soon as she saw her grandniece it became obvious to Miss Ida that God had a different plan.

There had not been one thing to say in the child's favor. She was abnormally short for her five years and resembled nothing so much as a small plucked bird. Her hair was thin and in the middle of her small face was a nose as flat as a squashed bean. She was sullen and ill-mannered. The years since the afternoon in New York when Miss Ida had taken the child's dirty and moist hand had been a battle of wills all the way, from the moment in the social worker's office when the child refused to give up the filthy teddy bear even though Miss Ida promised to buy her a new and bigger one.

As Miss Ida was turning out of the driveway in the old Ford she saw the black child running along the shortcut through the orchard. Jessie waved cheerfully. Jessie's mother, Sara Thatcher, lived less than a mile away. For years she had been coming twice a week to Miss Ida's, and one Saturday by chance she had brought Jessie with her and Carrington had taken an immediate fancy to the child. It was soon arranged that Jessie would come three afternoons a week and on Saturday mornings. Miss Ida gave Sara Thatcher money with the understanding it was to be spent on Jessie or put in the bank under her name. Jessie was the same age, but she towered above Carrington, who had hardly grown an inch in the years she had been with her aunt. Jessie was always polite and friendly, and Miss Ida was pleased with the arrangement, especially because Carrington went only with great urging to the home of schoolmates and never wanted them invited to her great-aunt's house.

Carrington leaned forward in the chair, thrust her neck out.

As soon as the Ford disappeared beyond the crepe myrtle bushes, she flopped onto the top step, closed her eyes and jerked her head back. Her aunt had cautioned her about exposing skin to sun, warning of the result, a toughness of complexion no lady should have. She cracked an eye briefly.

"Hey!" Jessie was breathless.

"You're late." Carrington kept her eyes closed.

"I couldn't come no sooner. Hog got out and I had to help git him back." She sat down by Carrington, then leaned over and with her fingers carefully wiped the dust off her shoes. She was a thin child but so swaybacked that her buttocks stuck out like two small melons.

Carrington continued to hold her face to the sun. "You know why school let out early, don't you?"

"Nor. Mama just said I had to git here."

"It's Crucifixion Day. Aren't you a Christian?"

"I dunno."

"You go to Sunday School, don't you?"

"Yeah."

"Then you're a Christian. Is my face getting red?"

"Nor, but you sweating. What you doing?"

"Nothing. I guess I'll do it some other time." Carrington wiped her face with the hem of her dress. She stood up. "Come on. We've got to sacrifice."

"Huh?"

"Give up something."

"How come?"

"For Christ. He gave His life for all Christians and on Good Friday you are supposed to sacrifice something for Him. Come on."

The children went into the house and upstairs to Carrington's bedroom.

"Ain't we having no tea party?"

"We can't. You're not supposed to have any fun on Good Friday. You're supposed to be sad. How would you like to be nailed through your hands and feet to a cross and die?"

"I dunno." Jessie squatted and began stroking the hair of a doll in a small wooden cradle.

Carrington rummaged in a toy chest at the bottom of her bed. "I'm going to sacrifice Anne. I love her the most."

"What you going to do?"

"Burn her."

"Burn her? With fire? How come?"

"Can't you understand? We have to give up something we love very, very much, or it doesn't count. Don't you think Jesus was enjoying His life and didn't He die for you and me?"

"I dunno." Jessie lifted the doll from the cradle and began rocking it back and forth in her arms.

"Well, He did. Aunt Ida said so."

"I ain't got nothing."

"Yes, you do. Your shoes. You're proud of them."

"My shoes!" Jessie looked down at her feet. "These is the onliest I got. Mama'd beat me sure."

"But Jesus will get mad if you don't give up something."

The room was silent. Outside a neighbor's cat darted across Miss Ida's barn lot trying to escape a mockingbird.

Carrington smoothed the hair of the doll she was holding, then tied one of its tiny shoes. Jessie looked up from the floor.

"You don't love her much no how, and you know it. You love him." She pointed toward the bed where like a stain on the white counterpane a teddy bear lay propped against the pillow. Its paws had been sucked and chewed and one of its ears was held on by a safety pin.

"I *don't* love him the best."

"You does, too. You done told me. And he ain't got no pretty hair nor nothing."

A few minutes later the children left the bedroom, Carrington with her arms gripped around the bear. In the kitchen she spoke to Jessie. "Get a paper bag for the cookies, please."

Jessie tugged at the bottom drawer of the cabinet.

"Try harder."

"I is."

Carrington put the bear on the kitchen table. "Watch out." She leaned over. "Jesus is just mad at you because you won't give up your shoes." She pulled several times at the handles.

Jessie grinned. "How come you can't do it no how neither?"

Carrington looked up and stuck out a small, pale tongue. "I'm going to tell Aunt Ida you were uppity and she won't let you come anymore." She gave up on the drawer and then looked at Jessie again. She reached out and touched Jessie's arm. "I'm sorry. I love you, Jessie. I wasn't really going to tell Aunt Ida. But you have to try to understand about Good Friday."

"I don't see nothing good about it." Jessie wiped her eyes with the back of her hand.

"It's good because Jesus takes away our sins. What we've done bad during the whole year."

Carrington pushed a chair to the cabinet and took down a box of matches. She picked up the bear.

"Come on."

Jessie hesitated. "Ain't you hot? I want water."

"Later. There isn't time now. We have to be through by three."

"How come?"

"Because that is when He died." Carrington glanced at the

broken cookies. "I guess we'd better not take the plate. It might get broken and Aunt Ida's be worse than a hornet. Make a basket, please."

Jessie held up the hem of her faded dress.

Carrington took a basin from a hook on the kitchen stoop. The children walked through the backyard into the barn lot, past what had been in Miss Ida's father's time a fine cutting and vegetable garden. Miss Ida could no longer afford to keep it up, but a few hardy perennials bloomed every year amid wild grasses and she, herself, managed to pull enough weeds from the bed to get a good yield of asparagus each spring.

Sometimes the children spent the afternoon in Carrington's room, sometimes they played house under the walnut trees, but more often than not they retreated to the barn, full of treasures. Empty jars and crocks, chipped dishes, coffee cans with odds and ends, pitchforks, rusty garden tools, an old saddle. Every now and then the children jumped in a small pile of hay left in the loft from the days when Miss Ida's father kept two horses and a cow.

Carrington marched through the open door into the barn's shadowed interior and straight to the ladder, where a shaft of daylight fell from a small hole in the roof. Jessie followed slowly, keeping her eyes on the cookies in her cupped skirt.

"Hurry up, please."

"I is."

Jessie started to walk faster and almost stumbled. "See what you done made me do?"

"I'm sorry."

Carrington flung the bear through the loft opening but not at enough of an angle. It feel back to the floor, stirring up specks of dust, which floated like dots of pale gold in the cone of light. She brushed the bear's matted face.

"Here. Dump the cookies." Carrington held the basin out to Jessie. "Climb up and I'll hand it to you."

Jessie looked down from halfway up the ladder. "It sure is hot. Can't we git no water?" She held on to the ladder with one hand and with the other wiped the perspiration from her face.

"Listen, we have to suffer some. Especially you because you aren't giving anything."

Jessie leaned over and took the box of matches from Carrington and pushed them onto the loft floor.

"Jesus was thirsty on the Cross. Didn't you know He wanted water?"

"Nor."

"Well, He did. Then I guess you don't know either what those people gave Him?" She handed her the bear, but Jessie pushed it away.

"Don't shove Teddy please."

"What it matter? You burning him."

Carrington ignored the question.

"They went everywhere until they found the sourest vinegar and poured in a lot of salt. How would you like to drink that?"

"I just want water."

"Don't you think I'm thirsty, too? Go on up, please." Carrington put her foot on the ladder rung. "Why can't you understand about suffering?"

On the floor of the loft the children kneeled with their arms crossed. Carrington looked at Jessie. Jessie was staring at the basin where the bear rested on the broken cookies and a handful of hay.

"You're supposed to keep your eyes shut when I am praying." Jessie closed her eyes.

"Jesus, please forgive Jessie for not sacrificing."

"I ain't got nothing."

"Be quiet or He can't hear me." Carrington paused. "She could give You her shoes, but maybe she loves them better than she loves You."

"I does love Him, too, but Mama'd beat me."

Carrington leaned toward Jessie. "Which is worse? Having Sara whip you or Jesus mad?"

"I dunno."

Carrington opened her eyes and gave Jessie a slight shove. Jessie began to rock back and forth as though she were some mechanical toy set in motion. Carrington thrust her head back and shouted. "I'm giving up what I love most in the world outside Jessie. Thank You for taking my sins away."

Hanging from the beams above the children a few cobwebs, no longer silver but shot through with dust, moved almost imperceptibly.

"Please take Jessie's sins away, too, even though she is being selfish." The skin on either side of Carrington's small flat nose was flushed. She reached for the matchbox. "Open your eyes, Jessie, and light the fire."

Jessie continued to rock back and forth. "I ain't going to light no fire. Mama told me not to when she ain't there."

"Looks like you could at least do that. He's going to hate you!"

Carrington took out a match and pulled it along the side of the box as if she were handling a snake. She tried several times to make it light. "You know what is going to happen?" She began to shout. "The devil is coming some evening and drag you out of your bed. He might even come tonight."

She stood the box on top of the hay and pulled the match down hard. It caught and she yanked her fingers back. Wisps of smoke began to emerge from under the bear. She suddenly reached over, gave Jessie another shove.

"What I done?"

"I *hate* you and so does Jesus!"

"I ain't done nothing."

"You've made me give up Teddy! That's what you've done!"

"I going home!"

"No, you aren't We haven't finished yet."

Jessie lunged at Carrington, pushing her down. Then Jessie rushed, stumbling to the loft opening. Her foot slipped on the top rung and she was unable to catch herself. A second later she lay motionless at the bottom of the ladder. Above her in the tunnel of light, flecks of dust circled like a host of minuscule angels.

Carrington stood up. Bits of dirt clung to her damp arms and legs. She looked down from the top of the ladder. For a moment she said nothing.

"See! He's punishing you! I knew He would." She leaned forward slightly. "If you ever push me like that again, I'll tell Aunt Ida for sure." She began running around the loft, flapping her arms as though they were wings. "He's punishing you! He's punishing you!" Several times she stamped her feet, watching the dust rise around her. With her hands no larger than magnolia buds placed on her tiny hips, again she looked down from the loft opening. "I know you're pretending. You just want me to feel sorry. Well, I don't." She flipped the basin over and shoved it into a corner. The basin left a sparse trail of cookie crumbs and ends of burnt hay. One of the bear's singed paws stuck out from under the rim.

Across the loft Carrington collapsed facedown onto the small pile of hay. A wasp bobbed lightly above her before rising to the rafter where its nest was almost completed. Outside the bird renewed its campaign. The cat had decided to risk the journey home.

A little later Carrington lifted the hem of her skirt, wiped her eyes and nose. She walked slowly toward the ladder, then she began to scream. A single flame was climbing toward the roof.

"Jessie! Come quick! It's burning!"

At the bottom of the ladder, she stooped and shook Jessie.

"Get up! It's burning. Please! Aunt Ida'll be mad!" She shook Jessie again. "I'm sorry I was mean."

Carrington grabbed an ancient milk bucket and ran to the spigot just outside the barn. By the time she struggled up the ladder with the water, the flame like a runner bean was pushing out in all directions. A minute later she leaned down, put her face against Jessie's. Overhead a rafter was beginning to snap and smoke to descend through the loft opening.

Carrington clutched the inert child by the armpits and started dragging her toward the barn door.

"It wasn't me, Jessie," she sobbed. "It wasn't me."

II

Alice and Me

A Novella

I COME THIS short hour after lunch before the young school-
children rush through the high iron gates toward swings and
slides and the Guignol, or run, hugging their sailboats, to
the pond. Always here to the same part of the garden, always to
the same place where the bushes curve. My church. My pew.
My need. It is only on the warmest days that I ever find my chair
taken. Perhaps the occasional change is good for me. The forc-
ing, the seeing of things from a different angle. I am deprived of
my usual view.

And of course the routine is broken when I meet him in London or Geneva, Rome, but most often here in Paris. In between
I seek the garden. I leave behind my husband to take his rest and
I spend these minutes alone. On rainy days I go up narrow streets
to the workers' bar with its four tables and extra bench along the
wall. Most of the noon customers have left by then, and the
woman behind the bar, dressed in a blue smock (the same material from which workmen's jackets and trousers are made), is
rinsing glasses. The first time I entered (the bar is scarcely more
than a slit in the wall) she glanced up, worried. Someone crossing the wrong frontier. Now she accepts me. She understands

I am not there to interfere in any way with those lingering drinkers: the black street cleaner, the Algerian carpenter, the occasional worker from le Marché St.-Germain, sometimes the husband of the concierge across the street. Perhaps when she pulls herself up from tangled dreams, when she wakes in the morning and hears rain beating on the roof, perhaps there comes to her mind an image of me just outside the bar, shaking drops of water from my umbrella. In those scant seconds she allows herself to linger under the warm bedcovers, as she feels the dampness against her lined face. Perhaps she murmurs, "L'Anglaise will come today." She provides what I need, shelter and anonymity. I pay for the service.

And it is the same with the clochards who sit near me in the garden. Always the same two. No, that is not quite accurate. Once there was a third and they quarreled. Was that not inevitable? The world is based on two. Plus and minus. Hot and cold. Night and day. Respect and scorn. Love and hate. Would we not move awkwardly with three legs, embrace clumsily with three arms? And would not a third eye add immeasurably to our already hopeless inability to see clearly with the two we have?

The clochards are always there when I arrive. We have never spoken. But we nod; we acknowledge each other with our eyes, theirs half closed and bloodshot. The red wine is placed equidistant between them like a pact, but I have never seen either one raise the bottle to his lips. It is as though they too were suspending their usual routine for those few minutes. Nor have they ever once asked me for money. We are equals. Is this not what we want, what we seek, if not always consciously, throughout our lives? To be equal. If we give, to receive. If we receive, to give. And in equal measure. Or is it?

You see, what once appeared so simple now obsesses me with its complexity. I speak of love. That is, of lust. I study lust. I seek out films of sexual carnage and in newspapers I feed on stories of misplaced love. A Parisian art collector is murdered by his pickup, a youth of seventeen. When the British lord resigns from the cabinet, indiscretions with a nightclub dancer, he defends himself, "One needs a change." "How can I stop a woman in my office from touching me every time she passes my desk?" a female secretary asks in "Advice to the Lovelorn." And Picasso at ninety still drew over and over the primal act.

Yes, I investigate lust. In literature I search for answers. Othello and Phaedra made desperate. Ophelia pushed to madness. The aging poet envious of the young in each other's arms. And old Karamazov awaiting the nubile Grushenka, his head thrust through the open window into the Russian night, a smile on his lips of "greedy expectation."

Yes, I ponder lust. And sometimes love, though I scorn those of us dedicated to that. So each day I come to this garden or I walk through rain to the workers' bar and I confess and I judge. I stretch out my life and the lives of others and I listen. And where better than here in Paris? Where better than in this City of Light?

Today in this city of strangers, I left my husband. Standing there in the long corridor, confronting him and then the girl who finally emerged from our bedroom, but what else, after all, could she do, I suddenly split in half, one part of me taking control, cracking the whip, jerking hard on the reins, the other obeying, turning around full swing, galloping off in the opposite direction, vanishing into unknown territory. If you say this can be a fresh start, a new beginning, how little you know of commitment, how little you understand the curse of total allegiance. Because those of us who love too well are set apart. And yet there are differences among us. Standing there this morning, even had I the strength I would not have strangled Harrison. It was myself I wanted pushed into oblivion. It was my mind imprinted with the image of that girl, my inner eye condemned at will to her slow and perpetual movement toward me. And yet, just after I looked past them, past Harrison, past her, down the dim corridor at the tiny rectangle of sun, the small window open wide on the autumn day, the spot of brightness, I was not indifferent to the sound of the whip. I heeded the order to turn. I did, after all, choose to survive, to withdraw at least figuratively and in a whirl of motion.

If Harrison had only had the wit to lie, then I would not have been in this hotel room weeping off and on like an idiot. I would simply be another wife unknowingly betrayed. And with so little effort, he could have feigned impatience instead of the debasing embarrassment, the small boy caught with a handful of forbidden sweets. It would have been easy to say he was having difficulty with a page of dialogue. I would have believed him and come back in an hour or so. I am happy when Harrison is at a desk writing or at least trying to.

At twenty-one I eloped with him but not because he is particularly handsome. He isn't. But Harrison has a subtle, commanding power and a certain charm, born I'm sure of shyness, which from the first I found compelling and which still binds me and always will. I was committed the moment I saw him. I am almost certain of that. I had not the slightest doubt that his destiny was also mine. At least that is how I remember it. I can explain my love in no other way.

If Harrison had asked me, I would have come back later and gladly. I am willing to do anything at any time to nourish Harrison's talent. You have to believe in something and for almost eleven years now I have clung to that cliché, Harrison an artist forced into prostitution. A banality which in this case happens to be true, like the banal situation we found ourselves in this morning, the soap opera triangle. You might be tempted to label our *petit drame* a French farce, but that would not be quite accurate because I do not have a lover waiting in the wings, impatient to take me for a weekend to Monaco or Marrakech. Nor do I want one, although I have been reared, nourished you might even say, by infidelity, the infidelity of others. Before Harrison there was my mother. And I have had my share of friends confessing their own pathetic and often vengeful affairs. But I cannot imagine betraying Harrison. If you are committed, then to survive you have to disregard, fail to see, practice selective inattention when contradictions are hinted at, corruption exposed in the person you love. How many of us dare acknowledge a wrong choice? We grab at any protection against anguish, against pain because we do not want to know. We do not want to see. But this morning Harrison forced me to look. That was his mistake. Without some measure of pride we are nothing.

Beyond that, there was the other thing. He was betraying his own commitment. He was breaking faith with himself. We came to this city which he loves and to which I have dreamed of returning, where he would again have a chance to write all day. Why had he allowed the need to invade his working hours? Why had he suddenly become indiscreet? He has seldom flirted in front of me, placed wet kisses on the mouths of my friends. And he has always assuaged his extra lust far from our bed; I am grateful to him for that.

But I must confess to one thing. This morning before I heard the sharp crack of the whip, before my sudden and swift retreat, I did for a few seconds feel detached as though I were watching the three of us standing in the corridor and I wanted to laugh.

Harrison so looked the part, his expression, all six feet four inches of him reduced, the child clutching forbidden candy. Only what he had did not seem to be made of sugar. It was the plainest of doughs and had been somewhat misshaped in the baking. If the girl had been beautiful, if there had been any grace in her movement, then perhaps? But who knows? There was nothing that I could see to recommend her or if so it was well hidden. No, that is not quite accurate. There was one thing. Her extreme youth. Was that the best Harrison could do, my husband who spoke perfect French? All day long only a few blocks away on the Boule Miche attractive young girls look out from soft eyes, challenging. Surely among them are those who like older men, who seek in lovers their own fathers? So, I confess my scorn. I have always imagined my rivals as beautiful, certainly poised, even witty. This morning at breakfast Harrison ate the last yogurt. I do not like to think of his standing in the kitchen tomorrow, his hair mussed (or will he have combed it for her?), his dressing gown belt only loosely tied, bending, a giant peering into that tiny refrigerator. Perhaps it will be the girl with her dull eyes, those eyes which look as though they had been cooked, maybe it will be she who discovers all the yogurt gone, who rushes out for more. Or will it be Harrison who hurriedly, who gallantly pulls on his trousers, who goes forth to fetch it, and freshly baked croissants? I don't know. But I do know that I see her chubby knees moving toward me and it is that I resent, the image forced, the image bursting without warning into my mind, that wretched child giving lie to my fantasies of Harrison's long legs tangling with legs as shapely and almost as long as his.

That was the small straw. My scorn. That must have been what sent me whirling with my suitcase to this hotel. But I shall go back. To be honest, I can imagine Harrison without me, but I cannot imagine myself without him. I shall, perhaps, go back for another reason, too. This morning he might have been counting on my coming home early. He might have been trying to say he had had enough, that he no longer welcomed my silence, my acceptance, my looking in the other direction. Is it so far-fetched to see his not turning me away as a desperate appeal to save him from himself?

I shall go back. Maybe tomorrow. Maybe the day after.

Alice bends over the basin and splashes water on her face. She hurriedly applies lipstick, is more precise with the powder puff. After rummaging in the suitcase she pulls out a notebook. She looks in her wallet, takes dark glasses from her purse, glances at herself in the full-length mirror, picks up the room key.

The café at the corner is crowded with students. She scans the faces without breaking her stride, then pauses for the light to change. Several minutes later, as she is crossing a narrow street, someone calls. It is the Spanish maid waving from a third-floor window in the hotel where she and her husband had stayed before they found the apartment. The maid wants to know how Monsieur and Madame are.

In the Luxembourg the leaves are beginning to burn. Nearby, deep in the still thick foliage of a chestnut tree, a bird calls, its sparse notes clear against the muted roll of traffic. From time to time a slight breeze lifts the ends of her hair. Halfway across the garden she picks up a yellow leaf caught in the seat of a metal chair. As she walks along she twirls the stem between her fingers.

At the exit beyond the iron gates, a workman with a broom made of sticks pushes trash along the curb in the stream of gutter water: used Métro tickets, plastic bottle tops, a child's torn handkerchief, bits of dead grass, a few curled pigeon feathers. She walks down several streets, turns corners twice. She passes a café announcing sandwiches *variés* and *bière d'Alsace,* a shop with plucked geese and fowl hanging by their feet, another with a row of skinned calves' heads, encircled by ruffs of parsley. She walks by a store displaying handbags, gloves, umbrellas, swirls of scarves, and a window offering pâtés, fish in aspic, cheeses, snails ready to serve. In another window, beyond a striped awning, eyeglass frames of every shape and color float, held in midair by almost invisible threads. Outside a café next to *Jacques, Coiffeur*, on a sidewalk table, someone has left a franc in an ashtray advertising Cinzano.

Later, several blocks away, she glances at her watch and hurries into the building. She almost collides with a gentleman wearing a turban. On the third floor at the end of the corridor she turns the knob slowly. The door creaks. Several people look up. She takes a seat in the back row and opens her notebook. There is a new student in the class, a young man sitting in the front row by the window. At the blackboard Madame Berné is writing words relevant to the assigned conversation topic. She turns around, brushes the chalk dust from her fingers.

"Bonjour, tout le monde."

"Bonjour, Madame."

"L'Amérique has a new coiffure. It's very becoming."

"Merci, Madame. I had to do something drastic. This morning I found my husband with a young girl. I've moved into a hotel."

Everyone in the class turns around, looks at her. Madame Berné tilts her head slightly.

"I'm so sorry, l'Amérique. You feel hurt, of course. That goes without saying." Madame Berné pauses. "But remember there are many fish in the sea. I think you have the same expression in English, *n'est-ce pas?* You must find a new lover immediately."

*

At the end of class Alice leaves quickly, hurries down the hall to the door marked *Dames*. A soiled towel has come loose from its wooden roller. She picks it up and lays it on one of the basins. She goes into a cubicle. Scraps of torn paper bearing the imprint of dusty shoes are scattered around the base of the toilet. The walls are covered with scribbled comments in a number of languages, including Arabic and Japanese. Hearts enclosing initials are squeezed among words of advice.

> Now that we're in the month of May
> Why not fuck the livelong day?

Above the toilet-paper rack a huge penis drawn in purple radiates the names of famous men, some living, some dead, as well as a few unknowns. As Alice leaves, several young women speaking German come into the bathroom.

Alice glances down the hall. It is empty. At the head of the stairs on the second floor she passes two dark-skinned men talking. One carries a worn briefcase held together by an elastic band. They both look at her. One smiles. In the foyer near the main entrance several persons are gathered around the bulletin boards, reading announcements of concerts, job opportunities, the hours for the phonetics lab. A large poster with a colored photograph of Chenonceaux advertises a day tour to the Loire country. The new person in the conversation class is among them. He looks up as she hurries past into the courtyard.

"Madame!"

Alice turns around.

"I was waiting for you." He speaks with an English accent.

"For me?"

"I want to commend your courage. What you said in class."

"Courage? I made a fool of myself."

"Not at all. I wanted to say so then, but I thought it might embarrass you."

"Frankly, I was so appalled at myself I could hardly make it through the hour."

"Appalled?"

"Yes. As though I didn't have an ounce of pride."

"That's just the point. Your openness. Your honesty."

"And you British? I'd think you'd be horrified by such public confession, exposing myself like that. I'll never go back to class."

"You're so wrong. If only my mother had acknowledged my father's infidelities." He reaches out as though to touch Alice, then withdraws his hand. "Several students were talking right after class. They all admired you. Just as I do." He smiles. "I'm John Botsford."

Alice introduces herself.

"Alice? My mother's name was Alice."

"Really. Well right now I wish I were the famous one. If only I could nibble something and disappear."

"Are you free by chance for an apertif? Dinner?"

Alice looks at her watch. "No, I'm sorry. I'm meeting my husband in a few minutes. We have to make certain arrangements."

"Perhaps another time?"

"Perhaps."

Just before she turns the corner, Alice glances back. John Botsford is walking slowly in her direction.

There is one calf's head left in the butcher shop. Its parsley ruff is in disarray, a few sprigs missing. The gelatinous eyes have only the glazed tips of the pupils showing, as though the animal had at the last moment looked heavenward.

In the Latin Quarter people are crowding the sidewalks. Alice buys an evening paper, a copy of *Vogue*, and at a delicatessen near the hotel a ham sandwich and bottle of Perrier.

There is no message in her hotel box, only the key. When she reaches her room she does not turn on the light. She falls across the bed and rolls herself up in the velvet counterpane as though in a winding sheet.

I do not think I slept at all. The girl kept moving toward me over and over like the waves that summer when I was twelve, those waves which suddenly changed from friendly hands tossing treasures for me to find on my parents' beach to monstrous fists pounding, "Dead! Dead! He's dead!"

That girl brought back those waves, she with her dull cocked eyes. Again and again I saw her enter the hotel as I listened to the sound of cars racing to a stop and students calling to each other on what might be the last warm evening before the cold autumn rains begin. She crept toward me through the brief silence, between the drunken shouts of a late café customer and the rumble of early delivery trucks. I saw her leave Harrison. I watched her pad up narrow alleys. She stopped for a moment across from the hotel waiting for a large vehicle to inch by, its twirling sweepers cleaning the street. I followed her past the dozing concierge and into the elevator, I heard her turn the knob of my locked door, felt her breath as she bent to whisper, "Me! Me! He's with me!"

Yes, I spent the night confronting the girl, except for those few moments of relief, if you can call it that, when I managed to reenact my humiliation in Madame Berné's class. None of the students could have been more surprised at my public confession than I. That I should lose control like that! No, I do not think I slept at all.

When I bought *Le Monde* and *Vogue*, I intended at least to read the headlines and look, if briefly, at the latest styles. But when I ordered the sandwich, even before the woman, her hair piled in a peak like yellowed whip cream, began slicing the ham, I doubted I would eat the sandwich and I almost told her so. "I shall, Madame, in all likelihood throw what you are making now into the wastebasket of room thirty-eight in a hotel not far from here because I am a betrayed wife." She could not have cared less about someone so stupid as to be suffering from infidelity. Her own husband, no doubt, accustomed to stroking the legs of willing *filles* and she, the wife, glad of it, thankful that her Marie-Antoinette coiffure was not subjected more often to his clumsy hands.

The first night I did not undress completely. What possible good could have come from feeling through my nightgown that emptiness stretching like a desolate pain outward from my breasts and stomach, my knees? During our years of marriage the warmth of Harrison's long body has become for me as necessary a prelude to sleep as bedtime prayers for the devout. The occasional night he works late and stays in New York or is away on a trip seeing a client, I never sleep well. But there was the other reason I did not undress. I hoped Harrison would call before the evening was over. If he telephones I shall be ready to go back.

Toward dawn I got up. I looked in the bathroom mirror and noticed for the first time two faint lines on my forehead. There was a heaviness in my stomach. I could not imagine ever wanting to eat again. Yesterday after leaving Harrison I went to a restaurant where we planned to go as a celebration when the first fifty pages of his novel were complete. Going without him was an innocuous form of revenge. But at the time it made me feel better.

Yesterday after the girl left, I put some things in a suitcase. Harrison carried the bag down and found a taxi, not that there was any feeling of good riddance or of speeding the parting guest. He did, actually, ask me to reconsider. But the horses had already felt the whip. They were galloping and I could not stop them. My quantum of pride had to burn itself out. Now I am certain Harrison was asking for help.

This morning when I went out the night was dying. Mist shrouded the Luxembourg, muting the trees save those close to the fence. The heavy gates were not yet open. I felt chilled. I took a scarf from my purse and wrapped it around my neck. On the rue de conde a concierge was about to carry an empty trash can back into the courtyard. She waited for me to go by. Her face was serene, her dark eyes untroubled. Was her husband in their cramped quarters snoring, sleeping off a drunken evening spent with some prostitute? The woman was used to it. She no longer cared. And when does one no longer care? When all rage is spent? When all love has gone?

I see the girl again. I see her in bed with Harrison. But I quickly transform the image. They are not making love. Harrison never wants to on the mornings he intends to write. But perhaps he won't write today. Perhaps he pans to rent a car and take the girl to Fountainbleau to see the foliage. Will they wander first through the forest and then visit the fish pond?

Seeing an aged carp rise to the surface, Harrison is sure to make some remark about the passage of time.

On the Pont du Carrousel I looked down at the Seine. How many anguished Frenchmen and despairing foreigners have found oblivion in its waters? Recently there was an article in *Le Figaro* about the number of prostitutes dragged each year from the river. And only last week I read in a guidebook about a group of Gallic warriors. They were so disgraced by their leader's defeat that they leapt in full battle dress into the Seine at the small island settlement not yet called Paris. Later near the same site, did some legionnaire weary of gray days and metallic cold, longing for aqua seas and olive groves, for bright sun and the crowded streets of his native Rome, jump into its icy waters? Or was it because he received news of an unfaithful wife?

I looked up the wide allée stretching toward the Concorde like a carpet unrolled for a bride. At the far end two people, a man and a woman, moved across the empty space like puppets on an empty stage. I felt tired and went no farther.

On the way back to the hotel I stopped at the Café de Cluny. I went there for the first time with my father. It was his favorite café. Something propelled me toward the table in the corner where we sat midafternoon on Bastille Day. It had been the last free table. My father smiled.

"Again, Sugar. The luck of the Irish."

My father was not Irish. It was a joke between us. Nor was he lucky.

I watched a charwoman, her face expressionless, come down the stairs and disappear with her mop and pail around the side of the bar. There is comfort in the first sip of coffee, in the warmth as it touches the tongue.

Two days later Alice is lying on the hotel bed. She picks up the phone before it rings twice. It is not Harrison but John Botsford and she asks him how he knew where she was. It was easy. He followed her at a safe distance when she left the Alliance Française. He is calling now from the café across from the hotel and would like to take her to lunch.

She accepts.

"I'll meet you in the lobby in a few minutes."

John is sitting in a chair facing the elevator. She tells him she has to be back by three. Harrison might call.

They go outside.

"The car's right here," John says. "I was lucky to find a spot so

close." He opens the door but Alice does not get in. She stares at
the elegant automobile.

"It's beautiful. Where did you get it?"

"In Dublin last summer. At an auction."

"I wish cars still had running boards. Nineteen thirty isn't it?"

John looks surprised. "How did you know?"

"My father collected antique cars."

On a narrow street leading to St.-Sulpice they are slowed by
pedestrians hurrying to lunch. A woman wearing a henna wig
and carrying a toy poodle rushes toward a bus stop. John almost
hits her.

"Old idiot!"

Alice does not comment on the woman or John's reaction to
her.

"My father had a Packard roadster exactly like this one only it
was blue not white."

"So your father and I have something in common."

"At least one thing."

The white walls of the restaurant are decorated with circus
scenes, simple black lines like cave drawings of tents, clowns,
balloons, horses prancing in a ring, lions attentive to their master's whip. The maître d'hôtel hands them menus and presently
they give their orders.

"Your French is excellent. Why the conversation class?" Alice
asks.

"For fun and to meet people who aren't French. What about
you?"

"For something to do, I guess. And to improve my accent."
She pauses. "May I ask you a personal question?"

John smiles. "I won't promise to answer it."

"How old are you?"

John hesitates. "Thirty-one."

"Really? You look younger."

"That's good. And may I . . ."

"I'm almost thirty-two."

"No, not that. How long have you been married?"

"Eleven years. I was a senior in college. We eloped." Alice tells him that Harrison had come to Bennington for a three-day conference on the arts. "It was only a few months after his novel appeared. Several critics said he might be a new Faulkner. Faulkner, you know, is one of our best writers."

John nods. "I've read a couple of his novels."

"Which ones?"

John hesitates. "I've no memory for titles. How did your parents react to your eloping?"

"My mother was furious. She's never forgiven me."

"And your father?"

"He died when I was twelve."

When John asks if Harrison has continued to publish Alice shakes her head. She tells him that Harrison started on a second novel the year they were married. A friend lent them a house in Vermont but nothing happened. Some kind of block.

"Our money ran out and Harrison did what some writers at home have found themselves doing. He took a job with an advertising firm. It specializes in television commercials."

"And they have a branch office in Paris?"

"Actually they do. But Harrison is on leave. His psychiatrist urged it. He's taking the year off to try fiction again." Alice looks straight at John. "You're clever, making me do all the talking. I know nothing about you except that your mother and I share the same name and we both chose husbands who would be unfaithful."

"There's not much to tell."

"What do you do?"

"I'm an artist. Portraits mostly."

"I'd like to see some of them."

At the hotel, before leaving, he asks if she is going back to Madame Berné's class tomorrow. She tells him she isn't sure.

Her box is empty except for the key. In her room Alice goes directly to the window. John is looking up, scanning the hotel's facade. She steps back. Several minutes later when she looks again he has disappeared.

I stood by the window not wanting to feel sorry I had insisted on being back at the hotel by three in case Harrison had called. I was not ready to admit I found it exciting, the slight tremor in what I thought was solid ground, being the one pursued after having for so long done the pursuing. For that is exactly how it has been, and almost from the beginning of our marriage.

At first I could not believe it. When John said, "Here we are," and opened the door of the Packard, I thought it was some kind of malicious joke. And when he closed my door the years fell away and it was Sidney, who kept the cars polished and in running order, waving us on, my father and me. We would be heading toward the end of Long Island, or if we turned in the opposite direction without the picnic basket, without the binoculars, it meant we would have the whole day in New York. Just the two of us.

What a travesty, riding in John's unknown yet familiar car. The first thing my father always did when Sidney closed the door was adjust the rearview mirror, clamped to the metal casing on the spare tire on the left side. I loved the twin spotlights and sometimes at night my father would let me play with them. I would circle the beams in the branches of trees, pretending I was catching a burglar. When I got into John's car I noticed the spotlight on my side was missing. There were scratches on the elegant dashboard and the floor covering was worn. But worse than being confronted with John's Packard were my revelations to him, a stranger. For Harrison knows next to nothing about my childhood. Nothing of the Packard or the other automobiles, many of them antique, parked in the converted stalls where my grandfather's horses once stood. I wanted to erase the first twenty years of my life and Harrison has respected my wish. He has never even met my mother.

I liked the Pierce-Arrow and the black Hispano-Suiza but the Packard Eight roadster was my favorite and my father always ordered it whenever we went on our expeditions. Sometimes on those special journeys I felt myself a princess rescued from a mother, not my own but an imposter. I did not tell all that to John. Actually I raised only slightly the window on my past, but I am annoyed I allowed even that small glimpse.

Last night before I fell asleep I made two decisions. I would not go back to Madame Berné's class and I would not see John again. But this morning when the girl lumbered by on the edge of my mind I reneged on the second. Why shouldn't I see John? For one thing I'm curious to see his paintings. At sixteen in boarding school I had a vague ambition of becoming an artist. But I'm convinced now that my art teacher praised my work because he was in love with me. If I had made my escape with him instead of Harrison . . . ?

On the isolated farm in Vermont I tried to paint but I didn't do anything that pleased me and gave up. I learned to cook instead and spent long hours in the kitchen making some complicated dish. At times the snow was so deep it reached halfway up the ground-floor windows. I was happy enclosed in that small world with Harrison, happy that he was upstairs writing. I did not know then that for all the days he sat in that room he produced only a few pages. Those handwritten sentences brought forth at a snail's pace were transformed to ashes in the living room fireplace one May night while I was asleep. It took one match and a few minutes of flame to destroy the evidence of his failure in that house which for me was a kind of heaven but for him became a form of hell.

Yes, I was happy in Vermont. I had escaped the destiny my mother planned for me and I felt secure the way I had felt with my father on our excursions. Surely those ten months in Vermont were a glorious journey?

That winter when Harrison and I made love, whether upstairs or downstairs on the rug by the open fire, our bodies seemed to curve around the earth itself. Outside the fields of unbroken snow stretched to the edge of the woods and sometimes in the cold silence they reflected the pale light of a full moon.

Alice parts the curtain slightly and looks at the café across the street. John is there. A folded newspaper and a café filter are on the table in front of him. Alice slips on a jacket and picks up her pocketbook. On the floor below she finds the *femme de chambre*. The maid looks surprised but locks the door to the room she is cleaning and leads Alice downstairs to the cellar lit by dusty lightbulbs. They walk past a carpenter's bench on which rests a half bottle of unlabeled red wine and a chair in need of upholstering. Near the door marked *Sortie*, several worn automobile tires hang from the ceiling like hoops for trained animals to jump through.

When she steps into the alley an emaciated cat with tits poking from matted fur darts in front of her, then stops at a distance and begins to meow. A block away Alice goes into a butcher shop. When she returns the cat has disappeared. She calls "Mieu! Mieu!" first in one direction, then in another. She leaves the bits of meat on the paper by the alley wall. At the corner she glances back. A yellow tom with broad scarred face and thick neck is gulping down the scraps. The end of his tail slowly twitches.

Alice walks toward the Seine. The strip of sky above the narrow street is deep blue. From the Petit Pont she looks down at a barge moving in the direction of Le Havre. The gold letters on the stern read *Hela, Hamburg*. On its deck a woman is hanging up a man's shirt. A small dog stands near the laundry basket and watches.

Alice crosses to Notre Dame and looks up at the facade for several minutes before she goes in. Later she walks through the garden behind the cathedral to the Île St. Louis and moves along slowly, studying the facades of the elegant houses. At the end of the quai she turns back and retraces her steps until she reaches a massive door embossed with nails. She pushes the buzzer.

In the four corners of the vaulted entrance, wide enough for a coach to pass through, there are statues representing the four seasons. The tip of Winter's beard is missing. A concierge appears in the small window overlooking the passageway. "Madame wishes?"

"Monsieur Fletcher? Is he still here?"

The concierge shakes her head. "He left a long time ago. He was a friend of Madame's?"

"Of my father's. I came here when I was a child." Alice looks across the courtyard. "The fishpond. It's still there!"

She walks toward it, the concierge following. "And the frogs! I'd forgotten them."

On a raised rock in the middle of the pool, two iron frogs,

their bodies flecked with moss, sit back to back. Water trickles from their mouths.

"We gave them names, my father and I, but I can't remember what we called them." Alice glances up at the building. "Which was Mr. Fletcher's? I know we climbed a stone staircase."

"The top floor" — the concierge points — "where the sky-light is."

"Of course. His studio. Now it's coming back."

Alice walks along the Quai aux Fleurs and wanders around the flower market. There are chrysanthemums everywhere, patches of color in cans of water and in pots and jardinieres hanging from stalls. She consults a vendor.

"It's not the season, Madame."

A cigarette butt hangs in the corner of his mouth. His black apron is streaked with mud and the visor of his cap all but hides his eyes.

"Perhaps you could find some at a florist where the rich live, but not here."

He picks up a pot of yellow chrysanthemums. "Don't these please Madame? They last a long time."

"They're lovely but I wanted white violets. My father always bought them for me."

The vendor shrugs his shoulders. "Too bad." He crushes the cigarette stub with the toe of his boot.

"Perhaps I'll take a few of those."

The vendor lifts a bunch of white chrysanthemums, shakes the water from the stems.

"That's too many. I'm staying in a hotel."

"Ask the *femme de chambre*. She'll get you a vase."

He squeezes the stems gently with a rag, then wraps the flowers in paper.

Alice opens her pocketbook.

"No, no, Madame. With my compliments. After all, you didn't find what you wanted."

He tilts his head back slightly and smiles.

Later Alice sits down in the Luxembourg several chairs away from a young woman who has on a heavy white cardigan and a string of amber beads around her neck. Blue eye shadow accents her eyes. The ends of her hair are slightly curled. Two clochards doze on the ground nearby, their heads against a tree, a bottle of red wine between them. The woman smiles and Alice addresses her in French. "What a lovely part of the garden."

"Yes, isn't it. I come here for a little while almost every day unless it's raining."

She nods toward the clochards. "They seem to like it, too. They're almost always here." The woman switches to English. "You must be American."

"And you French and have spent a lot of time in England."

The woman laughs.

"Actually I'm English and have spent a lot of time in France." She stands up. "I must go. I've already stayed longer than I should have. But the foliage is so lovely now and once the rains begin it is never the same."

Alice picks up the chrysanthemums. "Please won't you take these? I don't know why I bought them. I'm leaving Paris today and I can't take them with me."

After the Luxembourg I went back to the apartment. I had to confront Harrison. And the girl, too, I suppose. I had to know. Madame Germaine, the concierge, was standing in the doorway talking to one of the women who works at the corner laundry. As I approached they seemed to look at me with exaggerated curiosity.

"Madame has come for what Monsieur left?"

Before I could answer, Madame Germaine disappeared and returned with a brown envelope, addressed to Harrison from his agency. He had scratched out his name and written mine above it. He was off to London for two weeks and hoped I would move back into the apartment. He had to get away for a while. "Forgive me, Harrison." Seeing his name written out gave me a strange feeling. He has never, in cards or letters, signed anything but the initial H. It was as though something fundamental had changed between us.

I wanted to ask Madame Germaine if Harrison was alone when he left. But I hesitated, fearing the answer. And yet what was one more infidelity to her? She knew who came and went and when, which wives received lovers, which husbands brought in young girls or the wives of their friends when their own wives were away. Perhaps Madame Germaine assumed I too was having trysts and so I pretended indifference and asked.

"Oui, Madame. Monsieur was alone."

But that was only momentary relief. Maybe the girl did spend the night, left early before Harrison, went to her apartment or her family's, hurriedly packed a bag. That's what she must have done. I see her with a suitcase get out of a taxi at St.-Lazare and pad through the station. She finds Harrison standing near the quai where he said he would be, looking anxious, waving her on. She guards the baggage, he rushes to a telephone and leaves the message at my hotel. When he rejoins the girl he puts his hand on her shoulder as though to guide her through invisible dangers and then picks up the suitcases. Harrison never uses porters when it is a question of only one or two bags. His long arms and his strength. They disappear into the train, she perhaps to see London for the first time. And then I see myself those years ago in the middle of Trafalgar Square close to my father, imitating him, bending slightly forward. Several pigeons are taking grain from our outstretched hands. I am wearing a favorite coat, navy with silver buttons.

When I opened the door to our apartment, the scent of Harrison's aftershave lotion hung in the air. That we should be so vulnerable! That a stranger's stoop of shoulder or smile can bring back someone else. That a snatch of music or a particular food, a sound like a pistol shot, will re-create whole stretches of our lives. That without warning the past can strike and we are defenseless. Standing in the silent foyer, assaulted by that familiar scent, I felt only anger. But if someone had asked me whether against Harrison or my father or myself, I am not sure I could have answered. Perhaps against all three because we were each of us cursed by failure.

I went into the bathroom and opened the window. Across the courtyard in an apartment two floors down, a young woman was working in the kitchen. She glanced up at me. Did she know?

There was only one cup and saucer, one plate on the sink drainboard, and no new food in the refrigerator. The goat cheese I had bought several days before was gone. Could Harrison have spent the night by himself and gone to England alone?

I hesitated in the doorway to the bedroom. The iridescent silk on the headboard and the bed's matching counterpane reflected the sun in quivers of shifting light. How different the bed now from the afternoon the real estate agent had shown me the apartment. I had felt the mattress to see that it was firm. Occasionally Harrison has trouble with his back. A football injury.

And the bed, the piece of furniture so involved with our destinies? That small space where most of us begin and take our final breath. Where lust is spent or held in fury. Where we betray or are betrayed or dreaming transform our personal histories and relive in nightmares our private terrors. But how often do we imagine our bodies immobile? And yet a third of our given time is spent in sleep, oblivious to those we love and those we scorn. It is the self in motion, always in motion that the mind nourishes, that the ego demands, a ball on an elastic string, propelled outward from bed each morning, snapped back each night. We deny our slumbering body with its semblance to death.

I walked across the room and lifted the edge of the covers. There were only a few swirls of dust under the bed, no forgotten stocking or bobby pin. And no flecks of powder on the bureau. Nothing in the room betrayed the girl's presence. But when I looked at the bed, it was she I saw there with Harrison, not myself.

I closed the window in the bathroom. The young woman across the courtyard was setting a table in the room next to the kitchen. Her left arm held a baby whose tiny buttocks straddled her hip as though seated on a small saddle.

Alice has almost reached the hotel when John calls to her from the café. He has been there all this time like a detective spying on her. He strides across the street.

"I thought you'd be gone," Alice says. "I saw you in the café hours ago."

"I never give up. I came to take you to my studio. But how did you get out of the hotel without my knowing it?"

"I'm sorry. There was something I had to do. But I do want to see your paintings. Will you wait while I speak to the concierge?"

She tells the concierge she will be checking out later that afternoon. She rejoins John outside.

"The car's on the rue de Tournon. Do you mind walking that far?"

"I think I made a mistake this morning. I went back to places my father took me. Adam and Eve weren't at all the way I remembered them."

"Adam and Eve?"

"On the facade of Notre Dame. I could have sworn they were together, their arms around each other as though a bolt of lightning were about to strike. But they're alone, separated by the rose window. My father murmured something like, 'It's with those two, Sugar, all the trouble began.' He whisked me into the dark interior before I had a chance to ask him what he meant and by the time we left the cathedral I decided I didn't want to know. At that age I already had the convenient habit of plunging my head into sand. At least the fishpond was there."

"At Notre Dame?"

She laughs. "No, no. In the courtyard of a house on the Île St. Louis where a classmate of my father's at Harvard lived. Actually, he was an artist."

"What's his name?"

"You wouldn't know him. He's not famous. I was hoping to find him, but apparently he left some time ago. Then I went to the flower market looking for white violets. Once my father used to buy them for me. But it isn't the season. I settled for white chrysanthemums."

"You didn't have them with you just now."

"My God, what are you? A private eye? It's funny about people. I could walk a mile with Harrison with my arms full of flowers and he wouldn't notice."

They reach the Packard. He closes the door on her gently.

"Will you excuse me a moment? I just remembered that I have to make a call to someone about a bet I lost on the races last Sunday at Chantilly."

"You are not telling the truth, John. Harrison and I went to the races last Sunday. They were at Longchamp."

"Of course. Why did I say Chantilly?"

"It doesn't matter."

"But what did happen to the chrysanthemums?"

"I gave them to a woman in the Luxembourg. She was wearing a beautiful string of amber beads. For some reason I felt drawn to her. I said I was going to London and couldn't take them with me."

"So you don't always tell the truth either."

"Not always. Anyway, maybe I will go to London."

"When?"

"Perhaps tonight. Who knows?"

The studio near the Champ-de-Mars is a small room, one end all glass, with a bed, cabinet, desk, two easy chairs covered with faded twill, a philodendron in a wooden bucket and four easels. There's a small kitchen and a bathroom whose mirrored ceiling reflects a tile mermaid beckoning with open arms from the bottom of a sunken tub. John says he rented the studio because of her.

From the moment I arrived I found myself moving from easel to easel, back and forth. I could in no way relate the portraits, all heads of women, to John. He obviously had talent. There was a controlled simplicity about the pencil strokes. But each of the faces, two were of adolescent girls, was twisted in some grotesque way. And they all had something else in common, the same nose. The short strokes jutting outward from static gobs of paint and the bold colors, mostly shades of red and orange, gave the heads a striking texture. Two of them seemed to be gasping for breath. Once I turned, as I moved from easel to easel, to find

John looking at me for approval. But during those few seconds, seeing his guileless expression, it was I who felt reassured. Then confronting the tormented faces again, I became uneasy and turned away with a feeling of not getting enough air. And yet I would be less than honest if I denied the edge of excitement that circled my uneasiness. I wanted, I needed to understand the connection between John and the portraits.

"They're striking, beautifully rendered, but why the terrible agony?"

"I'm fascinated by the suffering of women."

"By their suffering? Why?"

"Why not?"

"Men suffer, too."

"Their suffering doesn't interest me. More often than not they manage to wriggle free without cost. But women embrace suffering, struggle with it. It's the spectacle I find fascinating."

I wanted to believe he was joking.

"Admiring the capacity for endurance," he went on. "What's wrong with that? Besides, I enjoy my fantasies of rescue."

I wanted to respond to his view of women with sketches of my own. I asked him to give me a drawing pad and some charcoal.

"You need a normal face around here if only to give more meaning to your victims."

He could not have been more surprised. "You're an artist?"

"I wouldn't go so far as to say that."

"Why didn't you tell me?"

"If you don't have charcoal, a pencil's fine."

"I do."

John pulled out a drawer in the cabinet and held up several pads.

"That one. My head has to be as large as possible to challenge yours."

Before I began to draw the face, I went to the bathroom. A door at the end of the room opened onto a small space where a ceiling spotlight flooded a statue of Shiva and pots of ferns at its base. One of the god's feet rested on the crouched body of a small calf with the head of a girl. At first I did not see the full-length portrait on the wall behind Shiva, a beautiful young woman in a black evening coat with an ermine collar. I recognized the eyes at once and then the other familiar feature. Each of the women in John's paintings had the same delicate nose.

Alice holds the pad upright, firm against her knee, and looks at the sketch. John is reading *Le Monde*.

"Is Shiva your favorite household god?"

John lowers the paper. "I suppose. Virgin and Devil rolled into one. Aren't all of us destructive or regenerative depending on the situation and the persons involved?"

"I guess so. But those extra arms, they're repulsive."

"You don't like distortion in any form?"

"That depends. Picasso's three-faced women, yes. They're psychologically interesting. But not Shiva's arms."

Alice makes several short strokes with the charcoal.

"I think it's finished."

She holds the sketch away from her and then hands it to John. He studies it for a few seconds.

"She's normal all right" — he looks up at Alice — "and wonderful."

"You think so? It's the first thing I've tried in a long time."

"Why?"

Alice shrugs her shoulders. "No confidence, I guess."

John continues to scrutinize the drawing.

"You must begin again. Immediately. Working here."

"And what will you do? Sit in cafés all day?"

"We can work something out."

The doorbell rings three times.

"It's Madame Vivien, the concierge."

John opens the door on a middle-aged woman. Her nose, wide at the bottom, is flat against a sallow face. She hands him a box wrapped in gold paper and tied with a fancy bow, then leans slightly forward and lets her eyes rest on Alice.

"Bonjour, Madame Vivien."

The concierge hesitates as though about to make a comment but turns away murmuring, "Bonjour, Monsieur, 'Dame."

John hands the box to Alice.

"For me?"

Alice unties the ribbon held in place by a gold seal bearing the name of a florist on the rue Montaigne. She lifts out a bouquet of white violets resting on a ruff of dark leaves. She smiles. "So your bookie runs a flower shop."

John nods.

"Shall we have a glass of Vouvray to celebrate your new career?"

Alice follows John to the kitchen.

"How did you know I liked Vouvray? It's the first wine I ever tasted."

"My luck. I get it from a vineyard near Tours whenever I'm down."

"Tours? Do you go often?"

"That depends. Actually, I have a small château nearby."

"How wonderful!"

"Not really. It's in terrible repair."

Alice and John sit facing the wall of glass and look across the tops of trees, their autumnal leaves moving gently like small flames. John fills their glasses again.

"How old was your mother when that portrait was painted?"

"Why do you assume it was my mother?"

"The eyes. You have the same beautiful eyes."

"Suppose I told you it was an aunt."

"It is your mother, isn't it?"

"Yes. She was twenty-three."

"How old when you were born?"

"Nineteen." John pauses. "You know, as a matter of fact, I was thinking of going to Tours this weekend. Would you like to come? The foliage is at its best."

"I'm probably off to London."

"To London? Why?"

"Why not?"

"For how long?"

"I don't know."

"How about dinner then? We could go to the Coupole. More celebration of your new career. It's still a place where artists hang out."

I am a compass with needle gone wild. I can hardly believe what I did this afternoon and after I had made up my mind not to see John again. I accepted a key to his studio. "Why not come here for at least a few hours each day to see what you can do?" To be honest, I was surprised at how good my drawing was and I did it with so little effort. It was as though someone else was guiding my hand.

I do not want to see John again. Those portraits! Can you really separate dancer from the dance? And the violets! And his insistence that throwing myself into painting will help me through the crisis with Harrison. I resent his intrusion into my private life and prepared my escape with another falsehood. At the moment London is the last place I want to be unless I knew Harrison was there alone.

John wanted to drive me back to the hotel but I insisted on a taxi. Then later last evening, lonely, I almost telephoned him, to say I'd changed my mind about dinner.

Only last week Harrison and I went to the Coupole. The atmosphere was exhilarating. The animated faces and interesting clothes, the snatches of conversation, waiters rushing about. Just before we left, a young woman arrived and caused a wash of silence across the room. Her blond hair fell to her shoulders, and the tiny stars pasted around her eyes glittered as she floated to a table in the back. Her escort was a stocky man almost bald.

People nodded, others waved, and she responded gracefully with her slender hands. I imagine John would know who she was.

There is something about John that attracts me. At least he talks. My life with Harrison has been laced with silence. For ten years now, five days a week, Harrison has been around people talking. At home he needs a change. I am not complaining. I have managed to walk an interior landscape and with my fantasies remake destinies. My own and those of others.

Yes, John does interest me, and yet there is something about him that makes me uneasy, like the unexpected shadow of a bird streaking across the day's brightness or the solitary ring of a telephone in the middle of the night. I felt it when we were having lunch and for an instant yesterday afternoon when I asked him about the portrait of his mother.

Last night I slept on the sofa. As soon as I arrived in the apartment, I emptied the suitcase and hung my things in the living room. Perhaps before Harrison returns I'll put them back in the bedroom closet. I did make one quick foray there. I was curious to see what he took with him. Only one suit and two jackets. And his typewriter. He must intend to write. But will the girl let him? She may not have the imagination to go around London by herself. Does she even know English? During our brief encounter she did not speak. She emerged from the bedroom, her dull eyes staring, and padded past Harrison and past me. She pulled back the heavy door as though she had done it many times and, with her right arm stretched behind her, shut it. And all this without once looking to the left or right.

John protested my taking a taxi but I stood my ground. He held the violets while I got in. When he handed me the bouquet, he leaned over as though to kiss me. I turned my head slightly and he stepped back.

"If you don't go to London please feel free to come anytime. I may be here. I may not. No matter, you have the key."

"I'll call first."

The taxi pulled away. I looked back surprised that John did not wave. He was obviously hurt and must have realized I was already moving out of his life. Looking at him, seemingly transfixed as he watched me disappear, I felt for an instant the same excitement I experienced leaving Harrison. The car gathered speed, escaping. And yet the circumstances were hardly the same.

Alice crosses the boulevard St.-Germain. A few minutes later she goes into an art supply store and buys charcoal, felt pens, paper and a collapsible easel in aluminum. Then she goes back to look at the tubes of acrylic. Suddenly she picks up the easel and paper sack with the outline of a palette imprinted on it and leaves the store. In the apartment house she does not call the elevator but runs up the two flights of stairs. She opens the telephone book and dials the Alliance Française.

"My address and telephone number are not to be given to anyone."

And then she telephones the Paris office of the Universal Agency and gives the same command. She explains that her husband has begun work on a novel and does not want to be disturbed. Under any circumstance.

The young woman in the apartment across the courtyard is sitting in an open window drying her hair. Alice put up her easel and begins sketching the woman's head with its thick hair falling over her face. Almost half an hour later she goes into the living room and props the drawing against the mantel mirror. She studies the sketch for a moment and then returns to the window. The young woman, following the sun, has moved to another window and is sitting with her back to the courtyard. Alice continues to work with swift, unhesitating strokes. In one of the sketches the woman holds a baby over her shoulder. The infant's face is a simple oval without features.

Alice lies down on the sofa and falls asleep. She wakes up shivering and rubs her arms. She turns on a light, looks at her watch. She is hungry. She wants a filet mignon and fresh bread.

Downstairs she hesitates in the doorway before crossing the street. She turns the corner by a small café. She goes first to a *boucherie*, then to an *epicene* for green beans and a bottle of wine. At a *boulangerie*, reaching from floor to ceiling, mirrors face each other. As she joins the line of people buying bread she sees reflected from the mirror behind her the white Packard creeping slowly down the street. John is looking straight ahead at the pedestrians, most of whom stop to stare before crossing in front of him. She rushes to the pastry counter at the back of the store. She is frightened. She stands at the counter pretending to deliberate, but she knows what she wants. Her father often brought macaroons home to her mother and he always brought some for her too.

Back in the apartment Alice turns off the light and goes to the window. Without taking her eyes off the street, she pulls the paper ribbon from the box. She has eaten five macaroons before she finally lets the curtain fall back into place.

I continued to sketch. Again as in John's studio some outside energy seemed to sweep my hand along. While working I managed to push Harrison and the girl out of my mind, but for a moment before falling asleep I saw them in Kensington Gardens, dwarfed, yes even Harrison, by the huge trees. Hand in hand they walked toward the pond, the foliage behind them brilliant against a darkening sky. But when they reached the water they stood a little apart, decorously, and watched a child and her father throw bread to a family of ducks.

Perhaps he was bored with the girl even before they reached Calais. After Dover, did he deliberately choose a compartment where there were other passengers so as not to be alone with her? Perhaps by the time they arrived in London he was desperate and wanted to return to Paris as soon as possible.

I was tired after the hours of sketching and fell asleep again. I awoke in the dark shivering. I had been dreaming of an empty automobile rolling on its own down a country lane lined with bare poplar trees. When it reached a fork in the road, it sniffed like an animal, first in one direction, then in another. Suddenly it veered left across a newly plowed field and disappeared.

Just before I fell asleep, it was not Harrison or the girl I was thinking about but myself. I was walking into a gallery on the rue Jacob with a portfolio of my drawings. And before she had seen half a dozen of them, the directress was murmuring, "It is not impossible, Madame, that we can arrange an exhibition."

Three weeks later in the early afternoon Alice walks down the rue Alberic Magnard and finds an empty chair in pale sunlight near an entrance to the Jardin du Ranelagh. Nurses walk by holding the mittened hands of small children and push baby carriages with immaculate lace covers reaching to the chins of sleeping infants. When a swoop of wind twirls around her feet Alice stands up and pulls her coat collar tighter.

She sits down in a café on the rue de Passy and opens her sketchbook. She does not unbutton her coat until she has several sips of cognac. Presently, unlike the other well-dressed pedestrians hurrying against the cold, a middle-aged man in a cashmere overcoat walks by as though it were a summer evening and he had hours to squander. For a moment Alice catches his eye. She watches him as he retreats slowly, and when he turns around and starts back, she picks up her drawing pad and begins sketching the profile of the waiter standing near the entrance to the café.

The man comes in and sits at a table next to hers. He removes his gray suede gloves and orders a *café filtre*. Presently he leans forward. "May I see, Madame?"

Alice turns the sketch toward him. The man glances at the waiter.

"You have talent. You are English?"

"American."

"You're married?"

"Recently divorced."

"Me too. Was it difficult?"

"Not really. We simply developed different interests. We parted friends. And you?"

"Hell, Madame. I crawled through hell."

The man gestures toward the empty chair at her table. "May I join you? My name is Jean-Claude Mercier."

It is dark when Alice gets into a taxi in Passy and gives the address of John's studio. Madame Vivien is in the courtyard.

"Monsieur isn't back yet from London."

"Oh?" Alice pauses. "Did he say when he would be?"

"He wasn't sure. Madame didn't know he had gone?"

"He probably tried to reach me, but I've been out a lot, all over Paris doing sketches."

Alice opens her pocketbook and holds up some keys. "Monsieur Botsford told me to use the studio anytime I wanted."

"So Madame is an artist?"

"I'm working at it."

Madame Vivien looks directly at Alice. "Tell me. Does Madame like Monsieur's paintings?"

"They're interesting."

Madame Vivien hunches her shoulders. "Me. I know nothing about such things."

Alice unlocks the studio, finds the light switch. She walks to an easel and picks up a comic drawing of her face. She smiles and puts it back on the easel. In the small space between the bathroom and kitchen, she stares at the portrait of John's mother, then runs her fingers along one of Shiva's arms. She leans over and feels the dirt in a pot of ferns at the god's feet. In the kitchen she lifts a watering can from its hook.

Later Alice pulls out the top drawer of the desk and sees a large manila envelope. She starts to close the drawer then hesitates. A minute later she opens the envelope and lifts out a sheaf of newspaper clippings.

*

So we both have our private nightmares, spawned in child-hood, John and I, and his perhaps more horrendous than mine. I at least was not witness, though I have lived the scene a thousand times. I did not see the beach grass stirring or the waves restless under the threatening sky. I did not hear the shot. I was at Faith Higginson's birthday party. Nor did my mother. She was most likely off with some lover. It was Sidney who ran down to the beach and found my father. But John? He must have been awakened by the angry voices, rushed to his mother's bedroom and opened the door the moment his father reached for her throat. Then followed the father's attempted suicide that ended in paralysis, a trial, the surprise acquittal because of a technicality. And later the move to France.

I understand better now John's evasions. For I too have imagined changes in my childhood and adult life. For some of us those fantasies are necessary.

John and Harrison both in London, one to escape, the other to find me! How strange. Does John really think it possible in that city of six million? I am flattered. Perhaps he has walked by Harrison and the girl in Green Park or passed them in a taxi on the Strand. I see the three of them side by side fingering scarves at the Scotch House. They might sit only a few feet apart on the upper deck of a bus going along King's Road. John looks down scanning the pedestrians, hoping he will see me. Does he notice when Harrison stands to get off with the girl at Sloane Square, how he has to bend over to keep from hitting his head?

John might be back at any moment. But I shall wait several days before calling him. I hope Harrison stays away longer. These hours of uninterrupted work sketching faces in all parts of Paris until my arms and eyes ache! I can now envision a different kind of life. Yesterday in Passy the hour of lovemaking in Jean Claude's apartment liberated me in a way I desperately needed.

A nice man. He wanted my telephone number. I refused. He begged me to take his. Perhaps I'll call him sometime. At any rate he was grateful. I hope my gratitude will last as long as the image I now carry of his nose and its several protruding hairs. Already in my imagination they have grown longer and thicker.

Alice looks out at the sky. She puts on a raincoat, stuffs an umbrella, sketchbook and *Paris par Arrondissement* into a canvas bag. She has gone only a few steps along the sidewalk when she turns around and looks toward the workers' bar. John waves and crosses the street.

"My God! How on earth . . . ?"

"I was stupid not to have thought of it sooner."

He had gone down the list of advertising firms in Paris. The second one he called informed him that the Reynolds' address and phone number were unlisted. Then he called the New York office, hoping she had failed to alert them.

"And I had. I'm not known for efficiency. What would a psychiatrist say?"

"That you wanted to be found. Is your husband back?"

"Not yet. But I don't feel as sorry for myself as I did. I've been working like mad for days. Madame Vivien said you were in London."

"I was. I just got back last night. My father isn't well."

"I'm sorry. I hope he's better."

"Not really. He has a heart condition. And did you go?"

"Only for a few days. London's for playwrights, Paris for painters. After all, it was you who put a drawing pad in my hands."

"And wasn't it a good idea?"

"I don't know. I'm having fun. Each day I go to a different part of the city and sketch faces. Actually I rolled up several of my efforts and put them in a closet in your studio. Would you like to see them?"

"You were on your way somewhere?"

"That can wait."

Madame Vivien is standing in the doorway. She stares at Alice and John. In the elevator Alice lowers her voice. "That woman is terrifying. She makes me feel guilty when I have nothing to feel guilty about."

The drawings are propped against the walls in the living room. John stops in front of some, picks up others.

"They're fantastic!"

"You think so?"

"I know a couple of people who own galleries. We must get busy."

"Don't exaggerate. This may be it, all I'll ever do. I'm having trouble now, some kind of block. It began several days ago. That's why I went to your studio. I thought I might get started again."

"And it didn't help?"

Alice shakes her head.

"But I had a good laugh at the crazy sketch you did of me."

"Those sudden fallow periods, they're frightening. I know. I've had them myself. You've been working too hard."

"But I've loved it. I've felt alive in a way I almost never have before."

"You need a change. Because of London I didn't get to the château. I was thinking of maybe tomorrow for a few days. Why don't you come?"

Alice does not answer immediately.

"May I think about it? If I let you know this evening, say around six?"

John nods.

"I'll call you at the studio?"

"Yes, I'll be there. But you will have dinner with me, won't you? No matter what?"

This morning when John called to me, I was surprised how glad I was to see him.

I hate my dissembling. It is not true that I am having difficulty. Far from it. I feel myself a small river gathering strength and without the possibility of sinking back to dry and dusty bed. The two drawings John liked best I did yesterday in a café at the place de Clichy. A young woman sitting near me. She was obviously a prostitute. But I felt I had to justify, even if it meant lying, my going to his studio after not using it at all during these past three weeks.

And I felt guilty when he tried to comfort me. As if I know nothing of the agony that comes with the sudden inability to create. I hope the girl is allowing Harrison to work. Perhaps being away from me will liberate him just as his absence has helped turn my life around.

Why are emotions so seldom pure? Disappointment tempered with relief. Joy tinged with sadness. How satisfying this total immersion in work. And yet after days of hearing nothing from Harrison and not seeing John, I began to feel lonely. I called John's studio several times. Then when Madame Vivien told me that John was in London I was disappointed but also relieved that he had not pushed me from his life as I had him. When I failed to telephone he must have decided that I had in fact gone to England and followed hoping to find me.

I went to the studio because I wanted to look at those portraits without John's observing me. I wanted to find them less frightening. I hoped the terror in their expressions, the agony I felt on first seeing them, was not there. But the easels were empty except for one. On it was a sketch of myself drawing, my features exaggerated in happy fashion. And in the corner was scribbled, "Rendering of a young artist by a young artist."

If the portrait of John's mother is in no way idealized, she was devastatingly beautiful. The thick dark hair, the eyes and long neck. Looking at the painting one feels that even the slightest movement of her body, the simplest gesture, would have been graceful. Just as one is sure her voice was low, and behind each soft and lilting phrase a playful irony seductive in its hint of life's possibilities. Her name was not Alice as John claimed. It was Pierra. I found this out from the newspaper clippings.

I was surprised the ferns around Shiva's feet were so dry. John must have left for London in such a hurry he forgot to ask Madame Vivien to water them.

Alice takes a taxi to the rue St.-Honoré. In one shop she finds boots and a pocketbook to match, in another, an Irish sweater with a hood. She buys two nightgowns, two silk blouses, an orange scarf, and gloves. She returns to the apartment and lays the things out on the bed. In the bathroom she looks across the courtyard. The young woman is on a sofa in the living room, leaning forward, and the baby is crawling slowly toward her.

A little after four Alice takes a taxi to John's apartment. Madame Vivien is nowhere in sight. The love duet from *Tristan and Isolde* is on full blast. Alice rings several times, then lifts a key from her pocketbook.

Water is running in the bathroom. Alice goes to the desk where the sketch John drew of her is lying by a new copy of William Faulkner's novel *The Sound and the Fury*. A sales slip from W. H. Smith, rue de Rivoli, is inserted at page twenty-three.

Alice gently closes the door to John's apartment. She almost bumps into Madame Vivien at the entrance to the building. The concierge is carrying a string bag in each hand. A loaf of bread protrudes from one, a bunch of leeks from the other. Madame Vivien greets her. "It is nice to have Monsieur back, isn't it?"

Alice walks in the general direction of her apartment. On the rue de Sèvres she goes into a small café and orders a coffee. The two other customers have left when she takes a franc from her purse, flips it in her cupped hands and lays it gently on the table.

"It came out the right way, didn't it, Madame?"

Alice glances up. The man behind the bar is drying a glass.

"I suppose so, but how did you know?"

"You were smiling."

"Was I?"

The summer my father and I were in London and Paris we were more often than not with one or another of his friends, but when he took me to the Loire country we were by ourselves for five days. As a child I had fantasies of living in a world of castles, of knights and rescues. So what excitement my first glimpse of Chaumont! I peopled the towers with maidens, their skin soft as lilies, and at Chambord I walked among the ladies of the court waiting to welcome François Premier back from the royal hunt.

Somewhere in the Long Island mansion if my mother has not thrown them away, are movies witness to those five days. I have not seen my mother since nor have I ever returned to that house. I was in a hurry, the afternoon I eloped, and forgot about the films or I would have taken them with me. In one of the movies I am skipping down the long allée under the thick arch of trees leading to Chenonceaux. At Ussé, near the round pool, I stand watching a peacock unfurl its tail. My father and I are together in the film at Azay-le-Rideau. It was taken by a young French woman named Louison. I was sure she was a reincarnated princess. We went through the château together and when the tour was over she offered to film us. We walk slowly, my father and I, over the Indre, the green of deep summer all around us, and we stop halfway across the bridge to look at the château's reflection in the water. I ask if I may invite Louison to lunch. But her fiancé is waiting in a café outside the grounds. They're off on his motorcycle to visit a cousin in the country.

I did not know then the truth about François Premier, that he was arrogant and mean, vengeful and dishonest. I did not know how different he was from my father until I wrote a paper on the French king when I was a freshman at Bennington. In the intervening years they had become linked in my mind. At Chambord, when the guide pointed to a window and my father translated, I took the legend as truth and saw the unhappy king alone in his bedchamber looking out at heavy rain. The beloved Duchess d'Étampes had been unfaithful again. Because of the storm it would be impossible for him to seek solace in hunting, to temper his agony even for a few hours in the excitement of the chase. In despair he grabs a diamond and carves on the windowpane, "Women are fickle and those trusting in them are fools." In time my father's tragedy seemed to echo the king's.

And at nine I could hardly be aware of Touraine's full history, and its tradition of chastity, for instance, besieged by fleshly lust. For me it was a fairyland of soft skies and green countryside where the Loire moved along gently. Sometimes we would stop and look for a moment at one of the small islands in the river where willows dipped into the water and the silver leaves of poplars stirred faintly like the sequins on the gowns of dancers.

And we stopped at caves for my father to sample wines. It was at one of those that I tasted Vouvray for the first time.

One day we had a picnic in an orchard where the gnarled trees were heavy with apples. I especially remember that night. During intermission at a concert in the theater at Tours, a young woman had an epileptic fit. I did not know what was happening. She sank to the floor and began to writhe. Her skirt became bunched above her waist, revealing pink underwear and a garter belt. She was like a corpse, exposed, bereft of all dignity.

I remember, too, the flowers. The columbines, delphinium, the hollyhocks and huge dahlias. And roses were everywhere, climbing above stone doorways and along ancient walls. And there was a black swan. It glided on the moat of a small château we happened upon. The château was on a back road and privately owned.

This morning when John invited me to go to the Loire country, I was evasive. I was not sure I wanted new images mingled with old or certain memories violated.

Alice glances at her watch then looks down through the falling rain to the street where rivulets rush toward underground drains. In the bedroom she eyes herself in the full-length mirror, reties the new scarf loosely around her neck. She goes back to the living room window and shortly after in the entrance hall picks up a suitcase.

John is standing by the elevator when she reaches the ground floor. "I was coming to fetch you."

"I wasn't sure you'd be able to park."

"Pure luck. Someone pulled out just as I turned the corner. Here. Let me take that."

"Thanks. I'll try Madame Germaine again. She wasn't in earlier. I thought I should tell her when I'll be back."

"And when will you?"

Alice looks surprised. "Three days. Isn't that what I'm invited for?"

In a corner by the entrance John picks up a large umbrella. He steps out onto the inundated sidewalk and opens the umbrella.

"My God! I never saw anything so huge."

"I had it made to order. It's great for knocking Frenchmen out of the way."

They are driving toward the outskirts of Paris. The car's windshield wipers clear arcs of visibility while its tires spin water outward with a hissing sound. All along the avenues the cafés are brightly lit against the dark day but the faces of their midmorning customers are blurred behind the walls of steamy glass.

"Are you warm enough?"

"I'm fine."

"What damnable weather. I called the Auto Club. It's raining all over Europe and not much hope for a change tomorrow."

"I love rain. Anyway, what difference does it make?"

"For walking."

"What's to stop us? Especially with that circus tent of an umbrella."

For a few minutes they ride in silence.

"You might want to stay longer. You may find you can work. There are empty rooms."

"What about supplies?"

"I have some at the château and there's a good store in Tours." John pauses. "I hope you'll at least consider the models I can line up even though they aren't Parisian faces. Émile, for instance. Old Snaggletooth. Wait until you see his mouth."

"Fangs?"

"Practically."

"You recommended I take a vacation."

"That's true. But you might get bored."

"Who's Émile?"

"He tries to keep the place together. But it's a losing battle."

"How long have you had the château?"

"For centuries. My mother's family."

"Where does your mother live?"

"She's dead. An infection from a miscarriage. She and my father were traveling in a remote part of Peru. They didn't get back to Lima in time."

"How awful."

"Would you like some music?" John turns on the radio, twists the dial.

"Vivaldi?" she asks. "How appropriate. Whenever I hear this I think of some king like François Premier riding back from the chase. Trumpets, banners, plumes, and blood dripping from the still warm stag."

"Is François Premier a favorite of yours?"

"Not particularly."

"In Paris I have a sword and according to family legend he gave it to one of my ancestors for some service rendered."

Again it was a strange feeling to be riding in a 1930 Packard roadster, a car so familiar with its handsome grille and headlights, its elegant wheels and dashboard, eerie to look at the driver and see a profile not my father's.

John and I were pushing through rain with fields on either side blurred to a narrow gray horizon. I was mulling over the fact that he had lied about his mother's death and wondering when, if ever, he would admit the truth. We reached a stretch of straight and empty road between rows of bare trees and my dream came back. I started to mention it but instead I told him

I looked forward to sitting in front of an open fire and listening to the rain. I was sure there were fireplaces in the château.

"One in every room, though some of the rooms are shut off."

I wondered if there was a moat.

"A small one. It isn't impressive."

We reached Blois in time for a late lunch. The river was rising but the rain had let up somewhat and there was a fringe of light at the bottom of the dark sky. In the ladies' room I looked at myself. I was pleased with the new scarf. The swirls of orange and pink went well with my complexion. Already Paris seemed far away.

John was not at the table when I returned. He was telephoning Émile to say we would be there in time for dinner.

I asked if on arrival we'd find a wild boar browning on a spit.

"It's possible."

My mentioning a wild boar reminded John of one of the few things he claims he remembers from his ancient history class. On the days Antony left Cleopatra, the queen would order a lamb or calf, a young pig, whatever, started over a fire every half hour, so that one of them would be perfectly cooked when Antony arrived. At fourteen, John confessed, that seemed to him the epitome of love.

I said I never imagined Cleopatra letting Antony out of her sight or his wanting to be. And then when John suggested it was probably only occasionally for the ecstasy of reunion, I saw Harrison returned from London embracing me in the hall of our Paris apartment, the hall down which the girl had padded silently. But I felt no joy, no twinge of desire. And no regret at feeling nothing. Rather, as in Passy days ago, I sensed that I had pushed open another door on my way to a freedom I never imagined possible or even thought I wanted.

While we were waiting for the first course, John asked me

why I had not come into the studio the afternoon before. Madame Vivien had reported seeing me. I did after all have the key.

It was a chance to confess, to tell John I knew about his mother and father, the murder, a chance to set things straight before our idyll if our days at the château turned out to be that. But I let the chance slip by. I told him I had rung several times. That was the truth. The record blaring? That must have been the reason he had not heard the bell.

"I might have opened the door and found you standing on your head."

"And would that have been so shocking?"

John asked me where I was when I telephoned to say I would go with him.

"In a café on the rue de Sèvres."

And that, too, was the truth.

When we left the restaurant, the rain had begun again. Perhaps it was the steady sound beating down on the car along with too much wine at lunch that made me wish I was already at the château and in bed with John. In spite of the heavy rain he began to drive faster and I wondered if he were wishing the same thing. Why is it we spend large portions of our lives with our bodies in one place while in our thoughts we are somewhere else?

Across the Loire the tower of Amboise rose in the wet air. We would visit it, John said, on our way back to Paris and pay homage to Leonardo if not to one of John's ancestors who took part at Amboise in the slaughtering of Protestants, in the disembowelments, the quarterings, the lining up on the ramparts of severed and bloody heads. When John commented on the savagery of the sixteenth century, I reminded him that the savagery was pale compared to our own.

It was dark but the rain had almost stopped when, some miles beyond Tours, John turned onto a side road and then onto a smaller one leading almost immediately into a wood. Some half a mile later before reaching the clearing I saw the dim lights of the château through the bare trees. We crossed a narrow drawbridge, drove under a tower into a cobbled courtyard, and drew up beside an old Renault. At the far end there was a dovecote and near it a fig tree.

Even before John cut the motor, I heard the dogs. A pack? Only two. Tristan and Isolde. Mother and son. Gentle as a spring breeze once they knew you. A second later they bounded across the courtyard in front of a man who hobbled toward us, slightly bent, smiling, and whose mouth did seem to contain an amazing set of teeth. Behind him, standing in the doorway, was a short woman with a blotched complexion and puffy eyes. Mathilde, Émile's daughter and, it seemed, an excellent cook.

Alice ties her dressing gown sash and draws back the heavy velvet draperies.

There is a knock on the door.

"Bonjour, Mathilde."

The young woman puts down a tray. "I brought tea and coffee. Monsieur Jean wasn't sure which Madame would want."

"The brioche look wonderful. Did you make them?"

"Of course, Madame."

"The dinner last night was delicious. I hope you enjoy cooking."

Mathilde shrugs her shoulders. She makes no move to leave.

"Does Monsieur Botsford come here often?"

"Not often. But he was just here for two weeks. I was surprised to see him so soon again."

"He was here? These past two weeks? The whole time?"

"Oui, Madame. Then Madame has not known Monsieur Jean for long?"

"No, not long. I suppose when he does come, he brings friends?"

"Hardly ever. He paints and hunts. But this last visit he stayed mostly in his room. Madame is English?"

"No, American."

"Monsieur Jean's father was English. He didn't like it here, but Madame his wife was always arriving with friends. My mother said she had many lovers."

Mathilde gives a faint smile as though somewhat embarrassed by the revelation.

"Did she bring him too, Monsieur Botsford, when he was a child?"

"Sometimes, but never without his nurse, Mademoiselle Allard. And when Monsieur Jean began school in England he was hardly ever here except for a few days during vacations. The last time was at Easter right after the war. He gave me one of his eggs. I still have it. You peep in one end and see rabbits." Mathilde pauses. "Monsieur Jean did not want to go back to England. He hated the school. We made plans for him to hide in the stable. I was to bring food each day, and to prepare for our adventure I began to steal from the kitchen. I hid bread and cheese in my pockets. Once an apple."

Mathilde raises her arms and then lets them fall. "The ideas children have. We were crazy, Monsieur Jean and I."

"So your plan didn't work?"

Mathilde shakes her head and stares at the floor as though reliving the scene.

"The afternoon Monsieur Jean was to leave we went to the loft and I covered him with hay. Mademoiselle called and called. She questioned me. I lied. Madame was furious. Finally she telephoned the Gardes Champêtres. They came with a dog. I was sure Monsieur Jean would be bitten and tell on me."

"And did he?"

"No, Monsieur Jean has always been kind."

"How old were you then?"

"Eight. The same as Monsieur Jean."

Mathilde seems pleased with the fact.

"Did the dog find him?"

"Yes, Madame. It barked at the bottom of the ladder. Monsieur Jean said he had fallen asleep. Madame was so angry she slapped him. For lying, she said. But my mother told me the real reason was because Madame would be late for a party in Paris. My mother did not like her."

"Was this Madame's room?"

"Yes, but my mother said Madame liked the tower room best and spent many of her nights there."

"The tower room?"

Mathilde points toward the door. "At the end of the corridor and up the steps."

"Is Monsieur Botsford awake?"

Mathilde suddenly brings both hands to her mouth. "Oh, I forgot! Monsieur Jean said to tell Madame that he would not be back until late afternoon. He left early this morning to hunt."

As soon as Mathilde leaves, Alice pours herself a sip of coffee and takes a bite of brioche. In the corridor she walks along a strip of red carpet, in places worn thin. She glances at the portraits on the wall, then stops briefly to look at the tapestries on either side of a Venetian mirror. In one of the hangings a dozen dogs surround a doe, their front legs arched above the animal as though held in place by leashes. In the other a unicorn bends to its reflection in a pool.

At the end of the corridor, Alice mounts a circular staircase and opens a door. A huge bed almost fills the room. Its head-board is covered with pleats of pink silk radiating from the bottom like a fan. The covers are flung back as though someone had recently slept there. A white lace nightgown yellowed with age is draped across a boudoir chair. On the small dressing table are several almost empty perfume bottles, a gold hand mirror, black evening gloves and a pair of opera glasses. Alice walks to one of the leaded windows.

Back in the bedroom Alice dresses quickly. She finds Mathilde in the kitchen scraping carrots and Émile oiling a gun. She asks for the phone. A few minutes later she tells them that a relative has suddenly taken sick and she must leave immediately.

"Can you drive me to Tours, Émile? The trains to Paris run often, don't they?"

Somewhere in the distance dogs are barking. Or is it a dream? I struggle as though slowly climbing stairs through darkness or rising at a snail's pace to the surface of some unfathomable sea. I do not know where I am. I open my eyes to an edge of gray light around draperies.

I get up and look out. The falling rain is so fine it makes no visible mark on the moat's black water. At the far end of the courtyard a few leaves still cling to an espaliered rosebush.

The bathroom is immense. It must have been a dressing room or antechamber before the tub with its enameled garlands of leaves and grapes was installed. Two people could easily bathe and not feel cramped. The assemblage of brass pipes looks like a Léger painting.

Last night when Émile left our suitcases in separate rooms, I was surprised. Aristocratic mores or appearances? When dinner was over, we went on a tour of the château. John could have, I thought, waited until today for that. Then, the rain had stopped and the moon was out, he suggested we take a walk. And finally there was the conversation in the kitchen surrounded by Mathilde's copper pots and strings of peppers and onions hanging from beams.

Most of the rooms are closed off. The painted ceiling in the ballroom is peeling, many of the gilt chairs along the wall chipped, and some have broken seats. Even though the chapel was restored in 1910 by John's grandmother, a pious woman it seems, it too has an aura of dust and decay.

There are several salons and a library. I did not see all of the rooms, but the furniture in most of those I saw was covered with bolts of cloth and gave off the chill of years. The room John uses as a studio is empty except for several easels, an easy chair and a table with art supplies.

Later when the walk was nearly over — we had followed for some distance a lane between fields — we stopped to look at the château under the three-quarter moon. Tristan and Isolde were bounding and circling in front of us.

"The view of the countryside from the tower must be spectacular."

"Probably." John's breath was white in the frosty air.

"You mean you've never seen it?"

"I used to go up there occasionally when I was a child. It was empty. Cobwebs and wasps' nests. I don't remember the view."

"It's the kind of tower I imagined Yolande de Goulaine looked out of."

"Who in God's name was she?"

"You don't know? You, with Touraine ancestors?"

I told John her story. Besieged by the English, and about to jump from a tower in her father's château because she preferred death to dishonor, she saw in the distance the glittering lances of her countrymen and her father come to rescue her.

John made some remark, but I don't know what it was. We had reached the moat and suddenly I was years away in time, not with Yolande and her father but with my own and the black swan.

I beg to feed it. My father says I must hurry. He does not approve of trespassing on private property. I grab the end of bread left from our picnic. The swan turns its head, hesitates before gliding toward me. The air is still, the only movement, the swan and a small white butterfly hovering above a clump of wild grass near the moat. Something compels me to look up. In a window at the top of a tower I see a face, a beautiful young woman with dark hair. A second later she is gone. My legs refuse to move, and the space between my father and me seems to grow wider. When at last I reach the car I can hardly breathe. I am terrified, sure if I say anything I will fall under an evil spell, that either the black swan or the face vanished from the window will seek me out. Which is the witch, which the enchanted maiden?

I did not mention my memory to John.

In the kitchen when he opened a special bottle of Cheverny, he asked me why I didn't leave Harrison.

"How can I leave him when to all appearances he has left me?"

"You know what I mean. He'll come back and you'll be waiting."

"Perhaps I love him."

"How can you love someone who treats you like that?"

I broke in. "Is love ever so simple?"

"It can be."

"Doesn't that depend on the persons and the neurotic paraphernalia they drag along? Didn't your mother put up with endless infidelity and choose to ignore it?"

It was I who past midnight made the advances, though it

turned out to be a seduction manqué. John's fumblings, the anguished whispers, and finally his uncontrollable sobs. I lay awake a long time after he left the room.

Why should so much depend on that simple but personal act, whether fantasized or achieved, which spawns more often than not wars both private and public and with which we try to prove something to ourselves or to others? John's tragedy and Harrison's. Which is less fortunate? One unable to drink at the fountain, the other capable but never finding relief for the thirst.

Were those months in Vermont really an idyll?

Almost from the beginning of our marriage, Harrison was restless. Each week in the town where we went for supplies, he would appraise the female faces, glance at them furtively as though he were seeing something sacred and forbidden. I took to walking several steps in front to give him free range without my scrutiny. And often when driving and without slowing down, he would turn to stare at some girl walking along the road. More than once I feared an accident. Harrison is different from my father. But is that not what some of us do in choosing a wife or husband, a lover, flee incestuous longings?

In the kitchen Émile puts the suitcase down. He lifts a jacket off a hook and pulls a woolen cap from one of its pockets. Tristan and Isolde leap up, their tails wagging. Émile raises his hand. "Stay!"

The dogs settle on their haunches, their eyes still on Émile.

"Monsieur Botsford told me they were great hunters. Why didn't he take them with him?" Alice asks.

"Monsieur went to hunt with an English friend, Monsieur Hankins," Émile answers. "He has dogs."

Mathilde stands by the narrow back entrance, wiping her hands on her apron. "Madame should go out the front door."

"No, it's bad luck not to leave the way you came in. Haven't you heard that, Mathilde?"

Alice puts out her hand. "Good-bye. Be sure to tell Monsieur Botsford I left because I didn't want him to feel he had to drive me back to Paris when he had counted on staying here several more days."

Émile opens the back door to the Renault.

"May I sit in front with you?"

Émile looks embarrassed. His lips move nervously over his protruding teeth. "Madame will be more comfortable here. In front there are drafts."

"I like fresh air."

Mathilde waves from the narrow doorway.

They have crossed the moat and are entering the woods.

"Émile, were you by chance at the château in July nineteen thirty-nine?"

"Yes, Madame. I had already been working here for five years before the war broke out."

"Was there a black swan?"

Émile raises his hand and lets it fall back on the steering wheel.

"There was! There was! But how I wish there hadn't been. It belonged to Madame. She adored it. A German officer killed it."

"Germans were in the château during the Occupation?"

"Happily, no, Madame. Only for a few hours, two days before the surrender. They were looking for French officers they claimed were hiding. But it was not so. Only me and my wife and daughter. I wanted to kill him, the last German to leave, the one who drew the pistol. But I feared for my wife and child. Madame adored the swan. La Dame Noire, she called it. But she never knew the truth. Thank God for that. By then she was safe in England. Her husband was British."

"I know."

"The last thing she did before she left was to break bread and feed it piece by piece to La Dame Noire. Her husband and Monsieur Jean and Mademoiselle were already in the car with Jacques, the chauffeur. I can hear him now, her husband, calling, 'Hurry up! Hurry up!' He was not a man of patience. Madame embraced me. I do not think her husband liked that. After the war he was seldom here. I was not sorry."

"Why did the German shoot the swan?"

"For no reason. Meanness. She was swimming toward him when he fired. But the bullet grazed only part of her head. Around and around she spun. '*Voilà la France!*' he shouted. 'She's dying!' That's what he said, the swine. I begged him to kill her. 'She's suffering!' 'Waste a bullet? *Nein*.' So it was I who had to do it. It was I who ran to the kitchen for my gun."

"How awful, Émile. How awful for you."

"And when Madame came back after the war, the first thing she asked about was La Dame Noire. When I told her that one morning I found the swan dead, she turned pale. 'I will die young, Émile. I know it. I will die young.' And she was right. But how did Madame know about La Dame Noire?"

At Tours Émile puts the suitcase just inside the station. "Wait here, Madame. I will park. There is time and then I will put Madame on the train."

Alice picks up the suitcase. "Thank you, no, Émile. It's not heavy. I can easily manage."

"Please, Madame. Monsieur would want me to."

In Paris when Alice gets out of the taxi, Madame Germaine is standing in the doorway to the apartment building. "Monsieur just arrived."

"My husband?"

"Yes, Madame. Monsieur has been ill. But no doubt Madame knows that."

"Ill?"

"Yes, Madame. Ill."

"I can't believe it."

How strange life is. Three weeks ago in the château when I telephoned the Paris apartment and pretended to speak with someone, had I called a little later Harrison would have answered and I would not have been involved in another falsehood.

It was obvious that John left the château that morning, who knows whether he went hunting or not, to give me a chance to go back to Paris, hoping, I'm sure, that I would. Since then I have tried to write him, but I can't seem to get the proper words onto paper. I think if I could talk with him I might be able to express my feelings, my gratitude. After all, he is responsible for my "new life." Even though I feel closer to John now than I did before, I do not want him yet to know where I am living. Soon I'll telephone and ask if we might meet in his studio or in some neutral place. I think I can persuade him to get help. If I confess my own deceptions and my knowledge of his? For days I have been carrying on silent dialogues, taking his part as well as my own. And yet in those imagined rendezvous or confrontations, if they be that, are we always able to follow the projected scripts? For aren't others as unpredictable as ourselves?

It turned out that Harrison, soon after arriving in London, came down with hepatitis and spent two weeks in a hospital. I stayed with him about ten days in our Paris apartment, sleeping on the sofa, until he felt strong enough to go to Nice for warm weather and again with hopes of getting back to the novel. I did not mention the girl, nor when I arrived with the suitcase did

Harrison ask me where I had been. He has never pried. The closest he ever came was the afternoon in Vermont when he told me he wasn't really a writer, that he had applied for a job with an advertising firm. Then he stared at the photograph on the living room table. It is the only family picture I have. My father, his polo hat still on, is smiling. He's happy. His team has just won. He has his hands under my elbows as though he were about to lift me up. I am leaning against him, horses and people in the background. My mother is standing a little apart. She is smiling, too, but not at us. At Brandon Epes, who is taking the snapshot. Probably her lover at the time.

Harrison picked up the photograph in its silver frame. "How old were you?"

"Six," I answered.

"It was already evident whom you would resemble most."

"Yes, but I have my father's eyes."

And then as though talking to himself, "Did you really grow up with all that money?"

My grandfather left a trust, not as large as you might expect, but adequate for me to live reasonably well. Harrison and I could have managed with it. But when I suggested we stay in Vermont, that he should not give up so easily, he refused the offer. Harrison has pride.

Harrison seemed sincere when he said he thought my drawings were impressive. He asked me to go to Nice, but for the present I am staying in Paris. I think I am free at last of the legacy my father imposed on me, that stubborn and romantic belief in fidelity. In my new apartment across the hall there is an architect. We have nodded to each other on the stairs and this morning we had a conversation while standing in line at the bakery. It is not hard to imagine him my lover.

From my apartment I look down on the marché de Buci with

its carts and stalls of fruit and flowers, fish and cheeses, and the waves of Parisians and strangers come to buy. As for art galleries, I need never go beyond my own street and the rue Jacob for enough to satisfy me. And the Luxembourg is nearby. I can imagine an almost daily pilgrimage to seek its sun or shade, its open spaces. The English woman I saw there, is it so inconceivable that we might become friends?

This part of the street even has its own clochard. I think of him as Georges. Georges wears a yellow wool cap and an orange scarf, both faded and moth-eaten. He is always alone but he is not without acquaintances. The other afternoon while I was sketching him from my living room window, a young man, his hair matted, his face encrusted with the dirt of days and nights, threw up his arms when he saw Georges and then leaned over and embraced him. Slowly Georges lifted an almost empty bottle from under his coat and the young man finished it off. I was moved by Georges's generosity. This morning when I passed him he was spruced up slightly. He was leaning against the stone bench where the rue Jacob meets the rue de Seine, where the pigeons fluff their feathers in the fountain, then sun themselves on the small grassy mound. Georges was holding a newspaper, his eyes bleary, scanning the headlines. What he finds there will hardly persuade him to give up the life he has chosen.

I sit in this garden now beneath gray sky and under bare chestnut trees. Their branches, exposed and lacking in ambiguity, have a cruel beauty. No limb or twisted twig is hidden by new spring or dusty summer green or bright autumnal shade, and I am forced to muse on death as well as lust and love. Across from me my nameless friends, my two clochard companions, sit side by side. No April gnat demands they raise a hand or sudden shaft floats down to rest on their unwashed hair. Do they, eyes closed against the chill, ponder their final fate?

And I? I glance toward oblivion too, for I am dying in this month of nearly spent November. No letter from London, no word from Rome. No call from Cairo or nearer by. Is he with someone else? Until I hear my lover's voice again, until I see his measured hand across a page, I'll breathe a living death. And if silence still follows silence? Then I'll but breathe and walk that death until death itself forbids me breathe and walk again.

The news today brings a paradigm of tragic horror. Here in this city a woman, an American, was found decapitated, a ruff of white violets around her neck, and near the body lay an ancient sword. And in the same apartment an Englishman, drugged, lay drowned in his sunken bathtub. The police have not yet released their names.

But is not this what love exacts, what love in the end demands? Sacrifice. Sorrow. Despair. Except for a minuscule number, those few destined to unite in love.

I must leave this garden now. My gentle husband, though some might not think him so, is waiting. His afternoon rest is almost over and he will soon be lifted from bed to chair and the board put between us. Then, grateful for a faithful wife, he will smile at me across our game of chess. He can smile because love is blind. But not as blind as death. For who loves when the heart is still? Who lusts when the flesh is cold?

III

And Silently Steal Away

FROM GRAY SKIES and damp streets, from western gales
and promise of snow, I left for that timeless country where
camels move silently under full moon across the desert's
sands. I left for those clean white cities reflecting the sun, for
miles of wide beaches where golden fish leap in aqua bays and
the pink heron pauses in the shadow of a sacred mountain. I left
for green fields, for lambs and strong young goats frolicking to
shepherd's tune, for strings of succulent tangerines hanging like
orange beads in the market squares.

In the cool and shaded medina I will bite into odorous figs
and watch workmen, cross-legged, their heads in turbans, weave
rugs of brilliant colors. I shall marvel at artisans beating trays of
silver, hammering rare necklaces of spun gold, and perhaps I
will buy a small round box encircled with precious jewels. I shall
seek sweet coconut and long evenings of sensuous song and,
dreaming in the ruins of an ancient and forgotten town, I may
trace with my finger intricate mosaics of a floating Venus and
five unicorns. I shall refresh myself at oases. I will lean against a
young palm and watch veiled and perfumed girls come at sunset
to fill their thin vases. I will see them bend in the soft evening air.

I left behind those dark clouds churning storm and came to
this land where the people, I thought, needed me.

There was only one taxi waiting and so small that I had to lean way over to climb in. Through rips in the cloth roof I could see dried leaves hanging from dying palms and there were so many holes in the ruined floor that I was forced to hold up my legs. As we bumped along swirls of dust rose from the road, making me cough. It settled in a fine powdery ridge on the greasy collar of the driver's shirt. A half mile from the hotel the engine sputtered and died. The chauffeur said nothing. He leaned against the inside of the dilapidated door and fell asleep. I was not able to wake him, but I left what I thought fair in coins on the floor by his shoeless feet. I left them among discolored peanut shells and a gob of axle grease flecked with the hairs of a goat.

I perspired in the morning heat, though my one suitcase and small typewriter are both light. Of late, I have traveled with only the barest of necessities. The hotel sign was crooked and several of the neon letters missing. There was no doorman, but a porter sat on the floor against the desk with his eyes closed. Frankly I had not expected such a modest establishment. The lobby was extremely small and what had been carelessly thrown down the day before had not been swept up. Cigarette butts of Egyptian tobacco, shriveled tangerine skins, a small handful of soiled and uncarded lamb's wool, several unwanted numbers of "Wireless Guide," last year's calendar with a camel yawning above the missing days of July. Aside from the two desk clerks and the sleeping porter there were no other people except for three ladies, unfortunately in advanced middle age and with sallow complexion, sipping coffee from small cracked cups.

The two clerks smiled as I approached the desk, put down my typewriter and suitcase. "Je suis Monsieur . . ."

And then they smiled again as though trained to retract the lips just so much and no more. Why do they smile? Not at my accent, for I have none. My French is impeccable. I had a private tutor as a child and then a whole year in Paris. They feigned interest in my work. They feigned it, I know. I am not here, mind you, to throw my weight around. But when I asked for the Director and by his full name, they jumped.

The Director is obviously a man of parts, not pulled from some hole in the medina and dressed up in a suit. Monkeys, those other two. Look at their teeth. Those not missing, black. But the Director, I would say, is a man of distinction, although his coat is not of the best cut and his unwashed hair needs styling. Still, his French is not bad. We should have no problems. I explain what I intend to do, what I can do for him and his countrymen. I show him an example of my work and then we bargain. These people are disappointed if you don't haggle. The guidebook recommends it. The verbal exchange creates excitement. And so we bargain about the price of room and meals. The Director is an impressive man but not, I soon discover, of subtle mind. There is a dull cast to his left eye. The right one is more alert. He does not seem to measure the range of my abilities. He offers me a room away from the sea, overlooking an abandoned field with a few blades of sandy grass, some dusty weeds and where a shepherd, a chronic victim of the national lottery, a poor fellow reduced to two ragged sheep, may turn up occasionally to enliven the landscape. I wonder how the Director can expect me to shed the best light on things, render justice to the region's vast possibilities, if I cannot have other views, if I cannot, for instance, look out onto the garden whenever I want. It is essential that I smell the night-blooming flowers and hear the throaty song of the national bird hidden somewhere among those virginal blossoms. Can I write about the effect of foreigners on this *pays* if I am unable to observe the long-legged Scandinavians, the loud and blond fräuleins stride down the path under shady palms to stretch themselves out on the sand? Or watch dainty geishas from Kyoto move shyly past the jasmine bushes and plant their frail parasols by the water's edge? I would also like to take notes as these young ladies mount the ancient camel kept on the beach for renting. The beast's knotty joints are covered with layers and layers of calluses from years of kneeling. Innumerable foreigners have climbed up to ride and for a pittance straddled the undernourished hump.

But finally I stop arguing. Perhaps in the end I will get more work done. The uninteresting shepherd, the two old ewes will be less distracting.

The porter's coat is much too large. The frayed sleeves reach almost to his dirty fingertips. He tries to wrench my typewriter from me. Once upstairs he would disappear with it around some corner and forever. An ill-fitting uniform is a crucial thing to watch for. The next time you travel, take a good look at the customs officers. If their trousers sag, if their jacket sleeves are soiled around the cuffs, if the fabric looks mussed as though sat in for days, tossed through countless humid nights — then be on your guard. Watch for the sleight of hand. I hold tight to my typewriter, follow the porter carrying my suitcase to the room assigned me by the Director.

I quickly learn that I shall not, at least during the day, be lonesome for human sounds. Three or four tiny nubile maids, tan, sweet and soft like the fresh dates one is served here for dessert, fly up and down the corridors together cleaning the rooms. Do they feel there is safety in numbers? That some male guest might take advantage? They chatter from time to time in their headquarters, a windowless cubbyhole next to my room, banging their mops and drawing pails of water. At noon they sit on the floor, giggling, eating from a communal pot, reaching with their fluttering fingers, no cutlery to wash, stuffing the bits of mutton between their wonderful little teeth.

My room is adequate. It is the desk, after all, which counts. I find on close inspection that it slopes, but several sheets of paper properly folded and slipped under the broken leg will take care of that. It has no drawers, but I shall arrange my carbon, pencils, eraser, my pens, my notes on a shelf in the wardrobe. And for a time one can survive a mattress that sags like a hammock, blankets into which are woven twigs, ends of thorn, burrs, small stones, slivers of date pits, fragments of tile. After all, can we hold these people to account? Most of them haven't the habit of beds. Centuries of sleeping on the ground.

The first lunch? I try to forget it. The slice of wild boar, considered a delicacy here, arrived with five bristles sprouting in the meat. But I shall be tolerant. I shall try to help these people. The only other persons in the dining room were the three unattractive women. I cannot determine their nationality. Their skirts are cut from the same dark material.

After lunch I brush my teeth, careful not to swallow any water. I decide to have a further look around. I lock my door, turn the knob several times, then push. But of course all of those young girls can enter my room anytime they please, rummage through my things, lift a pencil, steal a few pieces of paper.

The bar is no more than a hole off the lobby. It has several straight chairs and a barman slouched against one of them. I would hope he could mix simple drinks. After a hard day of writing, after hours of what can be a meticulous search for the *mot juste,* one enjoys diversion, a mild libation in a quiet corner with a charming young lady. The hotel's garden is not large either. But I welcome its intimacy. There is only one bench. The paint is peeling but it will be adequate to sit on in the cool of the morning while I plan my work for the day. I have already developed an affection for the little sparrows busy in the swaying and dusty fronds. I doubt there are hummingbirds among them. How much better these little creatures than exotic birds pretentiously screeching for attention, constantly displaying their plumage. In the past I have seen my share of them.

One small souk is attached to the hotel, just short of the beach. A dim light, low wattage, hardly adequate for enticing people in to buy. The only visible wares, a few faded postcards and some strands of shell beads poorly strung. The man in charge is dozing by the doorway. He opens one eye but only briefly. How does he know I am not a likely customer?

Here the sea is placid. There are no beautiful cliffs, no huge and majestic offshore rocks where wild waves break foaming. But the beach is surprisingly clean. After all the guests have left for the day there must be droves of little boys running back and forth across the sand picking up empty tubes of suntan cream, damp newspapers, Coca-Cola bottles and condoms. Little scavenger beetles scuttling at sunset.

But there are no long-limbed and blond Eves from the north, no flowered parasols sprouting by the sea, only the three *vieilles filles* who were at lunch. They lie side by side on large orange towels exposing their veined and gray thighs to the sun. The camel just beyond them, legs tucked under, proud head up turkey fashion, masticating, has more to offer than they. Its keeper, knees against his soiled rattan, leans snoozing on his charge. My shadow falls across his stubbled face and he slowly opens his right eye, then closes it sullenly. And how does this rascal know whether or not I was about to bargain for a short ride?

I amble at a safe distance around the beast's stained buttocks, past the dusty and tangled tuft resting like a woman's hairpiece on its rump. I have wondered if close inspection reveals where these animals store their water. Lifting the faded blankets folded over dirty rags, collected from God knows where, reveals no anatomical oddity except the hump. I drop the padding, look at the placid, unperturbed visage. I do not, frankly, like the way this camel chews, first on one side, then on the other. Over and over back and forth, never on the same side twice in succession. I do not like the predictability. I watch the jaws carefully. First one side, then the other. No concept that it might be done another way, that he is wasting energy. Have I unwittingly stumbled upon a symbol for this country?

I decide to test the animal's intelligence. Maybe it has the capacity to learn. I glance around and find a length of bamboo or perhaps it is a strip of sugarcane sucked dry by rotting teeth. I squat in front of this desert beast like a local nomad. Just after he munches on the left side I tap under that jaw, but he does not as I had hoped repeat the mastication. He shifts whatever he is chewing, if anything, to the right, then back to the left, as though my action were no more than the faint brush of a sand fly's wing. Each time he comes down with his left jaw I tap, increasing the strength of my blows. Water on a duck's back. Sand in a camel's eye. But I do not give up easily. Perhaps the right jaw is more sensitive. I switch my tappings. No progress! Suddenly the imbecile comes to life. He takes notice and opens those thin lips wide. He clamps down hard. Camel teeth. Me squatting, holding on, not giving an inch. He stubborn. *Têtu.* Then suddenly he moves again. He lifts me up, swings me around and around in the air as though I were nothing more than a child's circus toy, one of those little plastic birds whirling at the end of a thin stick. Sand, sea, sky and sun become one dizzying circle. Then the lips open and down I go, flung some distance from his slobbering mouth. I sit up, glance around. The three aged women have risen on their flabby elbows and are laughing.

I pretend not to see. The arrogant owner hasn't opened his beady eyes once, not since he was so sure about my inability to pay for a ride. I brush the sand from my trousers. Now insult to insult. The noise is indescribable. Have you ever heard a camel protest and with full force, blasting in your direction? At last the keeper opens an eye. The left one. He, too, lacks imagination!

Dinner was hardly an improvement over lunch. No bristles, but what the garçon brought was stringy and dry. Perhaps the chef never studied abroad. I may hint at this in what I write. Also the maître d'hôtel is sullen. I do not, apparently, exist for him. Tonight as I left the dining room, I deliberately stopped and stood in front of his huge wooden stand. He could not have failed to know I was there. I cleared my throat three times. He continued to pretend occupation with the reservation book.

I walk up and down in front of the hotel, hoping exercise will aid digestion. The garden in front is choked with weeds. Tomorrow I shall call from my window to the shepherd, suggest he bring his two miserable animals here. They will be able to feast for days, not have to scrounge in the rocky field for almost nonexistent blades of green. Why can't these people see the obvious? There are deep and dangerous ruts in the driveway. One must be on guard against the twisted ankle, the broken leg. Can you imagine suing this city for negligence? It could become a lifetime occupation.

I decide before going to bed to treat myself to one of the local brandies. I sit down in the bar. The garçon is leaning against the wall picking his teeth. I clap my hands. I whistle. Lost in his dull fantasies he continues to probe the recesses of his gums. I find a half-washed glass and pour myself a drink. It has the consistency of thick sweet syrup, but it burns my throat and the taste is bitter.

I had not seen them when I came in. I thought I was alone with the surly garçon, but they must have been in the corner all the time. As all three lean forward to suck on their tepid drinks, gold earrings in the pale light rattle against their painted cheeks. I leave the brandy unfinished and a coin on the counter.

The corridor of my floor is empty. The little maids have flown to their dark rooms in the medina. The door of their cubbyhole is closed and behind it silence. I turn my key. A rustling, a scuttling. I find the switch. Even in the feeble light I can see them, one extraordinarily large. Streaks of black. A small army vanishing into the secret hole around the pipe which extends from floor to ceiling. I come down with my shoe on the straggler, the large one, but he wriggles free. Courageous devil.

My body sinks into the soft mattress that curves like the new moon. Not the best arrangements for making love. I think of the little maids. Somewhere in the silent city they are sleeping, laughing perhaps in their dreams. Or are they? Are they restless on their thin pallets? Do they hear the donkeys breathing just outside the door, smell the goats tethered in the tiny courtyard? If I could choose it would be the one with the tooth. Winning the way she grins, opening her mouth wide, proud of that shiny gold. Her name, I'll wager, is Fatma. Graceful. A fawn. I have watched her. She moves her mop like a dancer gliding with an armful of flowers. Yes, it is Fatma I would choose.

I woke up suddenly, suspended in a black hole of Calcutta. Not so much as a sliver of moonlight came through the rips in the ragged curtains. I was being watched. I sat up, groped for the bedside lamp and in the pallid light of the forty-watt bulb saw him, the big one, squatting on my pillow as though he owned it, not two inches from where my head had been. He waves his long feelers, first one, then the other, circling them

above his head, unfurling them, a full ten inches in front of
him. Casting like those natives who make a single effort for the
day, hurl their lines into the sea, push the pole deep into the
sand and then retreat to sleep in the tall beach grass, not caring
whether they catch anything or not. But this fellow was different. He cared. Several times he waved his feelers in the air,
thrust them out in unison, wide apart like arms, then let the
ends touch as though he were shaking hands with himself. His
purpose was painfully clear. I picked up the pillow, flung him
into the air. He'd spatter. *La fin!* But not at all. That beetle is
obviously not the common pariplaneta you and I are used to
but of a different breed. He floated down slowly as though attached to a tiny parachute. When he touched the floor, he rose
on his hind legs, waved one of his tentacles in friendly fashion
and walked with great dignity to the no longer secret but now
quite visible hole encircling the pipe.

The room has grown smaller. When I went to sleep the foot
of the curving bed was not so close to the opposite wall. Or was
it? Perhaps in the excitement of reaching my destination, perhaps in the joy of knowing that during the day the little brown
girls would be hovering near me, perhaps in the levity of the moment, my quarters had on my arrival seemed larger. I stand in
the gray light, darkness is already giving way to dawn, and ponder my enemy. I do not think he will return in the next hours,
though I am sure he is not far away. I imagine him in some air-
less spot between floors, practicing, folding, unfolding the tentacles. But I will exterminate the brute! I will exterminate him and
all his relatives. I dress and in the freshness of early morning outline my day's work.

By one o'clock I had made so much progress that I decided to
take the afternoon off and have a look around the back alleys of

the old city. All morning my keys had clattered. Three whole pages, single-spaced: the annual rainfall and mineral deposits, average tonnage handled by the port, the number of dates consumed in several localities, sales figures for camels traded in four interior villages, the amount of wool sheared from black sheep, the intensity of summer sunsets. Little Fatma and her friends did knock on the door midmorning, but I waved them away, much as I would have liked to see their slender legs and tiny buttocks glide about the room, dusting, mopping, bending to shake and smooth the bedcovers.

After lunch I walk along the dusty road to town. The shepherd and his pathetic ewes are nowhere to be seen. I am glad my trousers are a bit outmoded, my nylon shirt faded and my shoes what some might speak of as worn. Not once during the afternoon do any of the little boys or the old street vendors approach me. I do not waste money on their stale slices of coconut or dusty dates, or on cheap rugs.

From one end of the medina to the other I inquire for cockroach poison. I push by goats and dying sheep and wailing children. I slip on rotting fish and stumble over the flyspecked and uncooked head of a suckling pig. Fat, oily stomachs shove me to one side and crusty elbows of greedy old women poke my ribs like thin sticks. Each souk owner to a man denies there are such vermin in this region. A wizened fellow, wearing a once white turban wound carelessly above crossed eyes, waves his bony finger in my face. "*Nous n'avons pas des bêtes comme ça, Monsieur. Nous n'en avons pas!*"

Another in striped bloomers, a portion of scaly leg showing above ankle sock too small and tennis shoe, is adamant. "We have never had them, Monsieur. I understand they thrive in other parts of the world. But here? *Jamais.*"

Retreating I vow to bring each of the gentlemen a sample of what they so confidently deny, even if it means borrowing Fatma's pail and sitting up all night. I will drown those roaches with boiling water.

Virtue is, they say, sometimes rewarded. Just as the medina gives way to the large square, at a souk on the corner, I see strips of flypaper hanging, black with victims. In no time at all I am negotiating for several rolls. If successful in trapping flying insects, why not on the floor to catch those that crawl?

I spent the rest of the long afternoon and early evening in the post office. It was urgent that I buy a stamp, see for myself a letter to my editor put into responsible hands for mailing. But the guidebook should have warned me. It should advise the traveler to take reading material and sandwiches, something refreshing to drink. For there is no system in the decaying foyer, no order, no concept of straight and well-disciplined queues. You lean over or raise your arm to swat a mosquito, and quick as a flash, turbaned head lowered or veiled face butts past and you are thrust back, back toward those long strands of wooden beads hanging in the doorway.

But at last I reach the counter. I am poised, ready to give my damp coin to the fat man whose buttocks are steaming, whose spreading flesh is draped over the sides of the tiny stool assigned him by the Director of Internal Affairs. His puffy fingers like risen dough tear and rip at the square sheets, the stamps already irrevocably stuck together, one sheet on top of another, the glue having melted and seeped into the improved portrait of that face, the National Leader's. Yes, I almost make it; I almost get the stamp. In that split second before I am suddenly and swiftly propelled backward again by yet another practiced and thrusting head, I see him. I see him for an instant before the damp coin is knocked from my fist, before it is snatched in midair, swallowed by anonymous fingers, my coin disappearing as though it never existed, vanishing as quickly as a gnat into crocodile jaws.

But for a brief moment I see the little dwarf, the smallest postal employee in this part of the world. He is the chauffeur elected by an overwhelming majority, the driver of the city's only mail truck, converted with some difficulty from an ancient Citroën. A Turkish towel obscures not only his undistinguished face but his whole body. It hangs in pleated folds over his tiny head, disguising him, the ghost of a midget prizefighter. As he bends surreptitiously, secretly gropes for the handles of the aged laundry basket into which outgoing mail is tossed, the towel suddenly wriggles free. It drops down, glides between the half-sealed envelopes, past packages of contraband dates, around the small vials of sample oil and dried goatskins, settles at last, hidden, comfortable, coiled at the bottom of the dilapidated hamper. The dwarf, bereft, enraged and frightened, makes no effort to hide his annoyance. The tug-of-war with the towel begins. But before he disappears squealing, before he is pulled down headfirst and suddenly, he heroically flings scores of letters across the counter into the restless crowd. His countrymen, too busy improving their positions, or too preoccupied with consolidating the ones they have, take no notice. The letters fall to the floor, are soon ripped and soiled by careless feet, torn to bits without so much as a readable word left.

And then I see the other one enter, an unobtrusive and insignificant figure. He enters, that is, when he knows that the dwarf lies defeated beneath what remains of the outgoing mail, buried under the broken vials of oil and forbidden dates. This other one moves silently through the hanging beads, searching for suspicious faces. He, too, has disguised himself, wound a camouflaged rag around his head and across his face. The rag? A piece of cloth found in an obscure and crumbling wall of a remote mountain village, put there with faith and twilight prayers in hopes of slowing the moan of a now forgotten sirocco.

This other one moves among the agitated postal customers unobserved. Suddenly he scoops up the disintegrated letters, all of them to the last invisible syllable. He scoops them up lovingly and stuffs the myriad shreds deep in his bosom. In areas, you understand, where the annual income is low, nothing can be wasted. But no one recognizes this man for what he is. Junk dealer manqué. He is a traitor. And the other one, too, the dwarf, now strangled, smothered, struggling with nightmares at the bottom of the abandoned basket. They are working together, these two. They work for us. Our men. I was so informed before I left home. But I shall suggest somewhere in my report that what they are doing is too little and too late.

At last the crowd has thinned, and once more I reach the head of the line. But the fat man has gone. Everything has been taken away. Only a discarded rubber stamp, gathering dust, only it and a faded sign, its letters splashed by warm rains. It advises in nineteen languages that the post office has moved to new headquarters. I turn and start across the silent and empty foyer. My feet sink into sand. I skirt an oasis with several functioning springs. I pass a small band of nomads unfolding their tents. I am afraid I will come upon the bodies of our two friends slashed by scimitars. But not at all. They are gathering reward for work well done. Reclining on cushions under a canopy they bite into dates rolled in marzipan. With the best French wines they wash down couscous and tenderest lamb and baklava made from the purest honey. The feast has been rushed to them by camel train from the capital. Nearby in an olive grove a dancer in gossamer skirt and golden veil, her stomach a burnished apple, waits to perform.

I have not been astute in my judgment. Those letters torn to bits were of no significance. Pieced together they revealed nothing. And that rag? Not abandoned or worthless material. It can fly at any moment, to any part of this territory and in a matter of minutes. These scandalous characters are worse than traitors. I know them now for what they are. Double agents!

As I walk past, the dwarf holds up his little fist. It is sticky with choice honey and crumbs of sweet almonds. He offers it to me for tasting while the other one proffers the vintage dregs of his goblet. A little farther down the road I find it, and no longer shiny. Scorned, discarded. *My* coin!

It was almost dark when I arrived back at the room. Only the faintest tinge of color left in the western sky. I open the door to the wardrobe. My suspicions are confirmed. I left my pens arranged in geometric design. The octagon replaced by a hexagon. I count the sheets of paper and carbon. Fifteen missing. It must have been Fatma. Yes, only she among those little butterflies would have the imagination, the desire and initiative to improve herself. I cannot be angry. I cannot condemn that lovely child. I am, in fact, delighted, and if there is time at the end, if I finish my work before the scheduled day of departure, I shall take her on as a pupil. I shall experiment with this ambitious little girl. I shall see how long it takes her to learn the alphabet and then summarize the results of our hours together, add it as an appendix to the main body of my work.

I look around. Nothing else is missing. Everything is in its place. My toothbrushes, deodorant, bedroom slippers, water glass, nose drops, laxatives. I make a quick decision. Tonight I will not dine at the hotel. I must observe the nightlife in the town as part of my effort to interpret these people to the outside world.

Moreover my strategy of extermination calls for absolute quiet. I carefully unroll the strips of flypaper, distribute them around the room. I tiptoe down the corridor.

I am not here, you understand, for my pleasure. I have, after all, a sweet wife and obedient children. I am here to observe only, talk with the madam, put a few questions to the employees when they are not too busy. I did not want to visit any of those large villas where the girls lay legitimate claim to royal blood. Nor was I interested in one-room hovels in which those offering their services cannot read or write. I purposely asked the driver to take me to one classified as average.

The madam, a marvelous mountain of flesh, once no doubt a practitioner of the art herself, sits with a green parakeet nestled like an emerald brooch in the folds of her shoulder. The bird, who speaks English but only a smattering of French, was left as collateral by an indigent British sailor on his way home from India. The madam is most cooperative. She is a shrewd woman quick to recognize what I might do for the business. I ask the most intimate details; she answers without hesitation. Height and weight. Size of feet. Whether the girls use camels or taxis. The length of veils and on what days they are laundered. The age of the oldest, the youngest. This I found a disturbing statistic. There seems to be no limit at either end of the scale. It does at least say something about the tastes of the men who drift through the ancient door of this establishment, drift like myriad grains of sand driven by desert winds.

From time to time throughout the night and early morning, clients from all over the world appeared at the heavily chained gate. But many of them were turned away. The yen of a businessman from Nagasaki were declared nonnegotiable. Nor did the gentleman from Calcutta qualify. Madam questioned his professed belief in the Prophet. A Peruvian and an Irishman fared no better. Cubans giving away cigars were not admitted. A Chinese delegation with valuable agronomic knowledge and Albanians manufacturing three-star goat cheese got nowhere. Some Russians may have slipped in the back door. Two of the Chinese and an Albanian came back disguised, but in one shake of the lamb's tail both Madam and the parakeet detected their true identity.

"Frauds!" the little bird shrieked, his feathers on end. "*Salauds!*"

And when Madam spat, the unfortunate ones jumped back. They retreated like the wind, and long before the two Chinese had reached the railroad station, the Albanian was at the port on the far side of the city, had booked passage on a freighter and was huddled behind a locked door in the men's room, where he stayed, mute and unfed, until days later when the rocky coast of his homeland came into view.

Around five o'clock in the morning, the little faun came loping down for the free drink of coconut milk. I could not believe my eyes. Fatma! Her dainty feet hardly touching the worn stairs, her tiny mouth moist and smiling, her eyes soft from the night's activities. I turned away, hoping she had not seen me. I did not need to linger. My notes were ample.

Dawn is breaking as I return with my heavy sheaf of papers. I find the two ignorant clerks still asleep, their eyes facing East, their heads resting on the counter like heads on a chopping block. They both wear dark glasses. The Director's door is not yet open.

Early morning light rolls with me down the corridor, and as I open the door slowly, cautiously, I do not hear any rustling, no scuttling at all, only strange music. Faint. Thin. An archaic tune.

I have always been a realist. When the chips are down I can

face facts. I do not have to measure to know what is true. My quarters have shrunk again. The bed now touching opposite walls, is shaped more than ever like a crescent moon and my desk has been sawed into pieces of identical length and stacked neatly by the wardrobe. I look in the bathroom. The toilet? Vanished! Only a dark hole left in the rotting floor, and the basin mirror is cracked and cloudy. It does not reflect even the bare outline of my face. I open my valise and find a neatly folded kaftan, a self-winding turban for those not experienced, an eight-foot scarf to use against desert winds, a tarboosh, a small prayer rug and a book, translated from the original: *How to Select a Well-Rounded Harem.* I fling the volume across the tiny room. It flies, performing arabesques in the air, and lands without a sound, right side up on the casement. I look at the typewriter. The ultimate horror! My alphabet replaced with theirs! And the flypaper has been transformed into a frieze, attached to the edges of the sagging blanket. All my days of research, my reams of writing, my statistics on camels and dates, on minerals and rainfalls, on the average size of a concubine's foot, all my pages have been delicately cut into the shape of minarets and, like those identical and endlessly attached paper dolls, fastened to the walls and hung from the ceiling.

As the sun leaps above the horizon I see him at last, the big one, ensconced on my pillow as on a throne. A Pan. His thin hairy legs, the hind ones, crossed at the ankles, his tendrils curled around a tiny flute. Arranged before him in two lines, swaying to the music, twelve of his young female kin, their tan bellies exposed, writhe, twist, bump on legs more delicate than the thinnest brushstroke. Is it possible that they all wear miniature dark glasses? Does this insolent creature, in fact, as I rush to leave, interrupt his sensuous tune to whisper after me, *"Bon retour, Monsieur, et bon courage"*? The music, insistent, compelling, begins again, winds itself around me like a serpent. I grab my hat and stagger downstairs.

The two concierges continue to sleep, their eyes still to the East, but the Director's door is open. His hair has been shampooed and cut, and his pin-striped suit is elegant. He sits at his desk, sunglasses on, quietly reading a comic book.

I have to know. I cannot leave without knowing. I hurry, a bit out of breath, through the fresh morning. The path is no longer dirt but an intricately patterned walk of flagstones. The souk owner has on a pair of dark glasses too. He is sipping mint tea by the tiled entrance to his shop, where everything is offered from Devonshire cream to pocket computers. Beyond the formal palm garden in which peacocks move with measured step, I find those other two where I left them, the keeper leaning against his immemorial beast. A huge beach umbrella protects against noon heat, covers them with its cool round shadow. He has acquired a pair of glasses for himself and a pair for the camel. I lean over, peer closely, but cannot see through the dark lenses. I cannot decipher the projected dreams of the master nor discern the plans in the other one's ageless eyes.

I would have been justified in not paying. My clothes stolen, my work destroyed, my dignity called into question. But have we not from the beginning of our history known ourselves as persons of honor? I did however draw the line. I refused to deal with the two knaves. I addressed myself instead to the Director, still at his desk, still reading the comic book. He did not seem to hear me. I spoke louder. In the end I was forced to climb over the counter and thrust the traveler's checks between his face and "The Adventures of Rasahid, Agent 732." He looked up and smiled but did not remove his dark glasses. All of his teeth were gold. "La note, s'il vous plaît, Monsieur. I wish to pay my bill."

He shrugged his shoulders.

"La note! I'm leaving," I shouted. "I'm leaving today. Right now. Your hotel. *I am going home!*"

With infinite poise, with incredible ease he gracefully gestured toward the checks I was holding like a torch in the air. He smiled again. "You did not know, Monsieur? Worthless."

I put on my hat, creep through the front door. I leave without suitcase, without typewriter. I leave empty-handed. They are there, I might have known, all three rocking in unison on the veranda, their old eyes covered in large and vulgar pink goggles of smoked glass. When I stumble down the front steps, they cackle and point their jeweled fans like arrows toward my back.

And he is there, too, just a hundred feet down the wide paved avenue, sitting with shades over his eyes, relaxing behind the solid ivory steering wheel of a custom-made Rolls, a Camargue convertible, camel color with gold trim. At the end of a silken cord hanging from the rearview mirror a jeweled model of the Great Mosque swings almost imperceptibly. The shepherd is parked by a field as green as Ireland's best, his flock of a thousand sheep feasting on tender lespedeza. In the backseat, languishing on cushions of the finest Moroccan leather, the two ewes, their fluffy heads coiffured and covered with ribboned bonnets, gaze down their soft noses through dainty harlequin spectacles, dark glass, of course, and made to prescription.

As I limp, as I come at last alongside the sleek metal body, the shepherd has removed his shades, replaced them with horn-rimmed glasses. Against the unconquerable steering wheel, he holds a book, bends over it like a scholar. Its cover is slightly worn.

Later, much later, I reach the headlights, those powerful eyes fitted with bulbs to penetrate the thickest, the most stubborn of western fogs. Lights which when urged can probe beyond the curve of earth, beyond the Hebrides, even beyond the Golden Gate. He calls me by blinking those lights, and I turn obediently. He points to the empty seat beside him and speaks in English, almost without accent. "May I drive you to your destination?"

I curse silently. I have always made it on my own and I intend to now. Somewhere in this inscrutable land there must be a way out. A two-seater plane? A galley, a felucca, raft, canoe, a patched 1915 Ford inner tube?

I struggle on, one short step after another. Suddenly, out of nowhere, out of the calm and silent midafternoon, a gust of wind whirls by me like a dervish, whipping sand into my eyes, lifting my hat as though it were no more than a jasmine petal, dropping it gently onto the shepherd's thick hair. The sun beats down on my widening baldness and the sand settling under my lids wounds the retinae.

I feel a twinge of nausea. My throat is dry but I am still moving. On my hands and knees. My chest, my stomach have not yet touched the ground. I can still see him faintly, sitting there, his sheep long gone, in the shadow of skyscrapers. But he is not alone. Fatma is with him, and it is she who wears my hat. Fatma, grown to full bosom and powerful hips. It is she who sits behind the wheel and who decides when to keep right, when to move left. As though suddenly remembering something — pilfering a gentleman's pen, paper, carbon? — she smiles and the new tooth sparkles. A diamond as big as Tangiers!

But they both caress it from time to time, the book, a first edition. She and the shepherd take it out on special occasions, on national holidays. They lift it carefully, gently from the jeweled vault, guarded by Old Pharaoh, the immemorial beast. He sits by the door on a chair made to measure of Tunisian eucalyptus and Lebanese cedar. His tuft is brushed daily, his buttocks kept immaculate. The old Patriarch waits. He listens. A machine gun lies on the marble floor by his manicured hoofs. The treasure itself rests under an immense white dome and is preserved at an even temperature by golden pipes through which sings a blend, refined and filtered many times over, of scented and multicolored oils.

The Face

I BEGIN WITH A commonplace, but there is no other way to begin. The world is divided into victims and victimizers and those of us who tread the thin line between. I shall be honest. I shall be direct. My husband is a victim. I have known him only a little more than four years and yet I do not hesitate to surmise that it has always been he who has been the hunted one, never the hunter.

He had an uncle who hanged himself. His own mother took an overdose of sleeping pills. His great-grandfather ended his life with a pearl-handled pistol which belonged to a cousin of the czar. I do not know how the pistol got to Boston. And my husband himself has had several so-called breakdowns.

Some people claim that inheritance is everything. I would refute this. I know that the strongest plant will die with scant nourishment, little sun and water. On the other hand, I have purposely chosen the puniest of seedlings and, by special fertilizing and constant care, eliminated their early handicap and produced blossoms which could take prizes at the most famous flower shows in Europe.

And so I discount inheritance. There is no question really of unstable genes, of what some might speak of as "acts of self-destruction" among those members of my husband's family.

Their sad histories can be explained by outside causes. The uncle hanged himself toward the end of 1929. This was not uncommon, I understand, among Americans who lost heavily on the stock market. He could no doubt be counted among those. If you will look at the pictures of my husband's mother, you will see her face is thin and drawn. She could have had leukemia. Can you honestly call it insanity when someone who is suffering, who wishes to spare her family the agony of pain, takes several pills too many? As for his great-grandfather, he was married to a woman of exceptional beauty. Her portrait was painted several times by one of the famous Impressionists, and while I have never seen any of the originals (they are all in Boston), it is not hard to imagine that she had many lovers. One needs only a little more imagination to understand what her husband, a homely but proud man, must have endured. Even the sanest of men can be driven to extremes by pride.

There is nothing mysterious about my husband's breakdowns. His brother and sister were responsible. Now, of course, they no longer control him. They must have been determined to make him pay for "youthful indiscretions," for those actions which in Europe are simply accepted as part of growing up. They were furious when he began having ideas of his own. There have been distinguished physicians in his family for generations, doctors affiliated with the best hospitals in Boston, and when he refused to study medicine, this brother and sister were determined to make him suffer. They despised him. They were pleased when he disappeared behind those iron gates where there are screams. They were delighted to see him vanish beyond the acres of well-kept grounds where there is silence. They enjoyed knowing he was condemned to badminton, reduced to checkers. They were glad that he had to make small clay bowls for which he had no use. But they did not learn that on certain days he was allowed to assist the gardeners, allowed to pull weeds and remove the heads of dead flowers. They did not know about the gardening and they did not know, of course, that all this time he was working secretly on what, with their total lack of judgment, they would fail to recognize as great, even if they had seen the canvases.

My husband is no fool. After his last enforced retreat, while he was still in the hospital, he must have been able to engage a brilliant lawyer. The attorney made the brother and sister agree on a financial settlement and he escaped to Europe. He will live here the rest of his life.

We have no children. We shall never have any. I very early made this decision. It took me no time to realize the extent of the damage done by the brother and sister. I knew immediately that I must devote all of my energy to restoring my husband's self-confidence, to nurturing his talent. Even with excellent nurses I would have had, at least in some small measure, to give part of myself to my children, and this I could not afford to do. You may feel this confining for me. I do not find it so. I enjoy the security of total commitment.

So it is I who make all the decisions. I was willing from the first to take complete responsibility. My husband must be left free from all practical concerns. One cannot create under any other conditions. I order Marie to prepare the vegetable which seems at the moment to be the best possible one for him. I do not in the least mind, for what is right for my husband I accept as right for me too. But most important of all, perhaps, he knows that I am watching. He is secure in the knowledge that I am on constant guard and that he shall never again be reduced to playing checkers, humiliated on the badminton court. He will not be forced to make things he cannot use. And, of course, it is no longer necessary to hide the easel or brushes. The oils are kept in the open, and there is always charcoal if he wishes to change. Because I am watching, he is free.

Money is no problem, not that I am extravagant. Only the vulgar flaunt their wealth. Only the wicked use their dollars for evil purposes. My great-grandfather did not lack brains. He sensed the direction of the wind almost before it began to rise, and by the 1860s he had made ample deposits in Swiss, German, English and French banks. And well before the turn of the century he left St. Petersburg for London and settled with his beautiful wife in a large brick house facing Hyde Park. My uncle died penniless, but my father's two sisters were spinsters and their part of the estate reverted to me. I am an only child upon whom my parents lavished an excess of love. When my mother and father died in an automobile accident, I came into a small fortune.

You cannot accuse me, then, of being a penniless European aristocrat who fastens onto an American for financial reasons. It was, of course, the other way around. Not that my husband needed money. It was a different kind of security he was seeking. And yet, in the end, it was I who sought him. I recognized at once his genius. I knew my destiny. The brother and sister have been unable to interfere. Their name and money may count in Boston, but here in Europe, among those who have been established for centuries, their dollars, their young family tree could not cause the slightest ripple.

From the beginning I decided my husband would not have any model except me. This is in no way fear or conceit on my part. But it is imperative to be consistent. The same face must be done over and over again if one is to succeed. It must be sketched and painted from every possible angle and under all conceivable conditions of light. It must be studied in bright sun, in rain, in mist and fog, in the shadows of the waning and waxing moon. Is it not, after all, the same clown who looks out at us from Rouault's frames? The same bearded uncle who floats in Chagall's masterpieces? Can you deny that the self-portraits done over the years are Rembrandt's best work?

And so it is my face which is created. I sit for my husband day and night, at all hours, even when I can hardly hold up my head. I sit whenever and for however long is necessary. And during those brief moments when I am not posing, he has the advantage of seeing me, as it were, off guard. At this time other facets of my personality are possibly exposed.

Sometimes, quite often in fact, if I feel it will save time, I ring for Marie to bring lunch or dinner, occasionally even breakfast, to the studio. And of course there are the studio beds where we can sleep if I decide it is too much of an effort to descend the stairs. You question a life so circumscribed? I would have it no other way.

But this winter we have stayed too long in the city. I should have noticed sooner my husband's fatigue. It has been a period of incredible creativity, and only a few days ago, for the first time, I saw how pale and thin he had become. I took account of the dark circles under his eyes. Because I am with him constantly I sometimes fail to detect the subtle day-to-day changes. I was not even aware of our clothes. His trousers are slick, the cuffs of his coats worn thin. My own elbows protrude from my cashmere sweaters. I am embarrassed by soiled slipcovers on the chairs, the floor with food stains and scratches. It needs scraping and sanding, a new coat of varnish, some fresh wax. Marie is discreet. She knows her place and never comments.

And so suddenly I see the dark circles, notice the listless way the brush is lifted to the palette, and I lose no time. I telephone my travel agent to send brochures. I order from my personal bookseller guides to the places I am considering. I must get my husband as far away as possible. He must go somewhere he has never been.

I telephone the couturier, the tailor. They arrive with yards of material in their arms, their mouths full of pins. They measure and snip. The sound of their scissors breaks the silence. Occasionally as they glance around the studio at the grease spots on the floor, the canvases suspended from the ceiling, a pin will drop and they hurriedly, furtively, put it back between their lips. We have the final fittings in the studio and during those minutes when I am not being measured, when I am not posing, I lie on the bed and look at the travel brochures. I study the guidebooks. I plan the vacation.

I know my husband dreads the journey. Perhaps he is reminded of the many trips he took as a child. His family must have traveled. All Americans do, if not to Europe, at least back and forth across the long stretches of their own country. He hated those vacations. The brother and sister made him miserable. They teased him unmercifully. They demanded his portion of the candy. They took his packs of Beech-Nut gum and, perhaps once, on the way to Bar Harbor, they threw his favorite book, *Russian Tales,* out of the car and held their hands over his mouth so he was unable to tell his parents until they had driven too far to turn back. And at night if the three were left alone in a hotel, they would twist his arm until he promised to give up his allowance. When the mother and father happened to witness any of these cruelties, they did not interfere. They nodded their heads to each other and remarked that everyone must be self-reliant, learn to take care of himself, work out his own problems.

Is it any wonder, then, that my husband welcomes the sleeping pills I always have for him when we travel? These trips are vacations in the real sense of the word. Not a brush or a tube, not so much as a piece of paper or an end of charcoal is taken. It is all left behind, all forgotten for the duration.

My husband will sleep through the whole journey. Sleeping pills do not work for me. I never take them. When traveling I sleep at best only fitfully. I worry for fear my husband will come uncovered, his pillow twisted or a draft develop which would leave him with neuralgia. I am elated when the powerful engines lift us into the night and we leave far below the blurred lights of the city.

I manage to doze for a few minutes. When I open my eyes it is almost light and I notice the copilot only a few feet down the aisle. There is a large brown mole on his left cheek. I find it attractive. He looks up and down at the sleeping passengers as though searching for someone in particular. When his eyes catch mine, he smiles and I know that he approves of me. Finally he turns away, disappears behind the door at the front of the plane. My husband breathes softly beside me. I enjoy being in a plane, detached from the world, high above the earth, plunging through pure air. I like being awake when everyone else is asleep. I think of the copilot, of the brown mole on his cheek. I am pleased that he likes me. But I must make it perfectly clear that he has no chance. He must be made to understand that I have only one commitment, one concern.

When we land, my husband is still groggy and is unable to take in the strange bustle around us. He does not smell the large ripe figs offered by a dark man in a turban. He does not feel on his wrists the warmth of the burning sun. And I do not think he notices the intense color of the orange flowers along the road as the hotel bus moves us between green fields into the valley. Here the air is so clear, the quality of light of such distilled purity that I can see the mountains, which I know are almost seventy miles away. Shadowed crevices like thin brushstrokes descend with mathematical precision the massive snow-covered sides. I am reminded of the light in Greece and in parts of southern Portugal. Perhaps it is like this in Marrakech.

I have studied the brochures. I am familiar with the plan of the hotel. I know we do not have to pass the game room in order to reach our floor. But I must be sure about the badminton courts. My husband slumps into one of the lobby chairs. I register and speak in a low voice to the concierge, a fat little man with crooked teeth. He assures me that no badminton court has been built since the brochure was printed and that for my information no courts will be built in the future.

I realize that it is the sleepless night on the plane, the excitement of being in a new and strange country, that has drained me of my usual energy. I leave strict orders with the concierge. We are not to be disturbed until dinner. It will do no harm to spend the first day in bed.

We are taken by elevator to our floor and then down a long and spacious corridor. Two pretty young girls in tennis shorts walk hurriedly by, but there are no other guests in sight. They must be in the large serpentine swimming pools or on the shaded golf course. Perhaps some of them left early this morning on a pack trip. Perhaps at daybreak they mounted strong Arabian horses and rode toward the distant mountains.

Our room is large and elegant and cool. On one of the thin-legged tables someone has left a bowl of white roses. I ring for the maid. She turns down the beds, draws the curtains. My husband falls asleep almost immediately. I myself drift off soon afterward, so tired that I forget about the roses.

I awake before the concierge calls, and when the phone rings I have already decided it is better for my husband to have this first meal in the room. I would, of course, prefer to go down. I would enjoy having a cocktail in the lounge, watching the chic women with their handsome escorts. I would like to wear the new low-cut black dress designed for me by my couturier. It would be fun to listen to the sophisticated conversation in the bar after dinner and slowly sip a vintage cognac. But I must think of my husband. After long and intense months of work it is difficult to face the world. And he has the added burden, the initial humiliation to which he must adjust each time. Before I get to know people, before I can remind them that it is what is behind the face that counts, there are the whispers, the stares of incomprehension, the bewilderment that I with my elegant beauty could tolerate such a homely man. And so I am not disappointed now. There is no hurry. There will be time for explanations. There will be other evenings to wear the black dress.

A handsome waiter brings the menu. His skin is soft and unblemished and his brown eyes are kind. He has a high forehead. It is he, too, who returns with the dinner. I have chosen what seems appropriate after our long hours of travel: a thin soup, a delicate fish which comes from the inland sea, a plain salad and a simple cheese. And, of course, a bottle of the region's famous white wine. I forbid the waiter to bring butter.

My husband is shy. He does not comment when the covered dishes are rolled in, but I know he is grateful to be spared the embarrassment of the first evening in the dining room. After dinner I read from the guidebooks, suggest trips we might take into the countryside. I list the important things to see in the capital. His face is white, the circles under the eyes wider. He is not interested. Although it is time for bed, I decide fresh air may do some good. I lead him to the balcony and we stand side by side looking down at the garden in the moonlight. But he hardly sees the apple trees and the hollyhocks.

He does not care about the birch grove or the cranberry bogs. He is indifferent to the fragrance of the white lilacs and the pale colors of the sweetpeas. Worse, he is unaware of the beautiful geometric patterns made by the paths and walks crossing and re-crossing each other. I have failed to understand the depth of his fatigue.

I undress as quickly as I can and turn out the light. I lock the door as I do every night and slip the key under my pillow. My husband walks in his sleep, a habit from childhood I have as yet been unable to break. I check his covers and pillow. I get into bed and am about to close my eyes when I remember the roses. They absorb oxygen which my husband needs. I get up and put them in the bathroom.

I awake suddenly. Moonlight sifts into the room past the draperies. I know without looking that my husband is not in his bed. I rush to the door and find it still locked. And then I hear the noise coming from the bathroom, a sound I know well, the faint scratch, scratch. As I run across the room I see myself in the full-length mirror on the door. I push the door open, and my husband's reflection replaces my own. He is leaning against the basin, the round moon over his shoulder, a small drawing pad in one hand, a half stick of charcoal in the other. I already know what he has done to the roses. Only the long green stems remain in the bowl. I do not have the strength to face him directly. I try to ignore the expression I see in the mir-ror. I cannot do what he demands. I cannot punish him for his indiscretion. And yet I must. I lean over, feel the hard glass against my face. In a few seconds I hear my husband creep silently past me into the bedroom. I would like to confess my miserable failure, but of course I cannot admit my weakness. I must appear at all times sure of my strength.

In a moment I recover. I go to my husband's bed. I do what I must. I reach down and find his eyebrows. I pull. My fingers ache, but I must not think of myself. I stand by his bed until the even breathing of sleep begins.

I return to the bathroom, pick up the pad. He has, of course, been drawing the torsos. The torsos. Mine and his. Headless. My breasts, my thighs, the small almost invisible scar which runs across my stomach. His narrow shoulders, his extended sex emerging from the mass of hairs. The forbidden torsos. Not forbidden, you understand, on moral grounds but on artistic. A genius cannot afford this kind of indiscretion. The torso must be left to lesser artists. Anyone can sketch the body. It presents no difficulties; it is endlessly the same except for proportions and sex. It holds no mystery. But the face! Have you ever seen any two alike? Even with identical twins there is always some difference, a slight twist of expression in one that the other lacks. It is the head, then, that the great artist must struggle to understand. It must be his only concern. It is, of course, his private domain. And yet, there are those others who try to challenge, who pretend to know what goes on behind the eyes. They are idiots and fools. Charlatans. Frauds.

I look into the toilet. Tiny balls of crumpled paper float in the bowl. I lift them out, dry each piece with a towel and spread the sketches on the floor. They are the same torsos with slight variations. In one my breasts are smaller. In another his bush of hair extends to the waist. In a third, the thin scar encircles my thighs. The bodies, of course, never face each other. They are always side by side.

I tear each drawing into bits and flush them down the toilet. Not even the smallest indiscretion, not the slightest evidence of my failure must remain. I watch the broken charcoal swirl in the water and disappear. I destroy the unused pages of the pad. I crush the cardboard cover and drop it into the wastebasket, where the heads of the roses are already withering. I know now when my husband slipped the small pad and charcoal into his hip pocket. It was just before we left the studio for the airport, when I had to turn for a second to speak to Marie. But that is not enough. I must know where he kept them once we reached the hotel. If I am to succeed, if I am to continue to help, if the marriage is to be whole, then there can be no secrets from me.

The moon is losing its luster. The night is dying. I glance around the bathroom wondering if it is here my husband hid the charcoal. I look at the old-fashioned tub with its wide faucet. My husband knows I never take baths. I am not a rebellious person but without pride one is nothing. Someone somewhere told me to take a bath. Ever since then I have cleaned my body with showers.

I lean over, run my finger around the inside of the faucet and when I withdraw it, I see that my suspicions have been confirmed. I look at the smudge, happy that I have gained control again. I have only the pad to worry about. I see immediately there are no shelves, and of course this old, elegant hotel was built before closets became fashionable. The radiator grille is fastened to the floor with four strong screws. I look under the tub; the thin layer of dust is undisturbed.

In the bedroom, I consider possibilities. It could not have been any of the drawers. I check them three times a day. I fold the clothes twice, or more often if I feel they need it. There is never anything in the desk. I have all the paper and envelopes taken away as soon as I move into any hotel. The suitcases are empty, but I shake one to be sure. I put a chair under the overhead lamp, and on tiptoe I peer into the glass bowl which diffuses the light of three bulbs: here, too, there is an even layer of dust without a mark on its surface. I step down and notice the edge of sheet hanging from my bed. I already know what I am going to find when I lift the mattress. The oblong outline of the pad is imprinted clearly on the box spring.

I raise my pillow, check to see that the key is still there. I no longer have to worry about the roses. I can lie down at last and close my eyes.

I do not sleep long. The watch on my wrist tells me it is not yet eight o'clock. My head is splitting. No doctor has been able to find anything that will stop these pains. I have on my own discovered that strong coffee will sometimes give me relief. I stand up, lean over my husband. I snap my fingers above his ear, whisper his name. He does not stir. The ache is unbearable but I do not dare order breakfast for fear of waking him. I am desperate. I can think of nothing but my head. I dress quickly. I shall ask the waiter to hurry, beg him not to delay. I shall stay only long enough for half a cup. I will take no toast or roll. Of course, no butter.

I hang the Do Not Disturb sign on the door. When I reach the dining room, I am thankful there are no other guests. When I am in such pain, I never feel like speaking to anyone. The waiter with the nice brown eyes is waiting for me. I explain the urgency. He understands. Almost before I sit down the cup is on the table. He stands by me, smoothing the cloth, arranging the flowers. A breeze drifts through the window, ruffling the thin white curtains. I take several swallows of coffee and the pain begins to ease. And then I remember. Then I realize the terrible thing I have done. Or is it the thing I have left undone? I am not sure. I try to be careful. I do not want to spoil the white cloth, but my hand is shaking. The coffee spills and burns my fingers. I am in such a hurry I forget to thank the waiter. I forget to tell him good-bye. The Do Not Disturb sign is swaying slightly, and I find the door, as I knew I would, wide open. My head no longer aches. My husband's bed is made, the pillow smooth, the coun-

terpane in place. I know he has gone and yet I check the bathroom and the balcony anyway. I take my time bending to look
under the tub, and I pause before raising my head. The dust is
still there. I open the door to the balcony. I do not expect to find
anyone. I stop to admire the empty deck chair, the even stripes
running at intervals the length of the canvas covering.

At last I can leave the room. I do not plan to take the elevator.
I am in no hurry. I push the button and walk away. As I descend
the wide stairs I count the steps. I am almost at the bottom when
I realize I have made a mistake. I do not in the least mind returning to my floor and starting over. This time I carefully pro-
nounce each number aloud. I have no trouble arriving at the
correct count.

I have not forgotten the sundeck. I remember from the
brochure that it does not open until ten o'clock, thirty-seven
minutes from now. But this in no way deters me. I summon the
elevator. It arrives empty. I enjoy the swift ascent to the top.
When the door opens I step into a bubble of light. Beyond panes
of glass, the white café tables with their garden umbrellas are
arranged in rows of equal length. I cannot decide which I shall
return to later. I am attracted by the large yellow umbrella, but I
am also drawn to the table shaded by the delicate parasol, the
kind one sees in Impressionist paintings. I have almost made up
my mind between them when I hear the muttering behind me,
the simple Russian phrases. I turn and see her in the corner, the
thin, haggard woman in black rubber boots, scrubbing over and
over the same square of blue tile. She raises her emaciated finger, makes a slow arc in the air from side to side and shakes
her head. "Nyet! Nyet!" yourself, I reply. I am pleased to be
able to answer, to put her in her place with her own language. I
rattle the locked door to annoy her. Wearily, she turns back to
the square of tile. As I step into the elevator, I fling a Russian

curse toward her corner. I am in no way sorry for what I have
done.

I have one more place to check before I can go into the garden where my husband is. There is time enough to find him. I
shall stand by his side and together we shall admire one of the
exotic flowers. We shall marvel at the color, delight and wonder
at its intricate structure. Perhaps a bee will sink into the soft
petals, become drowsy with the perfumed sweetness.

And my husband will no longer be afraid. He will come with
me quietly back to the hotel.

The game room is full. I knew it would be. Every chair is
taken. I slowly study each of the silent faces as they gaze at the
checkerboards. I do not, of course, find my husband among
them. He has made more progress than I dare hope for.

I stand on the front porch with its huge white columns, and I
try to make up my mind which path to take. I watch two women
in identical gray dresses rock back and forth in wicker chairs.
Perhaps they are sisters. I choose the walk which leads to the wis-
teria arbor. I look up at the large clusters of lavender blossoms
hanging over my head and see the flecks of sunshine like drops
of rain fall through the leaves and dance across my face.

I have been direct. I have been honest. Can I make you believe me now? I know that my husband is in the garden, but I do
not know that he is waiting by the elm, watching me leave the
arbor. I did not know that he would be here, the pearl-handled
pistol up, the tiny barrel pointing at my head. I refuse to believe
it. There is, I feel, some mistake, some misunderstanding. How
can the only person I love want at this very moment to kill me?
And yet I see his paleness, the thin body. I note the circles under
his brown eyes.

I long to reach out, to touch him, to assure my husband that
everything will be all right, but I have already said I cannot, for

his sake or for mine, indulge in sentimentality. I save myself in time. I am exerting my strength. "You are tired! You are very tired!" I hear myself speaking firmly.

I watch the delicate hand with the pistol fall, the distress move across the eyes. But I am not yet completely in control. He does not walk toward me as I expected, but turns and disappears behind the bayberry bushes. I am not discouraged. I can run as fast as he and without my shoes even faster. I am taking off my sandals. The handsome waiter rushes up. He grabs my wrist and tells me what I already know. The guests have been told to return to their rooms. I ask if it is because someone in the garden is not behaving according to the rules. He nods his head and seems embarrassed. I announce that I can take care of myself, that I am not afraid. He reminds me that I must comply with the directives. I offer to help look for the escapee. He explains there are certain personnel assigned to the task and there can be no overlapping of services.

You wonder that I do not argue? You are surprised that I acquiesce without protest? That I do not put up more of a fight for my husband? You see, I have traveled enough to know that in the long run it is better to observe the regulations, that in the end this observance may be a means for escaping them. As I walk along the path, the hard pebbles slip and slide under my bare feet. I do not tell the waiter I know who has disappeared in the garden. And I do not say that I am glad my husband is up in the maple tree, well hidden by the foliage. I cannot forget the waiter's kindness, how it was he who rushed the coffee to me. I do not want him to be embarrassed again. But if he were not a man of the people, he would understand that all artists are above rules and that from time to time they must be allowed certain indiscretions.

When I walk into the room, I notice that my husband's bed has been taken away. I go to the balcony, look down through the iron grillwork. I look down hoping to find him. And I do.

The pistol is no longer in his hand. He struggles in the late afternoon sun, digging his bare heels into the stones on the driveway. I do not recognize the four waiters who hold his wrists and legs. He is helpless against them. As they lift him into the white bus, he looks up. I wave, but it is too late, and I am so far away my voice does not reach him. I feel warm tears at the edges of my eyes. I would not have thought it possible. I would not have believed the waiter with the kind eyes could betray me. But I am not discouraged. I am already making my plans. I look down at my wrist to see how much time I have. My watch is gone. I do not know what happened to my wedding ring.

I am about to leave the balcony when I see them. They are standing on the gravel driveway looking toward my room. I should have guessed. But I am not by nature suspicious. They have managed again to corrupt with their money. They have been able to profit by their name. I lean forward, press my head against the grill to see better this despicable brother, this whore of a sister. They do not look like my husband at all. I touch my face. The hooked nose, the square chin. But the brother and sister cannot keep my husband from me. It is true that they have given money. They have corrupted again. They have corrupted the waiter with the high forehead, the soft skin. But now my husband has the strength to fight. He has a defense against this kind of indignity. He is no longer thin. He is no longer pale. The dark circles have disappeared and his eyebrows are growing back, thick and glossy.

They are clever, this brother, this sister, but not as clever as I. By evening my husband and I will be together. Once more I shall watch that he does not put too much salt on his vegetables. I shall caution him about the dangers of butter. And I shall be sure that his bowels move each day.

Yes, before the sun is down, before the moon is up, we shall be together again, lover and loved, painter and poser, artist and model, lost in the ecstasy of creating. And there will be other charcoals of my face, done in the light of a summer rain.

The Baker's Daughter

A Tale of Holy Russia

WHO AM I? A spinner of tales to help pass the time in this part of our country where, except for those few weeks in summer, the sun arrives late then vanishes, condemning us to darkness and the hunger of wolves. Yes, a spinner of unlikely histories. And yet what I am about to tell you did happen, though there are those among my countrymen who argue about which of the two endings is the true one. But while they may dispute the actual fate of Lisa and Alexis, of Boris and the Widow, there is no disagreement among my acquaintances about the talents of Madame F, the Moscow clairvoyant, about her uncanny ability to foresee the future. She did after all predict the violent and unfortunate end of our late czar, Alexander. But to the tale.

Some years ago in the town of Y— there lived an aged baker, a widower too old to carry his on trade, and his young daughter, Lisa. Lisa was not only beautiful and intelligent but also ambitious. She had early shown talent for baking, especially cakes and pastries, and her father, an enlightened man, saw no reason not to prepare her to take his place. While none of the townspeople had imagined a female baker, they gradually grew used to the idea and some even whispered behind the old father's back that they would welcome the day he put Lisa in charge. For the most part these were men who looked forward to touching the young woman's fingers when she handed them a warm loaf of bread or a delicately turned sweet.

Late one afternoon an extraordinarily handsome youth, Boris O, rode into the town of Y——. When he dismounted in the square to let his undernourished mare drink at the fountain, Lisa was there fetching water. At first neither spoke, but Lisa stood staring while her pitcher overflowed. Finally when she lifted the vessel, water spilled on her bodice and sloshed her slippers. Some swear that the baker's daughter never looked at another man. She soon sent her suitors packing, and they fled like roaches exposed to light. But Alexis, who was lame, continued to worship her in secret.

Because Boris wore a faded doublet of poor cut and shoes of cheapest leather, and had appeared on a starving mare, the citizens of Y—— wondered at Lisa's decision. To this day some argue among themselves. How was it possible that Boris, who came from so far away, knew about Lisa and her father? Or was it by chance that he stumbled upon the town? A few blamed Igor, the knife grinder, blind in one eye, who went great distances to ply his trade. Once it was six months before he returned, and the townspeople, cursed by rusty scythes and dull knives, spat when they spoke his name, but Igor denied having ever talked of Lisa or her father or ever having been in the village where Boris lived.

The truth was this.

One afternoon a regiment of Cossacks camped at the east end of the town of Y——. The next day when they rode on their way east, a young officer, Stephan H, brought up the rear. As he was crossing the square, Lisa emerged from the Widow B's house, where she went each morning to take the attractive widow a fresh loaf and read her appropriate passages from the Bible. Only after he had ridden a good mile beyond the town and saw an old woman, the only person abroad at the time, was the Cossack able to learn Lisa's name. The other townspeople on hearing of the approaching regiment had hidden the overworked horses and pregnant cows and rounded up their complaining hogs and nervous fowls. They fetched extra water from the fountain, snatched the frayed and still damp wash drying on bushes and the low branches of mulberry trees and finally retreated to their cramped cottages reeking with cabbage long boiled. Then they bolted doors and crossed themselves.

But the old woman? What had she, a toothless crone, to fear from virile horsemen? At the edge of a birch grove she was poking among the wet leaves for mushrooms and wild cranberries. Stephan had hardly addressed his question before she shaded her milky eyes and looked up at him. And she offered additional information, which Boris O himself would later hear from the young officer: Lisa was about to become the town's baker.

From the moment he saw Lisa crossing the square, the Cossack's life was never to be the same. Not that he had a long one. Soon after taking up his post in Siberia, he came down with a fever and died. But until then his thoughts were only of Lisa. Each evening in a drunken stupor and with comrades willing to listen he would praise in detail the baker's daughter. The lips, the dark hair, the neck more graceful than a swan's, the eyes, the breasts, her skin the color and texture of a pale rose. "The beauties I had in Moscow and Petersburg? Kitchen maids and slop girls compared to her." And sometimes he would smile and say with reverence and as though witness to the scene, "Even the Ruler of Holy Russia and the Empire, even the sainted czar himself, would surely swoon at the joy of parting Lisa's limbs." And the young officer would pound his head. "Idiot! Idiot! not to desert! How much better to live unknown in the town of Y——with Lisa than wear on my chest a dozen medals."

It happened that one evening Boris overheard the unsuspecting Cossack in a tavern where Stephan H and two comrades were drinking. On learning about Lisa and her father, Boris rushed into the night and leapt on his dozing mare without draining the last drop from the tavern's battered and unwashed tankard. He sensed his destiny, the road he was to follow. But since another's heart is unmapped territory, who can say whether Boris was attracted more by the possibility of becoming the husband of a baker with a steady income or the husband of a beautiful wife?

And so it was that this young man arrived at the fountain where Lisa was drawing water. Having refused to allow his desperate animal to nibble so much as one blade of grass along the three hundred kilometers, let alone drink from the many streams they forded, on reaching the square Boris relented and loosened the reins. The horse hobbled to the fountain. She plunged her parched muzzle into the cool water, then lowered her stiff neck to tear at a tuft of sweet grass nourished by spillage from the fountain. But so overcome by the unexpected generosity of her master, the animal in an ecstasy too much to bear dropped dead, her brittle and near fleshless bones cracking, the shrunken muzzle still damp and the deprived mouth clutching the clump of tender grass.

How many soon-to-be lovers have exchanged their first words over the body of a dead horse? There was no witness. But what Boris said must have been brilliant, perhaps unique, since the moment of meeting became the peg on which Lisa would hang all her happy fantasies, especially toward the end, when she could move only her eyes and those but slightly. She relived the evening at the fountain again and again, nimble, climbing up and across and down the unsteady terrain of the dead horse to fall into her future husband's dusty arms. Or she would envision gently lifting the defeated beast's head, cradling and stroking the rigid neck, or imagine covering the sad frame with the vermilion quilt made long before by her mother and singing soft lullabies to the inert animal as though it were the child she longed for but never had.

There is no need to dwell on those first hours when Boris was welcomed by the old baker, save to report that Lisa was awake half the night with the knowledge that only a thick wall separated her from the stranger. Likewise Boris lay sleepless, plotting.

Though his eyesight was failing, as well as his ability to hear, Lisa's father realized what was happening between his daughter and Boris. Lisa had shown little interest in her suitors, and he was afraid he would die without his child married to a kind and caring husband. That the young man's horse should have collapsed in the town of Y—— instead of some other place was one more proof of what the old man had long held: "Everything works out for the best." And when from the first day Boris began helping in such a willing and efficient manner, lifting heavy sacks of flour, measuring milk without spilling, separating eggs and not allowing a tad of yolk to contaminate the whites, and delicately sprinkling sugar on blackberry tarts, Lisa's father could hardly believe his daughter's good fortune.

When only a fortnight had passed and Boris asked for Lisa's hand, her father's eyes filled with tears as he embraced the future bride and son-in-law. The old man lost no time in removing a hearthstone and lifting up a sack of gold, secretly saved over the years. He gave the money to Lisa, who handed the sack to Boris. The youth after slight hesitation returned the gold to Lisa, who dropped the sack back into its hiding place, smiling at Boris as she did so.

No time was lost in preparing for the wedding. But Lisa's hope chest was empty save for the vermilion quilt. Unlike the other young women, she had put her hopes on becoming a baker, not a wife. Why waste time initialing fine linens or gathering down for pillows?

And the wedding celebration? Among other dishes there was roast goose and *kasha* and the braided loaf, *challah*. And there was *prianik* and other special sweets made by the old baker, washed down with pitchers of *kvass*. And all the while balalaikas were playing. After hours of dancing and feasting, the guests, snoring, beards mussed, petticoats awry, lay scattered across the landscape like bodies at Borodino. That day cows went unmilked and pigs were denied their slops, dogs barked at will and fowls roosted late.

But so much joy proved too much for the old baker, and only a few days later he was struck with pains in the chest. While Boris galloped to fetch the nearest doctor, Lisa held her father's once strong hands and fought back tears. Later when the Herr-Doktor — who had not distinguished himself at Heidelberg and who like others of his countrymen of questionable ability had decided to practice in Russia, where patients were easier to please and harder to kill, arrived — he found the daughter weeping by the dead father. When Lisa looked up, her face so moved the Herr-Doktor, he reduced his fee by half.

That night Lisa slept only fitfully. The next day she went into mourning, and such was the depth of her sorrow she could not think of working. But when three months were up, she decided to begin at last her career as baker, a position Boris had kindly taken on while she came to terms with her loss. That morning before dawn when Lisa arose, Boris was in a deep sleep. She gazed at the dark outline of her spouse dreaming under connubial covers and wanted to crawl back into bed beside him. But as she made her way down to the cellar her step quickened. After so many weeks she was glad to see again the shadows cast around the room by the coals of the banked oven. Then something struck her as strange. The shadows were not their usual shapes. Lisa lit the two lanterns and saw that everything had been changed. The sacks of flour were lying flat on the floor, and slit along their sides, making it necessary to bend over to scoop up the contents and easier for mice to inhabit. The spice jars were no longer in alphabetical order, and the spoons and spatulas were wedged into a crock while the knife for cutting fruit and the custard bowl were out of reach on a shelf. The slabs of butter put every night on the table to soften were outside the window frozen. As for the gallon of sweet cream left each evening by Fyodor G's retarded son, Alyosha, Lisa found it curdled on the stove. In addition, the wood box, the water bucket, the egg basket were empty.

But Lisa was not discouraged. She rushed to the shed and grabbed an armful of wood. She ran through the darkness to the fountain. She knew how to restore cream turned sour with prayers and a pinch of salt. And she remembered a St. Basil's Day when at noon there appeared out of nowhere a swarm of oversized bats. For twelve minutes they circled the onion dome of the village church and for twenty-four hours thereafter the hens in a five kilometer radius refused to lay. Her father had then taught her how to make pastries without benefit of eggs.

Lisa began to work like a fiend. She mixed, poured, stirred, scooped, peeled, kneaded and glazed. She fluted, twirled, twisted, stuffed, sprinkled. By the time the clock struck seven and the townspeople were banging on the door, she was ready to receive them. A few noted how pale Lisa looked but agreed the pallor enhanced her fragile beauty. Others remarked on the cast of sadness in her eyes but felt this added character to her face. Still others commented that the faint line across her forehead gave new interest to her countenance. And they were quick to forgive if they found a seed in an otherwise excellent apple tart. They overlooked lumps in the bread and pretended not to notice the lack of completed twists around certain pastries making them lopsided. The young bride had been through a difficult time.

When Boris finally came down, the bakery shutters were closed. He found his wife stretched out on the worktable staring at the low ceiling. There were flecks of flour in her hair, an apple peeling caught in her bodice, unleavened bread crumbs clinging to her skirt, sesame seeds under her nails and cherry juice stains across the soles of her slippers. She seemed lost in thought. Boris tiptoed past her to the front of the bakery. Most of the shelves were empty. There were a few loaves of bread left, one with a clump of oats baked into its crust. Hearing a faint noise he rushed back and found Lisa sitting upright and sobbing. While embracing her with one arm, he used his free hand to remove a broken cherry pit wedged between his front teeth. It was during those few seconds that Lisa decided to ask her husband why he had rearranged things, but just as she was about to open her mouth Boris kissed her, and she did not ask the question then or ever.

"My beloved *blin*, my little winter cabbage, you have returned too soon. You must rest another three months. I will carry on. Your father would want it so."

Suddenly through her tears, Lisa saw the old baker slowly descending the stairs, his bushy eyebrows standing on end, his shaky arms stretched toward her. When he reached the bottom step, he vanished. Lisa took her father's appearance as a sign of approval and not a warning and without the slightest protest allowed Boris to carry her upstairs to the bed, where she willingly swallowed a mixture of powders to calm her nerves and induce sleep.

At first Boris waited on Lisa night and day. He would bound up and down the steps, fetching her strong tea. He would fluff the bed pillows, straighten the rumpled sheets, rearrange the vermilion quilt or simply fling open the windows for fresh air. And each time without fail he would bring some delicacy from the bakery and plead with Lisa not to put it aside but to eat it while he looked on to gauge her pleasure or disapproval. Three nights a week he gave his wife a sponge bath. He rubbed her enlarging arms and legs, massaged her stiff neck, removed the tangles from her hair and was gentle in applying salve to her increasing bedsores.

In the early hours before dawn when Boris arose to work, more often than not Lisa would offer a suggestion for improving a certain pastry or a particular kind of tea loaf. He should use less of some spice or soak the raisins in brandy as well as rum. Perhaps additional egg yolks would improve the solstice sun cakes? After several days of insisting that Lisa open her mouth wider as he forced in a pastry, Boris would question her — "The flavor is subtler, don't you think?" — and when Lisa made an effort to nod her head, he would add, "I used less cinnamon." Or he would say that raisins soaked in rum alone were boring. If Lisa felt in any way that her ideas were treated by Boris as his own, she kept her feelings well hidden.

Boris never failed to see that the Widow received her daily bread. He took the loaf across the square himself, and occasionally he, too, found time to read her appropriate passages from the Bible. Shortly after the visits began, some of the more observant townspeople swore they saw the Widow, who had been reduced to a wheelchair after the sudden death of her husband, moving about her house, and with a step so light she seemed to float.

"One of God's miracles!" said Father Zaharov, crossing himself. The priest, jolly and overweight, served the town of Y——. His parishioners were for the most part devout, the only skeptics among them carrying traces of French blood left willingly if hurriedly by a free thinker in Napoleon's retreating *armée*. It was thanks to Father Zaharov that Boris became famous.

One morning after administering the last rites to a man who had loved the bottle too well, Father Zaharov stopped by the bakery and Boris gave him a solstice sun cake newly improved by a suggestion of Lisa's. The priest on tasting the cake ordered a dozen for the Countess K, an ill-favored but pious woman who lived nearby on a large estate and whose interest in the priest went beyond the spiritual. Of this the Father was not unaware. The Countess had eaten five cakes in rapid succession before Father Zaharov mentioned the need for another icon. She seemed not to take note, but when she had devoured the last cake she rose from her gilt chair and left the room. In no time the Countess returned with a bag of money, which she handed to the pleased priest. And the next morning she had an order placed with Boris for a dozen solstice cakes to be delivered daily.

It was then the fame of Boris as baker began to spread. The Countess gave cakes to her husband the Count and he to his mistress, a marquise, and she to her new lover, a baron, and he in turn to his favorite, a princess, who happened to play roulette for undisclosed stakes with the czar. In less than a year Boris was summoned by a special messenger in a glittering uniform to appear at the Royal Palace in Petersburg.

So it was that Lisa's husband came to be celebrated from Baltic to Black Sea, on large estates and small and by representatives of the twelve classes. In Moscow and Petersburg, in hamlets, villages, towns, under parasols on the beaches at Sochi, persons of note and privileged dogs were eating solstice cakes.

The town changed drastically. All of its inhabitants were employed at the bakery, all that is except lame Alexis. His was the only hovel left, the others having been replaced by houses, each boasting a brass samovar. The bakery, now devoted solely to making solstice cakes, expanded up one side of the street and down the other and for sanitary reasons was enclosed by a high wooden fence. This change served to create a number of disturbed geese and swine, no longer able as they had for generations to waddle and root along the muddy thoroughfare.

The Widow, completely recovered thanks to Boris, became his assistant and took charge of the bakery whenever he was away. On returning from his tours, Boris would remove his coat, sometimes silk, sometimes fur or velvet depending upon the season, and he would rush to Lisa and embrace some part of her now huge body. And then he would describe in detail how much he had won at a count's table or the concerts he had attended in the house of a great prince. He took special pleasure in recounting his rides with the czar on Nevsky Prospect, where at certain times of the day very important people strolled up and down.

And in the name of candor, Boris told his wife, whose body now filled the whole bed, about the women he had in Kiev and Kharkov, in Nimi, Novgorod, and Minsk. Sonia from Odessa had one blue eye, one green, a combination he found irresistible. When two large tears rolled down Lisa's fat cheeks, her husband took them as appreciation of his honesty.

Boris continued to stuff his wife and while he was away the Widow pushed the solstice cakes down Lisa's throat. And when home, Boris kept urging Lisa to think up new flavors for his product, and even though her body was sluggish and her voice weak, Lisa's mind still had the sureness of a crane's flight south in autumn. Oil of lavender. Smoked cabbage ground to a fine powder. Guinea eggs tempered with those of wild turkeys. Rose water. And until her fingers became too fat to hold a quill pen, Lisa spent hours drawing new designs for the cakes.

And so several years passed for Lisa and Boris and the Widow and the citizens of Y——. And for lame Alexis. Because Alexis did not work at the bakery, he became even more isolated than before and had less and less in common with the townspeople, whose conversations were now limited to talk of solstice cakes. But Alexis continued to long for Lisa, who had, of course, known all the while that he loved her. Whenever Boris left, Alexis tried to summon courage to call on Lisa, but each time his courage failed him. However, on the very night of the day Boris left for an extended tour of France, Alexis had a dream in which he and Lisa appeared with the Holy Mother. The Virgin held out an icon for Lisa to embrace and then turned it toward Alexis, who awoke trembling. The icon was the very one hanging over his bed of straw. It had been presented to a serf ancestor who rescued a young boyer from drowning in the Neva. The Holy Image was in its usual place but at such an angle it seemed to have been hung in a great hurry. And yet when Alexis had knelt and prayed before it only a few hours ago, it had hung straight down between the dirt floor and cracked ceiling. Alexis crossed himself and a feeling of bliss, unlike anything he had ever felt before, enveloped his body and he fell into a dreamless sleep almost before he had pulled up the worn and unaired bedcovers.

The next morning Alexis did not stop to eat his breakfast of pale tea and discarded solstice cakes, those judged by the bakery's inspector general to have some imperfection and tossed over the fence as a gesture of civic-minded generosity. After kneeling before the icon Alexis wrapped it carefully in a faded red shawl that had belonged to his great-aunt, now deceased. He left his hovel and with each limping step gained more and more confidence. When he reached the high fence protecting the bakery buildings, he left the gates wide open so the pigs and geese could once again be free to wander up and down the thoroughfare.

Alexis knocked on the door to Lisa's house, and when he heard a faint "Da! Da!" he went in and found Lisa in bed, the curve of her breasts and lithe body outlined beneath the vermilion quilt, her lovely face framed by dark hair. She turned toward him smiling. Then in a voice as clear and lyrical as the cuckoo's mating call she thanked him for his selfless love and spoke of a sack of gold she wanted him to have. Later when Alexis thought of his reply, he blushed. "I will buy a handsome troika and fine horses and carry you far away."

But that morning anyone else would have seen not what Alexis saw but rather a mass of flesh filling the room, a person whose feet and head had almost disappeared in an expanded body grown round like a solstice cake.

Because Alexis limped hurriedly to find the sack of gold, he did not hear Lisa's whispered response in answer to his plans for spending the money. And even if he had, he could not have known they were her dying words. He had no trouble locating the loose hearthstone. The space beneath it was empty. Boris had long since given a few of the gold pieces to the Widow, and the rest he had lost gambling with Prince L, a lateral descendant of Ivan the First. Alexis suspected dishonesty on Boris's part, but it was not in his nature to tell the baker's daughter that the gold was missing. Now he was all the more determined to rescue her.

He would not, as intended, give her the icon but sell it. Immediately after calling up to the dead Lisa that he would soon return he set out to look for Father Zaharov.

It is at this point in the story that disagreement among my compatriots occurs. One rich landowner from near the village of R—— was so adamant that he lost a thumb in a duel defending his opinion. He claimed that when Alexis, carrying the icon wrapped in the red shawl, emerged from Lisa's house, the Widow was looking out of a bakery window. Later as a witness at the trial, the Widow said she had no doubt that Alexis used the shawl to smother Lisa because she found traces of red wool where the nose and mouth of the victim had been. The Widow may have told what she thought was the truth. In fact the bits of wool were from the embroidery on Lisa's vermilion quilt and not from Alexis's great-aunt's shawl. But Alexis was found guilty and sentenced to die.

The night before the execution, Smerdinsky the jailer fell into a deeper sleep than usual and had a dream. The prisoner walked by without the slightest limp and in a circle of blinding light. At that moment Smerdinsky was awakened by Father Zaharov, who had come to give the last rites. But when the two men reached Alexis's cell the condemned man had vanished. Father Zaharov was the first to fall on his knees. "My God! Another miracle!" he said, and crossed himself three times.

And one Dimitri A, a well-meaning but ignorant man who worked hard all day in the bakery and drank with equal diligence each evening, claimed he was stumbling home the night before Alexis was to be executed when suddenly there rushed by him a golden troika and three fine horses driven by none other than the prisoner himself. And seated beside him wrapped in a vermilion quilt was the baker's daughter, laughing, her dark hair flying.

The hallucination of a sodden mind? Hardly, for soon other people in the town began to see the golden troika, on foggy days and moonless nights, its strong-legged driver and the beautiful daughter of the old baker driving across the sky. In no time at all the dark and gloomy cell where Alexis had awaited execution became a Holy Place of Pilgrimage with hundreds of people arriving in the town of Y——. Boris made the most of this. His already considerable fortune multiplied faster than flies and fleas. He built inns and casinos and spas with hanging gardens and even created lakes and filled them with such a variety of fish that the most fastidious of anglers were ecstatic. And he and the Widow lived happily until the end of their days.

But there are those others who shout, "Not true! As false as the Antichrist!" They swear that Alexis did not dream of the Virgin the night Boris left for France but months later, the night before he returned. They insist that after leaving Lisa on his way to find Father Zaharov, Alexis was limping down the main thoroughfare when Boris arrived in a dazzling coach, a present from the duc d'Orléans. Furious at finding the gates open, Boris ordered the coachman to lash the horses. Pigs and geese scattered to safety but Alexis was unable to get out of the way. While the driver pulled the mangled body aside, Boris looked out of a damask-curtained window and smiled. Now at last every citizen in the town of Y—— was working for him!

The Widow was waiting at Lisa's house to welcome Boris. They embraced discreetly. Just as they entered the bedroom there was a noise so loud it rattled windows in the Countess's domicile some five kilometers away. The baker's daughter had exploded! Bits of flesh shot through the air. One of the Widow's eyes was sealed by a strip of skin, likewise Boris's mouth, save for a small opening which thereafter resulted in hours of frustration because of slowness in eating. A lock of Lisa's hair dangled from the Widow's cheek, and teeth embedded around her throat formed a necklace. Minuscule shards of skin hung from their bodies in layers like feathers and waved slightly with each movement the Widow and Boris made. They stared at each other in disbelief, the Widow seeing only half as well as before. Near dawn they slipped out of the house and disappeared in the coach and were never heard of again in the own of Y——.

But sometime later had you lived in Amga or Maya, Namisy, Sangar, or Vilyuysk, you might have seen Boris and the Widow in a small circus making the rounds from one Siberian village to another. They were billed as the Unusual Sweethearts, embracing each other and blowing kisses while the shards of Lisa's skin waved up and down on their bodies and the loutish peasants guffawed. In the privacy of their unheated wagon, however, they snarled and cursed, each blaming the other for their misery. For a kopeck, members of the audience were allowed to fondle the lock of hair on the Widow's cheek or watch Boris lift his threadbare tunic to reveal a blinking eye embedded just below his heart.

As for Alexis, the day after he was killed by the galloping horses a crippled child dragged herself into his hovel to escape the rain and, as she told it, was suddenly able to walk. When Father Zaharov heard the news, he again fell to his knees and crossed himself innumerable times. "Another miracle. Another miracle. How blessed we are in the town of Y——!"

And how right he was. Alexis's hovel became a place of pilgrimage, and soon people in great numbers, especially the lame, were flocking to the town. Under Father Zaharov's guidance, the bakery buildings were transformed into shops selling holy relics and a huge church was built which housed a collection of icons rivaling those in Moscow and Petersburg.

And what of Madame F, the clairvoyant whose talent none

dispute, and her horrendous vision of what in half a century or more will befall our beautiful Petersburg? She claims that the city will be besieged over many months by a well-equipped and merciless enemy. Parts of Petersburg will be completely destroyed and thousands of the city's inhabitants will die of disease and starvation. But one day under a desolate sky there will appear on frozen Lake Ladoga a troika of ancient design, drawn by strong horses and urged on by a young driver standing upright on sturdy legs, and seated beside him a beautiful young woman, a vermilion quilt around her shoulders. The horses perform arabesques on the ice, then take to the sky, the troika behind them as weightless as a bubble of air, and then they disappear into the dark clouds. Soon after, a convoy moves across the white expanse, large and unfamiliar vehicles, each with a mounted gun but no visible means of locomotion. The city will be saved, Madame F claims, and the evil invaders pushed back toward the West, where finally their empire will collapse.

It is, of course, in Madame F's interest to keep her audiences alert and agitated. But she will not be around to defend herself if this prediction proves false. Nor will you or I.

The Journey

HE IS COMING now, coming in the yellow car, bought because yellow is my favorite color. As I watch him turn off the highway, where already, at only a little past ten, the heat waves shimmer above the asphalt, I understand why I have had to wait, sitting in the motel room on this unmade bed, between his suitcase and mine. The sun gleams on the hood. He has had the car washed, the dust and fingerprints of yesterday erased. Should I rush out and tell him it is not so simple? At this moment I cannot honestly say what I plan to do.

Yes, two days ago, we left Pasadena in the late afternoon so as to cross the desert by night. We rode in silence through Devil's Canyon and over the Cajon Pass. I was tired. We had lost sleep all week entertaining guests from out of town and, until we stopped at Barstow for a light supper, I lay back with my eyes closed. We would have a late dinner in Las Vegas. My husband had telephoned for reservations and was pleased that he was able to get a table on the edge of the dance floor. At last we were beginning our long-delayed honeymoon. When we married eight months ago, my husband, a lawyer, was working on the brief of a difficult case and felt he could take only three days away from the office. The trip to Santa Fe was to be our postponed wedding trip.

After Barstow we drove again in silence, across the desert and into the night. Once or twice, I opened my eyes to look at my husband. We were going quite fast on the straight road and he was leaning forward, his small body in the exaggerated position of a jockey. He seemed absorbed in his own thoughts and unaware of me, and I was glad, for I was beginning to feel guilty about my long silences.

We stopped at a gas station and he got out to go to the toilet. When he came back, I noticed a faint shadow on his delicate face. He had shaved just before lunch. I knew then that he too must be tired. His beard seemed to grow more rapidly when he was in need of rest. Ordinarily, he appeared younger than his age, but under the harsh station lights, he looked his thirty-four years. Just after we turned onto the highway again, I leaned over and kissed him.

It was almost eleven when we reached the outskirts of Las Vegas, but miles before, in the clear night, we had seen its lights reflected against the desert sky. There was a Sorry, No Vacancy sign at our motel, but as we turned in and stopped by the swimming pool, I noticed only two cars in the courtyard. This was, then, a real night city. At dawn the guests, happy, depressed or indifferent, would drift back toward beds all over the town. Already, I had decided I would not be among them. I had no desire to dance, and the thought of a midnight supper revolted me. Through the office door, I could see my husband signing the register. Beyond him, the head of the office attendant, her hair dyed, her lashes heavy with mascara, suddenly reminded me of the big black and yellow spiders that often appear in New England gardens in early fall.

Our room had a thick wall-to-wall carpet and soft indirect lighting. In an alcove I saw a small refrigerator. While my husband returned to the car for our bags, I took an ice tray into the bathroom. My face was burning, and I wanted something cold against my cheeks.

I did not like to disappoint my husband but I was, after all, tired. When I told him I did not want to go out, he turned away, but not before I saw the look in his eyes, magnified by his thick glasses. He said he needed a drink. He felt tense from the long drive. After telephoning to cancel our reservation, he withdrew to the bathroom so I could get to sleep.

I was putting on my nightgown when the cricket began. At first I found it cheerful, but after a few minutes it got on my nerves. Near the floor by the room's entrance was a small grate, part of the air-conditioning system, and I located the cricket's sound. I did not know how to get to the insect; I called my husband. He came out of the bathroom, his shirt unbuttoned. After poking a few times with a pencil, he fastened his shirt and went to the office. He returned with the blonde, who sprayed the opening.

"He'll make some more noise, but in a few minutes he'll be through and you won't hear nothing," she said, her voice harsh. After she left, my husband bent down, kissed my lips and neck and returned to the bathroom, closing the door behind him.

Despite the air-conditioned coolness, there was something oppressive about the room. I closed my eyes and the stillness pushed against me. Suddenly the cricket gave a bright chirp and then followed several twangs as clear as the first. I was on my back and turned to my side, but I felt uncomfortable. I tried lying on my stomach. Soon I found myself staring through the blackness toward the ceiling. My pillow seemed abnormally thick, but my husband's if anything was worse. Finally I admitted to myself what was wrong and leapt out of bed. If the grate would come loose, it might not be too late to rush the cricket into the night air. I slipped my fingers through the metal openings. I pulled and pushed and twisted. The grate did not budge. Suddenly the insect gave a feeble call, so faint I could hardly hear it. I put my head down and kept my ear over the grate for several minutes. There was only silence.

I had to get out of the room. I slipped on my clothes, left a note on the bed and shut the door quietly. When I reached the sidewalk, for no reason I turned left. I did not know where I was going, but I no longer felt tired. The night air was dry and warm. Several minutes later, I entered a casino in one of the large hotels. I moved from table to table, silently choosing someone, watching him or her gamble, giving as it were my silent support. I had no desire, myself, to take active part in the games. Several times I was approached. I was flattered; I was pleased. But I enjoyed even more watching the expression in the men's eyes when I said I expected my husband.

There was one gambler I kept returning to watch. I never saw him standing, but he must have been well over six feet tall. His face had an aristocratic reserve. Occasionally he smiled, not at anyone, nor in relation to what was happening in the game, but as if at some private thought. There was a large space between his two front teeth. Once or twice he looked at me, as though to acknowledge my support, but whether he welcomed it I could not tell.

Each time I thought about going back to the motel, I was more determined than ever to remain. I must have been in the casino over three hours. Toward the end I moved to the slot machines and lost rather rapidly about twenty dollars. It was then that I found myself looking toward the entrance. I heard someone behind me ask if I still expected my husband. It was one of the unattractive older men who had spoken to me earlier. I did not bother to answer. By then, I must admit, I was hoping my husband would walk into the casino and take me to our room. It was unreasonable, I know. In the note I had told him not to follow me. But I was annoyed that he did not understand me better. I imagined my note, unread, lost somewhere in the covers of our bed, and I thought of him going from nightclub to nightclub, from casino to casino, looking for me in the lights and the shadows of the city. As I put my last quarter in the slot machine, I knew I should return to the motel, but instead I found myself back at the table which had attracted me most. Although I must have stood there over a half hour, the man did not once look up.

As I passed the motel office, the woman glanced at me but said nothing. My husband obviously had not left any message with her. When I opened our door, I heard his soft breathing, and in the bathroom wastebasket, I found my note, torn to pieces, scattered over the empty whiskey bottle. My hands began shaking, and I could hardly undo my blouse. I pressed against my husband's small body and laid my cheek on his. His whiskers sent sharp twinges through me. "Forgive me! Forgive me!" I kept whispering. But now I cannot be sure I meant it.

We slept until after ten and before breakfast we had a short swim. For a few minutes we lay by the pool, our feet touching. My husband made no reference to my note and I was grateful. I let the recent hours withdraw to the edge of my consciousness. The swim had refreshed me. The warmth of the tiles on my breasts and stomach and the heat from the sun on my back seemed to meet inside me and burn. We returned to our room and there, on the soft rug, some twelve hours late, we began our second honeymoon.

In the afternoon we were driving slowly, climbing in the tunnel cut through rock on the side of the desert mountain. Every few hundred feet, level with the road, were large arched openings, each with a parking area for those who wished to stop and have a look at the canyon and the range of mountains. The sunlight drifting through these openings in slanting cones reminded me of divine light in medieval paintings.

I am frightened by heights. Feeling uneasy, I kept my eyes on the road straight ahead. We must have been almost at the top, the road seemed to be leveling for some distance, when we both spoke at once. A small light was flashing. As we reached the next open arch, a young man rushed toward us, waving a flashlight and gasping for breath. He stared at us for a second and then stammered that his wife just a moment before had lost her balance and fallen from the low stone wall across the opening. My husband turned off the road, drew alongside the man's car. I felt nauseated. I had the terrible sensation of the rock beneath us crumbling. I saw our car, sliding forward, turning over and over, rolling down the mountain to the bottom of the dry canyon.

My husband walked toward the stone barrier. I tried to follow but I couldn't move. I wanted to call, warn him not to lean over, but I could not open my mouth. A second later, I was ashamed, and relieved I had not been so tactless. The man, standing near our car, kept running his hand through his hair.

I saw the fist of his other hand open and close. By the time my husband was back, I had taken the small whiskey bottle from the glove compartment. My husband offered the man a drink, but he refused. He asked for water. I poured some from our thermos. His hand was shaking and as he raised the cup to his mouth, some of the water spilled. He wanted us to send help from the next ranger station, a short distance beyond the exit of the tunnel. In a voice so low I could hardly hear, he asked if my husband had seen his wife move. He said no, but that she might only be unconscious. Though I was almost sure he did not believe that, I clutched at the possibility.

The man was handsome. He was tall. I was sure he must be

about my age. He was wearing shorts and his open sport shirt was cut from expensive material. I suggested that he come with us. Nothing could be gained by his staying, since rescuers would have to approach from below.

At first the man refused, but a few seconds later, he seemed reconciled and got in the front seat beside me. We passed more arched openings, one of which I noticed had heavy wire across it. Had a whole car crashed through that stone barricade, taking its occupants to death? After we came out of the tunnel we twisted slowly down a steep road. I offered whiskey again, but again the man refused, asking for more water. As I handed him the cup, I noticed perspiration on his forehead. His fingers felt cold as they touched mine. I longed to comfort him in some way. I glanced down and saw the bright polish on my toenails. The scarlet color seemed suddenly frivolous, even vulgar. I pulled my feet back toward the seat as far as I could. I felt the heat of the man's body, and suddenly I had an image of him on a tennis court, his long arms curving gracefully in a powerful serve.

None of us spoke the first few minutes, then he told us how the accident happened. His wife's hobby was butterflies, and they had left on a camping expedition two weeks before with the hope of adding to her collection. Just as they reached the area where she fell, she had spotted in the arched opening a group of small butterflies, a species she had been hoping to find. She had screamed for him to stop the car and, grabbing the net, rushed after them. Before he realized what was happening, or could reach her, she had climbed onto the barricade. Swinging wide with the net, she had lost her balance.

I could see the beautiful young girl — she would, I knew, have to be beautiful to have such a husband — with lovely legs, gliding like a ballet dancer onto the stone railing, the tiny butterflies, harmless flakes of whirring gold, leading her on. What did she look like now? Was her body relaxed, her delicate hand still holding the net? And far below her, were the butterflies innocently fluttering among the pink boulders, on the canyon's floor? Only a few hours before, in the cool dawn, she might well have been in her husband's arms, their bodies pressed against each other.

We finally reached the ranger station and my husband walked quickly up the steps into the office. The man, his lips pale, thanked me. He even apologized for involving us in his trouble.

My husband returned almost immediately, jumped into the car and said we must get away in a hurry. I could not imagine why. I wanted to open the car door and rush to the young man's side. But my husband was backing out. A second later we were speeding away. He said there was no way of telling whether the woman had fallen accidentally. We should not get involved. We might be detained for a day, or longer, to testify — perhaps even called back for a trial.

I was horrified at his words. Was it possible I could have so misjudged my husband, understood him so little? That he could even remotely entertain such a suspicion frightened me. It was a thought from a twisted mind. Or, was this perhaps subtle revenge? Had he been so perceptive as to be aware of the mild attraction I felt for the man?

The argument which followed was bitter. I was positive no person could pretend such an obvious state of shock, assume such genuine grief. The man's face had been distraught; his body had jerked in agony.

We rode without speaking. When I felt calmer, I began again to imagine the lovely girl, limp in death, on the hot mountainside and her husband, gathering her into his arms while the rangers with their horses stood quietly by. I followed the party's slow descent down the canyon, the telephone call to her family, to his, the news release over the wires. I turned on the car radio several times, but there was no mention of the accident.

Later, I worked myself into another fury and finally broke the silence. If being a lawyer meant protecting oneself against human entanglements, then a plague on the profession! My husband did not answer. His smugness, I thought, made him immune to my protests.

When I woke this morning, my head ached and I had a bad taste in my mouth. The room was dark except for the tiny slits of sunlight around the edges of the heavy curtains. I felt the warmth of my husband's body against me. Worse than my throbbing head was the guilt which descended as soon as I was fully awake. Again I had failed my duty as a wife. Worse, my decision had not been made on the spur of the moment. It had been calculated. I knew, hours before, when we were speeding away from the ranger station, that I would refuse to make love. For a few minutes I continued to feel ashamed, and then I began to rationalize. Did he, after all, really have much to complain of? He was lying by me now. The blood in my veins was hot; I was alive. But the young man: could he reach out to his wife's soft body? And again I saw my husband, rushing down the steps, away from the ranger station, running toward the car.

I jumped out of bed, my head throbbing violently. I started for my purse to get aspirin and remembered I had taken the last one two days before. My husband would not have any. He never had headaches. I glanced down at him, annoyed at his inadequacy. He was looking up at me without his glasses. For a second I forgot my pain and admired his eyes. When I told him about my headache, he got up, dressed immediately and went to get aspirin and coffee for me. I asked him to buy a paper; I wanted to see if there was anything about the accident. Moments later, when he came back from the coffee shop, he told me the papers had all been sold.

While he shaved I lay on the bed, half asleep. By the time he left an hour ago, to take the car for an oil change, I was feeling better. My self-justifications still left me a little uneasy, and I found myself putting on the pink cotton dress I knew was his favorite.

After packing our bags, I felt the need of another cup of coffee, and I went to the motel coffee shop. I glanced around the room. I enjoy being in a strange place, among people who know nothing about me. Sitting at the counter, an Indian, his shirt open on a hairy chest, looked at me sullenly.

I was halfway through my coffee before I noticed the newspaper rack. Only two papers were left, but one, it turned out, was all I needed. There was a picture of the dead wife, a plain woman in her late thirties. She was from a wealthy Chicago family. The story was in two neat columns, near the bottom of the page. I hardly got beyond the headlines. Under questioning the young man had broken down and confessed. His wife had, in truth, climbed onto the stone barrier, hoping the butterflies would come back. But she had not fallen. He had pushed her.

I found it difficult to keep my hands from shaking as I folded the paper and returned it to the rack. So the man had betrayed me! I was glad his wife was old and ugly.

When I reached the door I felt like running. Instead, I walked as slowly as I could across the motel courtyard back to the room, my heart pounding, my eyes almost closed against the blinding sun.

And now my husband is coming and I get up from the bed and again walk with deliberate slowness through the motel door, though my body longs to move violently and quickly toward him. He drives the car into the parking space in front of our room. I reach for the door handle. The motor is still running. He looks up at me and smiles. The angle of his thick glasses makes his eyes grotesquely large. And I remember. I see myself standing in front of a fish tank outside a restaurant in Paris. A fish swims toward me and its eyes, suddenly magnified by some freak combination of light, glass and water, seem to be asking for help. I toy with the idea of buying the fish and setting it free. But the impulse was, of course, irrational. I kneel on the car seat and reach toward my husband. I grab his shoulders and I hear his glasses hit the rim of the steering wheel.

Death Is Where You Find It

HER HUSBAND said it was, after all, part of the culture, that she should give it a try at least once.

She looked across the balcony beyond the olive grove at a clump of early spring poppies growing wild on the side of a hill.

He told her it had to do with things the Spanish considered basic. Bravery, fate, death. That it had style and beauty, like a ballet. And he remarked that the bulls were treated better than the cows on her father's farm.

She protested. Their cows had never been mistreated.

He denied saying that. He had said the bulls were treated better. They were protected from the time they were born. They were put in the best pastures, fed special food. He wondered if a few minutes of frustration could not be dismissed in the light of so many months of good living.

She opened the desk drawer and took out her dark glasses. She told him she had to go to the bathroom again before they left.

He raised his voice to reach her through the door, urged she try to forget her Anglo-Saxon background for a little while. He assured her there was nothing drawn out about the suffering, that, even with the less skillful fighters, death was relatively quick.

She looked into the bathroom mirror and beyond her own face saw the thin white face of her mother, the eyes closed, the long hair, black as a crow's feathers, spread against the pillow. Then she heard her husband calling, saying they should leave. It would be too bad to miss any of the preliminary business. It was part of the show.

They were following the sea, driving along a stretch of road cut through red rock, and her husband said he couldn't remember whether she had read *Death in the Afternoon*. She told him she had started it once but that she hadn't gotten very far. It was the only thing of Hemingway's she had never finished.

She had fought the man, she had fought the writer. She had battled with him through his novels, his short stories, read him out of a kind of perversity, enjoyed her scorn for his prose, and his ideas, which seemed infantile compared to the richness and subtlety, the complexity of other contemporary writers. She had relished her hate for his narrow masculine ethic of enduring, whether it was failure or defeat or death. And she laughed at his simple view of women. But in the end Hemingway had won her. In his final despair, in his failure to follow his own arrogant rule of patient acceptance, he had at last become, for her, human.

Her husband said he thought *Death in the Afternoon* was the best book ever written on bullfighting, was likely to be for a long time, and she should give it another try. He felt Hemingway sometimes understood the Spanish better than they understood themselves.

The Mediterranean, pale blue, rose toward the bend of the horizon. She remarked on how smooth it was and her husband said it was the way it should be. Whitecaps meant wind, and *corridas* were never held if it was very windy. He explained why. He said there was so much more to it than the actual *tercio de muerte.* She heard about the signal for *paseo*, the ritual of throwing the key, what the ribbons on the bull meant. He described the three stages of the fight. He warned that sometimes one of the horses, gored by the bull, had to be dragged away, too, by the team of mules. He admitted that was an aspect of the *corrida* he did not like.

On a green hillside between the road and the sea, a flock of sheep were grazing. She noticed that a few of the ewes had new lambs clinging to their sides. It was several seconds before she saw the shepherd, blending into the brown boulder he leaned against. She wondered what he thought about all day.

It was only near the outskirts of the city that they had to slow down for other automobiles, for donkeys, for Spaniards in their worn and dusty clothes walking along the road. On the main avenue, shaded by palms, a one-armed attendant tried to wave them into a parking place, but her husband drove on, certain, he said, he could get closer. He found a spot on one of the small streets not far from the Plaza de Toros. He reminded her to lock her side of the car.

As they turned a corner they almost bumped into a man urinating against a wall. A growth like a small apple, a hard bubble of taut skin, protruded from his wrinkled neck. When she looked away, her husband took her arm. He told her she must try to accept, remember that she was not in Richmond, Virginia.

But walking down the narrow streets with dank odors drifting from behind ancient tile doorways with their curtains of beads, she knew it was not just the man relieving himself, not the idea of when in Rome, not simply a question of the moment. The problem had been defined long before when she crouched in the dark hall outside her parents' bedroom. *She will have a hard time coping. She may not be able to survive.* And walking now down the unfamiliar street in a city she had never seen before, she was tempted to accept the role prophesied for her, to beg off, say she had changed her mind again, turn back to the car. Instead she moved closer to her husband, struggled against her father's words, his protesting that her mother was protecting her too much, refusing to let her know the facts of life, that with two dogs, five cats and a bird, she did not need the damn pig too, that she should be told the truth, repeating again for emphasis, *She may not be able to survive.*

When they reached the Plaza de Toros she felt the need to be by herself, to confront alone for a few moments the ache at the back of her knees, the tightening in her stomach. She told her husband she would wait by the entrance while he bought the tickets.

Most of the people converging on the arena looked poor. There was no shouting from one group to another, no laughter. The Spaniards walked with quiet dignity. They might have been going to a funeral. She watched two old women move slowly by her, their milky eyes peering from under black shawls. Both of them had long white whiskers curling on their chins, and one made a soft sucking sound with her withered lips.

"Por favor, Señora?"

She looked down. A dark-skinned child held up a dirty hand. Where his foot should have been there was a stub with unformed knobs of flesh. She opened her pocketbook and took out a fifty-peseta piece. The child's grave face broke into a grin. "Gracias! Gracias! Señora!"

Her husband, holding the tickets, came up smiling as the boy hobbled away. He said the child would be able to retire on what she had given him, that now all the gypsies in the region would be alerted and on the lookout. Then he took her hand and told her they were all set.

*

When the gate opened and the black bull came rushing toward the center of the ring, she put on her dark glasses and closed her eyes. A few people around her shouted, taunts or advice, she supposed. Several times she felt the quick thrust of her husband's hip as he leaned forward. When finally she could stand it no longer, when she opened her eyes and saw the picador twist the lance, saw the blood trickle down the black hide, she told her husband she had to leave. He asked if she wanted him to come, too, and when she shook her head, he reached into his pockets for the car keys.

The fat Spaniard sitting at the end of the row shrugged his shoulders and smiled as she pushed past him. There was tolerance in his expression. It was to be expected. He had seen it before, pale, well-dressed Northern women leaving just as things were getting under way.

When she reached the bottom of the steps she hesitated, under the arcade, then broke into a fast walk, following the curve of the stands.

Twice she passed the blind beggar sitting in the dusk, saw each time his white eyeballs turned toward her, his hand held out. She noticed the pockmarks on the arena walls and columns. Some of the larger cracks had been patched with a darker cement. She felt the weight of her pocketbook flopping against her side, the sweat gathering above her lips, and under her arms, but the arena held her. She could not make herself turn away, seek refuge in the maze of streets beyond.

Then the slow rhythm began. The voices became one urgent sound, with each *olé!* soaring like the sweep of a giant bird, and she began to run, stumbling, catching herself, stumbling again. In her desperate circling she no longer saw the beggar's outstretched hand, the patches on the wall. She did not notice the dirty pieces of discarded paper scattered along the arcade.

She had been running the same way then, hurrying home from school, wind at her back, strong gusts pushing against her, tossing leaves in the air, blowing them along the sidewalk, and as she ran she noticed a leaf with a bright yellow center, ringed in red like a flower and she knew she could catch it, told herself if she picked it up before it was blown into the street, her mother would not die, but she slipped on the damp pavement and she did not reach the leaf in time.

She heard her heels hitting the hard ground. She stopped running and in the silence listened to herself gasping for breath, felt her body begin to shake. And when the clapping started, when a few bravos rose like released balloons above the steady applause, she bent over and closed her eyes and waited for the wrenching to begin.

A second afterward she realized she had smelled his sour body almost as soon as she felt his fingers. When she screamed, the Arab, barefooted, backed away. Several of his teeth were missing and his trousers were tied at the waist with a string. He turned and started running. She watched him disappear around the side of the arena.

The nausea was gone. She thought with detachment about fear, what effect it had on the body. But there were no animals around her now to smell the adrenaline, to profit or care that she had been afraid, only the old horses with their eyes blindfolded, their sides inadequately protected, only the horses and a dead bull. She wondered about the Arab. Perhaps he had simply wanted to help her.

People were beginning to leave their seats, moving down to walk along the arcade while waiting for the next fight. She hoped her husband was not among them. She crossed the square. She had no idea in what direction the car was, but she knew if she walked up and down the sidewalks as though they were spokes in a wheel, the Plaza de Toros as center, she would sooner or later come upon it.

As she went down the silent streets, past houses with their painted walls faded and stained, their shutters rotting, she smelled again the dank odors, the stench of decaying fish and human waste. Once as she turned a corner she caught a glimpse of the sea.

She had been walking almost ten minutes when she saw the small dog, so thin there seemed to be nothing between his skin and the bones beneath. He held one of his hind legs up close to his body. She remembered the box of crackers in the car, reached down, touched the dog's head and spoke to him. He turned and hopped along on three legs beside her. Finally she recognized the wall where the man had urinated.

If the car had been hers she would have lifted the dog in, let him eat on the seat by her, given no thought to fleas or the raw sore on his stomach. She spread a newspaper on the sidewalk and dumped the box of English tea biscuits. The dog gulped down the crackers, scarcely stopping to chew.

"Y yo, Señora?"

On an upstairs balcony three houses down a young girl in a red skirt, a white blouse drawn tight across her breasts, was making a mocking gesture toward her stomach. Then she swung her hips in a half turn, flung her right arm up and tossed her head. She laughed and made a sweeping exit into the house. She came back and began combing her long hair. She would have been pretty except for a flat nose. Behind the girl, on the wall by the balcony door, a small wooden crucifix hung above a vase with two plastic roses.

As the dog was finishing the crackers she remembered the half-eaten box of raisins in the glove compartment. When she emptied them onto the newspaper, she noticed the girl disappear quickly through the upstairs door. She was back almost immediately with two older women. They were fat and heavily made up. All three looked at the dog, then at her, and began to laugh. A few seconds later they went back into the house.

The dog finished the raisins and seemed to understand when she told him there was nothing more. He hopped across the sidewalk and flopped down in the shade. He laid his head between his front paws and looked at her. She folded the newspaper and put it on the floor of the car.

Then she heard it again, faintly, the rising voices. She picked up a map the automobile agency in Madrid had given them when they rented the car. She glanced at the dog. He had not moved, but his eyes were closed. There was no one on the balcony. She opened the map, began tracing the route they had taken south. Her finger paused at Toledo. She had been unprepared for the startling brightness of the El Grecos. She saw that Cordova was closer to Seville than she realized. She folded the map and wound up the windows. She put her head down on the steering wheel.

In a little while she opened her eyes. There were five women now, crowded onto the balcony, their lips and cheeks heavily rouged. They were all looking down at her. Then she realized what they were. One of the women opened her mouth, exposing two gold teeth.

They continued to stare, their eyes hostile, demanding that she justify herself. Justify her dress, the car, perhaps even her existence. Justify spreading a newspaper on the sidewalk so a diseased mongrel would not have to soil his mouth while he ate imported crackers and the most expensive Spanish raisins. Explain why she sat like an idiot on a warm afternoon with the car windows rolled up.

She wondered how far back the house went, how many

women worked there, if the girl in the red skirt was the favorite, the most asked for. She supposed there were saints' pictures on the walls and more plastic roses in cheap ceramic vases.

She had read about the city, how its history stretched back into antiquity, how this particular part of the coast had come under the rule of many different peoples. Phoenicians had set up a village for trading. They might have built a shelter on the spot where the brothel was now, built it for the female slaves they had brought with them. Perhaps Greek and Roman prostitutes had waited through the afternoons as these women were waiting now, waited for sailors, for merchants, for legionnaires to seek them at the end of the day. She imagined Arab concubines arriving with the Moorish conquerors, stretching their sultry bodies on the earth near where she sat in the car.

The distant *olés* were beginning again, another sword about to be drawn. She no longer cared what the women on the balcony thought. She found the guidebook on the back seat. She opened it at random and began reading. She learned that the Guadalquivir flowed into a marshy plain, las Marismas, and that in prehistoric times it had been a lake.

Almost an hour and a half later, the men began to arrive. She watched them go into the brothel. The girl in the red skirt was alone on the balcony. She called down to one of the men, and took the dancer's pose. When the man said something and laughed, she grabbed the railing, leaned over and spit. He stepped aside. He laughed again and disappeared through the brothel door.

Then she saw her husband coming, his smooth young face and seersucker coat a dot of brightness among the dark Spaniards. She half-expected him to turn and vanish into the brothel. The girl in the red skirt lost no time. She beckoned with snapping fingers. When he looked up she swung her hips and tossed her head, flinging her long hair.

He opened the car door and saw that she had been looking. He smiled and said he had not realized he had parked in such a select area but at least she was aware of who would take care of him if she wasn't nice. He leaned over and kissed her. She knew the girl in the red skirt was watching and she felt sorry for her.

Her husband asked if she had been bored and she told him she had studied the map, looked at the guidebook, and then she apologized for being a coward. He turned on the engine. He smiled and said that he had missed her, that he was sorry she had not managed to sit out the first one because he was sure she would have been all right after that. People claimed it took only one to get used to the blood.

When they turned the corner, she glanced back. Two more men were going into the brothel. The girl in the red skirt was no longer on the balcony. Then she saw the dog, hopping down the middle of the street, his head up, his eyes on the retreating car, and she wished she had not looked back.

As they drove past the row of palm trees, down the avenue, through the dark narrow streets at the edge of the city, he told her about the fighters. They had all been young and relatively unknown, but unknowns started in places like this. Pepe, he thought, might make it to the top. He seemed to have potential for the skillful ease of the great. He said again that it was too bad she had not been able to stay just a little longer because the first kill especially was quick, beautifully done.

A few miles on they passed a gypsy family. The father was riding a thin mare with a small boy clinging behind. The child had nothing on below the waist and his tiny buttocks moved from side to side with the motion of the horse. A pregnant woman followed on foot, holding the hands of two little girls.

Her husband laughed, said that was the way to treat the ladies, make them walk, and when she asked him if he would like her to get out, he smiled and said he would let her get her exercise later. She knew he could not have failed to see that the woman was pregnant.

He was driving fast along the road, sunk between fields of tall sugarcane, when they came suddenly to a narrow bridge and he had to slam on the brakes. The car skidded and she was thrust forward. He said he was sorry and she asked him why he was in such a hurry. He smiled and told her he had an engagement with a lovely señora some twenty miles ahead, a señora who might have a red rose in her mouth, and he did not want to keep her waiting.

Her husband was probably not thinking of her at all but of the girl in the red skirt, what it would be like to tangle with her fiery body. A rose belonged in the mouth of someone who could spit so far. He was joining the Spaniards, pushing through the brothel door, even though he had nothing in common with them, poor and ignorant men, their faces leather from long hours of work in the sun. He found the girl in the red skirt, and when he was done with her, he moved to another, and another, from prostitute to prostitute, leaving with each the memory of a kind of lover they had never had, a man whose skin was clear, whose mouth was gentle.

When she saw two goats and the pig tethered near a fig bush by the side of the road, without thinking she told her husband that she had once loved a pig. He began to laugh. He wanted to know if it had been a man-pig or a pig-pig. And when he asked her what happened to the animal, she simply said that it had been killed.

They were only a few miles from the hotel when the sun dropped out of sight, leaving the clouds above the mountains to the west a fiery red. In the distance she saw on a slight rise of ground an ad for a Spanish brandy, a huge wooden bull, painted black. Its massive shoulders supported a great head, with horns and eyes challenging the countryside. It was an ad she had seen over and over again when they were driving south from Madrid, in open fields, on the crests of hills. She wondered why she had not noticed this particular one earlier in the afternoon on their way to the city. She stared at the bull now, watching it grow larger and larger. Suddenly it was galloping toward her, filling the whole sky with its blackness.

When she heard the shower running she went into the room and filled a glass with whiskey. She left the empty glass by the bottle and went back to the balcony. The iron railing was plain, black like the one the girl in the red skirt had leaned over. She thought of the young whore, then gave her hips a twist, flung her arm up in exaggerated imitation of the prostitute. She understood the girl's repeated gestures. It was the fantasy which helped her endure. In those seconds the prostitute was no longer confined to the role of spreading her legs for any man who paid and demanded it. She was a dancer performing in the best Madrid hotel, able to choose and dismiss lovers with a snap of her fingers.

The railing began to shimmer. She sat down and looked beyond the olive trees. The beach was empty. There were only the waves. If she wanted to, she knew she could walk, one foot after the other, walk slowly, slowly, along the sand, follow the edge of sea and come to the place where the bulls were, where they lay stiff, their hides soaked with blood. But perhaps it would be too late. Perhaps the butchers had already begun to work.

It was almost dark. She pulled the sweater closer around her neck. The waves kept coming. There was no way to stop them. She closed her eyes.

He swayed above her, a towel tied around his waist. He wondered why she was still dressed. She tried to stand. She wanted to help. She saw his teeth white against the dark sky and felt his arms.

She ran after the bull but he was headed for the open sea. Her mother was sitting backward on the animal, straddling his rump. She screamed when she saw the bull raise his tail and lash at his rider's breasts, but her mother was laughing and did not hear her. The footsteps behind her stopped. She turned around. The baby lay asleep on the sand.

She awoke. He was beside her. They were naked and she felt his sex warm against her side. He whispered, "Bravo!" Spain had liberated her! He raised up on his elbow, began remembering the weekends before they were married when he had tried to get her drunk, so he could seduce her properly, and now at last she had done it for him. He kissed her. He told her that she had been great, that he would have to take her to Spain more often. He kissed her again. She wondered what time it was and he told her it was long past midnight, probably close to five o'clock, that he had been to sleep himself. He said he had tried to rouse her for dinner, but she would not cooperate. He had brought back sandwiches. They were on the bedside table, and when he began to unwrap one, she shook her head. He told her he thought she should eat something, but she said she was not hungry. He lay by her quietly and asked if she felt like it, if she would mind, for just a little while.

Her tongue was heavy and her left shoulder arched. As she

moved slowly, down the length of her husband's body, she saw another body, saw it collapsed on the floor, the muscles once carefully trained, the physique the man had been so proud of, saw it gone to fat, its blood spilled on that remote and desolate spot in Idaho. He had been right after all. There was only endurance and lust and death.

The Spanish night pressed down, darkness whispering all around her. . . nada. . . nada.

A Citizen of the World at Large

S HE HAD ALWAYS done what they wanted. She, a daughter
and only child born late to aged parents. It was they who
demanded the most, or perhaps in the end, the least. For
them she had the operation. For them she went to Radcliffe and
Harvard's Law School. For them she married Thatcher. The operation, she admitted, especially for those who had to look at her,
was a success. And no doubt about it, with the law degree she
would hardly be likely to starve. But the marriage could only be
counted a failure. And why, she wondered, why did she who
prided herself on seeing things as they were, why did she think
that by crossing an ocean she could, as is said, start a new life?
Could evade, even with the automobile accident and the other
death, even with the divorce removing the four persons to whom
she had been committed — two by birth, one by love, the other
by a ceremony — why did she think her days would be different,
that she could survive, could deny all commitment?

Somehow they had found her. The voice on the end of the
wire, urgent, his breath she was sure carrying scent of garlic and
fish, asking what time it would be convenient, as though there
were no question of her receiving him and today. And even before she punched the buzzer, even before she opened the door
to let him in she knew what he would look like. Short with fat

legs, beard, black hat, insistent. But the one who telephoned her was not the one who came. She had to look up at him, at Abraham, tall and thin, gentle, stooped, with eyes sunk in his skull and suffering. Far from having breath redolent of fish, she wondered if he had any breath at all, and when, if ever, he had put food into his mouth. She felt she should call a doctor. But when he began to speak, she forgot the gauntness, the ludicrous wisps of hair hanging about his face, and by the time he left she knew in detail about the group, what it was trying to do and had done. She knew where he had spent his early years, understood why no matter how much he ate he would always bear the mark of malnutrition, and she knew, too, without having to take a few days to think about it, she knew she would do what Abraham had come to ask, that she take money and messages secretly to Leningrad and Moscow. And almost without thinking she said something to him in Yiddish, learned from a friend, not her parents, who never spoke a word of it in her presence, and when he answered she saw herself joining a long human chain, the beginnings of which were lost in the blackness of time. She was happy and angry.

Yes, she was early subjected to the idea of an operation, her mother at first alluding to it only obliquely and then more openly until by the time she was sixteen there seemed to be no way of avoiding what her parents had their hearts set on, a Jewish daughter who did not look Jewish, but she never felt the reconstructed nose part of her real self and for months afterward her sleep was filled with humiliating and terrifying dreams involving her body.

And her parents made it clear to her, too, almost from the day she entered school, that it would be ridiculous to go away to college when the best university in the country was at her doorstep.

And so she went to Radcliffe and returned each weekend to Brookline as she was expected to do, and related in detail what she had done the previous five days. She spent hours arguing with her father, who was already talking of graduate study, trying to convince him that she could get into the Law School without concentrating in government. He would not be convinced until one of the deans at her request telephoned to assure him that his daughter was correct, that the Law School welcomed, even recommended, that prospective candidates concentrate in the humanities.

In the first semester of her sophomore year, in a Russian literature course, she met and fell in love with Patrick, and she lived with him for a year and a half until he fled to Canada. The same year she took an art theory course designed for interested but nontalented persons and discovered that she had a gift for simple comic drawings, human figures in which she would exaggerate some part of the body. A leg might encircle a neck, a shoulder hump or twist out of all proportion, a nose spill onto the ground or wave like a banner over a head, a toenail emerge ten times larger than the toe itself. She decided with Patrick to concentrate in Slavic literature, and long before she had to declare her thesis topic she knew what it would be: a critical study of Gogol's short stories with her own illustrations.

Yes, she submitted to the operation. She went to Radcliffe, which she did not regret, and she suffered the Law School, which she did regret. At the Law School she felt stifled by details, bored by endless facts, and she never accepted the principle of the discipline, the power of the law at what often seemed to her the expense of justice. Nevertheless she graduated high in her class and she knew secretly that except for the misogyny of two of her professors she would have been even nearer the top. The operation, Harvard and Thatcher, the boy she married

while she was still in the Law School, the Trinity as she sometimes thought of them, humorously borrowed from the adopted
religion of her parents and by extension hers.

Perhaps she and Thatcher could have made it, had some kind
of workable life together but for his parents, who from the beginning were determined that their son's indiscretion would not
endure. They began their campaign under the guise of generosity with the Cambridge house, bought and furnished to the last
detail, even the prints in the powder room, all done without so
much as five minutes' consultation with their son or daughter-
in-law. And there was the advice, given often, the rationality of
getting to know one another, of having free and happy years before the demands of parenthood claimed them. But she knew
the real reason for the furnished house, for the advice on off-
spring. They assumed their son's wife was bound to lack taste.
But beyond that and worse, they lived in terror of having a grand-
child, witness to the union of bloods. Thatcher's parents praying
for the marriage to break up before there was issue; her own parents rejoicing that their daughter had reached what they thought
of as a promised land.

But less than three years after the marriage, when her mother
and father were killed in the automobile accident, her mother
outright, her father living only a few hours, she fled the house
she never considered her own, the house where she hardly dared
change so much as an ashtray, fled because she no longer had to
play the role of pleasing her parents. Yes, she left that house, but
before she packed her bags she asked Thatcher to go with her.
Even as she was suggesting it, even then she was sure he would
be unable to make the break. His only and last rebellion had
been marrying her. Even if by some act of God his parents,
brothers, the aunts, uncles, cousins and friends were all swept
from the face of the earth, he would still be incapable of imag-

ining life anywhere but in Boston or one of its suburbs. And so she fled alone. She fled to Paris, where she intended to live for a while until she knew what she wanted to do with her life, if anything. She found an apartment on the rue de l'Abbaye. She joined a mime class with no motive except her own amusement, and she began to brush up on her French with a tutor at Berlitz. And she started drawing again, the little figures with the comic exaggerations. Several times a week she walked to a different part of the city, settled in a café and watched the crowds. She felt she had lived a long time, even that she had been born old, especially when she thought of her parents. It was as though they were her dead children. She was no longer ashamed of their shame, understanding better their need to deny the past and why they had longed for her, too, to shed the ancient identity and embrace a new one in the adopted country to which they had fled and where they wished to believe that hatred had expired.

But her need to deny all allegiances was as strong as their need had been to exchange one for another. She had seen in a history class, as early as the seventh grade, films of Nazi atrocities and of the Allied destruction visited on Berlin, on Dresden, on Hamburg, on Hiroshima. Like her contemporaries, she had been nourished on television accounts of violence in her own country, in the world. She had been unable to avoid pictures of assassinations, executions, burning children, civilians thrown into ditches and sprayed with bullets, pictures of innocent people in Belfast and London, in Israel and Lebanon, innocent people in airports, on trains, here and there, blown up because someone was blindly and totally committed. It was commitment that brought suffering. It was commitment that could ruin life for those who wanted to live and wanted others to live too.

And yet now she was committed. They had somehow found

her and she was committed for eight days. Something in Abraham's eyes, something in the stoop of his shoulders spoke to her and she was unable to say no. The instructions with variations in case of trouble had been gone over and over, memorized, and sitting in Le Bourget waiting with all the other passengers in the French tour group, the airplane already several hours late, she kept hearing the cadence of Abraham's English: "Fail I know you will not. Fail I know you will not."

But during the first weeks in Paris, before Abraham had appeared at her door, when she was walking to the mime class or the French lesson, when she was sitting in a café or alone in the apartment, drawing the comic figures, while her legs and hands and eyes did one thing, her mind moved back and forth across her life. She thought about Thatcher, wondered if he had already found someone to marry when the divorce was final. She thought about her childhood, about the houses she had lived in around Boston. As her father's business prospered they had moved, always to a better neighborhood and finally to the last home, the large modern colonial in Brookline. And sometimes she remembered herself in the Law Library surrounded by books, gathering facts, building arguments, and she remembered particular law classes, certain triumphs, occasional humiliations.

But it was Patrick she thought about the most, that her mind fastened onto and would not let go of, Patrick with his cascading words, his conviction that he was Yeats and Joyce and Pushkin all rolled into one. He often stalked her dreams, but she had tried to keep his memory from invading her waking hours. But now in Paris, away from the Square, out of sight of Leverett Towers (they had lived in a corner room near the top), away from Mount Auburn Street and Mass. Avenue, where they had bumped along on his eccentric motorcycle, away from those particular bricks, from that particular river, from the dirty snow and the elm trees, the censorship she had imposed on herself almost four years before lifted and she dared think about her months with him. About the classes they took together, the Slavic lit courses, the intensive Russian. About the special day, a Friday, when it was almost dark, when they had spent all afternoon in bed together and for the first time, when they were finally dressed and looked beyond the lights of Central Square and Kendall to the faint brightness above Boston, when Patrick, laughing because he was nothing if not ironic, swore with exaggerated gestures that they were the lovers Ivanov was describing in his poem. They were the two tree trunks smashed together by lightning, burning forever in the night forest. And she promised to marry him, though she warned she would never allow their children to be brought up Catholic, to be brought up anything for that matter, for by then she had already committed herself to noncommitment.

And at the end of the semester she would have followed Patrick to Vancouver. For she believed it, allowed herself the banal image, felt they were one flame and burning so brightly that no other part of life was visible or mattered. It was there, with papers piled around him on the floor and no doubt flung across the narrow bed, that he began to edit the mimeographed poetry sheets, the poems of deserters and conscientious objectors like himself. Then drunk or high or careless, she never knew which, he fell from the fourth-story window of the small room he had rented with its view of the bay, the room she knew in detail because he had described it to her in letters. The news of his death sent her reeling back to her mother and father, not that they ever knew she had left them, and she clutched at the life they had planned for her.

For two days she lay on her dormitory bed weeping and, like a fish out of water, gasping for breath. Then gradually she accepted the fact that Patrick was dead, that he was as mute as the ground over which she walked to classes. But for weeks whenever she heard a motorcycle she would turn without thinking, expecting to see him, helmeted, his long body straddling the steel. A mighty wind, he had roared into her life and carried her to a far country and she was sure she would never again feel such power, never again take such a journey.

It was months before she wanted to go out, much longer before she took a lover, and then there were several, but her only connection with any of them was loneliness and physical need. At the Law School she met Thatcher. She was still lonely and he fell in love with her. They had the law in common and with his Anglo-Saxon background he fitted perfectly the kind of person her parents hoped she would marry. From the beginning it was obvious that Thatcher's mother and father would not be overjoyed at having her as a daughter-in-law and so she and Thatcher were married secretly one weekend in Maine. It was some months later, when they found out, that Thatcher's shocked parents bought and furnished the Cambridge house and removed their son and his bride from the two-room apartment in Somerville.

But in those early weeks in Paris she could not help imagining over and over again what married life with Patrick would have been like, often trying to make the fantasies as unhappy as possible. If it turned out he was neither Joyce nor Yeats nor Pushkin let alone all three wrapped into one, if he finally realized he was only a fifth-rate poet, maybe not a poet at all, he would have become difficult. He would have become bitter. There would have been quarrels, recriminations. Their love would have died in the blackness of an unmapped forest. And yet she knew, she knew that was not the way it would have been.

When the memories, the fantasies became too painful, if she were in a café she would leave and rush into the first cinema she came to, no matter what the film, or if it were at night she would walk rapidly for an hour or so among the crowds on the Boule Miche and then circle back through the narrow streets to her apartment, always walking as though she had some destination.

The night before she was to leave for Leningrad, she did not sleep well. She kept waking up, afraid she would not hear the alarm, afraid she might sleep through Abraham's call. But she was up long before eight, long before she picked up the phone and heard his voice. Already she felt she was talking from a distance, already, even standing in her apartment in the middle of Paris, she felt she had left France, had disappeared from Western Europe, vanished into the mythic bear's mouth, those jaws stretching from the Baltic to the Black Sea. And what if she failed? "Fail I know you will not," Abraham had said. "Fail I know you will not," he had repeated as he was leaving the night before, and looking up she had seen his sad eyes come toward her, felt his skeletal arms encircle her back, his lips against her cheek.

And he was proved right. She did not fail, and eight days later when she saw him waiting, standing beyond the barrier at Le Bourget, she wondered if her legs would hold up, if she could make those last steps without collapsing, without tears. Yes, she had managed to get through the eight days, but not without moments of terror, moments when she waited for the knock on her door, expected a hand on her shoulder, a whisper close to her ear, "We know who you are."

Before she had even landed in Russia, when she was still in the air, she thought she had been found out, expected to be arrested when she stepped from the plane in Leningrad. Because at Le Bourget, while she and the other passengers waited through the afternoon and into evening for the plane to take off, a man glanced at her each time he walked past. The last time he went by before they left, his face was flushed and his thick hair in disarray. Earlier he had sat down for a few minutes near her and spoken in Russian with an old man excited because he was returning to Leningrad for the first time in sixty years. Finally when the plane was announced for boarding, the man was the last to get on. Swaying slightly, he walked down the aisle shouting in French, "Enfin! Enfin! They're getting off their asses!" And as he strolled by, he glanced down and caught her eyes. There were little beads of saliva in the corners of his mouth.

Later, on her way to the toilet in the back of the plane when she passed his seat, he reached out and grabbed her hand and spoke in English almost without accent. "You're too young to be a lawyer." She pulled away, sure he would detect the change in her pulse. She told him the first thing that came to her mind, that she had had her face lifted, and looking into the mirror, with the toilet door safely locked, her heart still pounding, she knew that her answer had been partly true. When she returned to her seat, he followed her, stood leaning over, his eyes bloodshot, his mouth loose, and she decided that he was not pretending, that he had been drinking. Each time one of the expressionless and wide-hipped hostesses would squeeze by, he would turn his head around slowly and look them up and down, address them in Russian. "What are you up to now, beautiful? No more of your Soviet wine, thank you," and he would turn his thumb up and then down in disapproval. They seemed not to hear.

When he asked where her husband was, she felt the pressure in her throat increasing. Obviously he had seen her visa application; and sure now that nothing made any difference, that she was doomed, she dared ask how he knew she had a husband, and he shrugged his shoulders, closed his eyes for a moment. "All beautiful young girls like you have husbands." And when she told him she was getting a divorce, he made an effort to straighten up. He reached in the inside pocket of his jacket and pulled out a passport, French, and opened it to the picture of himself with a pretty blond woman and two little girls. His wife was German, he said, and he claimed she had thrown him out of the house only the week before. And so, sure that she had been apprehended, she plunged ahead, asked him where he had learned his Russian, and he looked toward the top of the plane as though the facility had come from the heavens. And she pushed even further, asking what he did. He closed his eyes again and opened them slowly. "Me? I have a good time." And then quite suddenly, quite deliberately, she felt, he bowed and returned to his seat.

Perhaps he would not be her betrayer after all. Perhaps he was working for the French government, sent to check on some of its citizens traveling to the Soviet Union. Perhaps he simply had information on all the people on the agency tour, whether they were French or not. But later that night, or early the next morning rather, when she was standing under the bright lights about to go through the final part of customs, she saw him, now seeming quite sober, step up to the far end of the barrier and hand a large black briefcase across to a man who hurriedly disappeared with it around a corner and who was obviously not an employee of the French consulate. He looked exactly like a young Khrushchev. But no one came to arrest her.

Then almost two hours later, when she was falling asleep in the hotel in Leningrad, she heard faint screams from far down the corridor and she was sure someone was being dragged away. She wanted to help but her body would not move and she knew they would come for her, knew she would be next and she lay there waiting and she thought of Patrick and Thatcher. She thought of her parents and Abraham and then she woke up and it was morning. At first she did not know where she was and when she remembered she could hardly believe she had not been arrested. And she could hardly believe either that Nevsky Prospect was only a block away, the street which Gogol caught so beautifully in a short story. His stage, the Nevsky Prospect of early nineteenth-century St. Petersburg: a servant tossing stale tea cakes to early morning beggars, peasants with lime-stained boots hurrying to work, tutors, lowly clerks, mustached dandies, officers, elegant ladies with waists as thin as the necks of bottles, important people, people full of propriety, all strolling up and down the Prospect. She dressed and went to breakfast. Someone mentioned the screaming. An old lady had locked herself in the bathroom and had been unable to open the door.

She saw the Frenchman one more time, at lunch the first day after she had already delivered the envelopes. He sat down in an empty place by her, and she wondered if he were about to whisper that he knew why she had come to Leningrad. At first he said nothing, and then when she passed the bottle of wine, he shook his head and remarked rather seriously that he never drank when he was in Russia, only when he was coming and on his way home. She thought it strange, his confiding this to her. He asked if she were enjoying the city and then if she were free that evening. He knew a pleasant spot where there were balalaikas and good dancing.

This was the plan, then, to whisk her away at night, avoiding the spectacle of an arrest in broad daylight. She told him, and it was the truth, that she had a ticket and was going with some of the people in the group to the ballet. There were lines she had not noticed around his eyes and mouth. He fell silent and she could think of nothing to say. He left without eating any dessert. Under other circumstances she might have enjoyed an evening with him. He did not seem like the kind of person who would play with other people's lives. Yes, she would have liked, in fact, to talk with him frankly. She might have asked him why he was doing it, but she never saw him again.

And then four days later, that morning in Moscow, when Olga, the handsome guide whose green eyes with their slight Tartar slant seemed, though perhaps in her paranoid state she only imagined it, to have within them depths of icy cruelty, when Olga looked straight at her, who had not raised her hand for the tour to Zagorsk, and said, *"Tant pis pour vans"* as though she, Olga, knew why she wasn't going with the group to visit the monastery, knew what she was going to do instead, what her plans were for that morning. And she was sure Olga, looking straight at her, could hear her heart, knew about the sudden pains in her legs and was getting pleasure from the fear evident in her eyes. But she had been mistaken about the guide, too.

The actual deliveries turned out to be the easiest part of the trip, perhaps because she thought they would be the hardest. Those few seconds when she was handing over the envelopes she was in the calm eye of the storm. It was the hour before, the hour after, that she felt the pains, that her heart beat faster. In Leningrad at the Hermitage, in front of the Rembrandt portrait with her thumb holding a place, dividing almost equally the pages of the *Guide Bleu*, she glanced at the people around the painting and one of them gave the sign, then the second sign, which told her he felt safe. And she wandered off and a few minutes later walked down the steps to the cloakroom, her pocketbook already open, to ask for the sweater she had deliberately left with her raincoat and he was close behind her and when the old woman, the guardian, all but toothless and smiling, turned her back, she handed the envelopes to him, and when the woman turned again to fetch his coat, he gave her the small package and she felt his eyes embrace her.

Locked in a cubicle in the ladies' room she slipped the small package into the secret compartment of her pocketbook, safe only from a cursory search, not from a thorough one, and she saw herself in an espionage film, felt herself walking the pages of a novel of intrigue, and she wondered if the woman in rubber boots, scrubbing the floor, who looked at her in a strange way, already knew, had already been alerted. Perhaps there was a closed-circuit television camera hidden in the cloakroom.

She slowly climbed the wide marble stairs. She climbed up and up, swirls of gold and mirrors and statues all around her, and long before she reached the floor where the Impressionists were she expected a hand on her wrist, a whisper in her ear, but no one touched her or spoke. In the first room there was an empty chair and she sat for a moment and then she moved to one of the windows and looked down at the huge Palace Square, across which she had walked less than half an hour before.

With her own heart still not slowed, she did not find it hard to imagine the terror of those people in 1917 standing in the same spot, looking down on the Square, hearing the shouts, the cries, seeing the raised fists and not so much as a paving stone exposed, all of them to the last one covered by thousands of restless feet.

The Square was almost empty now, a few automobiles, a few people. Some soldiers, probably on leave to visit the birthplace of the Revolution, were sitting at the base of the Archangel's monument, their legs stretched out, their caps pushed back on their heads. For a moment she forgot her fear, and looking down from the Winter Palace she saw herself, her arms wrapped around Patrick's waist, her left cheek resting against his back, she saw him, she saw herself, mounted on the motorcycle, roaring around the Square. They circled the Archangel's column, and that angel with the face of Alexander I looked down at them and smiled and flapped his wings in approval. They zigzagged back and forth through the arches, back and forth across the Square and Patrick, without his helmet, his long hair flying, was waving all the while to the several soldiers, greeting them, shouting revolutionary lines from Pushkin.

Three nights later in Moscow she woke from a dream, she woke up laughing in the dark. Patrick, but this time alone, had defied gravity, had swept the whole length of Red Square, along the Kremlin Wall, he and his crazy machine, weaving arabesques in Easter egg designs and leaving rippling tracks like Christmas ribbon candy. Suddenly he had taken to the air, had cut the motor and floated slowly, silently in and around the striped and colored domes of St. Basil.

She spent the rest of the morning looking at the Impressionists, and after lunch she went to Pushkin's house and seeing the bed on which the poet died she told herself that a duel was almost as ridiculous as falling from a fourth-story window. She knew that Patrick would have charmed the guide, a girl with a thin face and long graceful neck who talked almost without pausing, giving the minutest details of Pushkin's life. Yes, Patrick with his matching flood of Russian would have charmed the guide. In the library he would have managed somehow to step over the barrier. He would have sat at Pushkin's desk, even dared to take down and read a few sentences from one or two, maybe three of the hundreds of books on the shelves. Yes, he would have done that and gotten away with it.

When the tour was over she went the two blocks to Nevsky Prospect and returned to Pushkin's house with some flowers. She put them in the entrance hall with bouquets left there by other admirers, the hall where his death mask was enshrined. She left them, the flowers, in memory of two poets.

No, the actual handing over of the envelopes was not the hardest part of the eight days. It was the hours before, the hours after. In Moscow there was no need either to fall back on alternate plans. It was in the subway at the beginning of the noon rush hour that she made the delivery, this time to a young girl who limped slightly and who was wearing a faded dress a size too large. She would have liked to talk with her, would have liked at least to give her something, her watch or her corduroy jacket.

In Moscow she saved until last the visit to the apartment where Gogol had died. Standing in the room where he had struggled for days with death, she thought of the feeble, the great writer trying to fight the leeches fastened flopping around his nose and the irony of the dying man having to submit to the orders of a German doctor, a member of that race whose citizens he had mocked with such wit in his writings.

Outside the house in which Gogol's apartment had been, she sat down on one of the benches near his statue, its head leaning forward, the enormous nose presiding over an enigmatic smile. She took out her sketchbook, drew her own version of that spinner of grotesque fantasies, exaggerating the already high weeds which the Russian earth he had loved so much was supplying abundantly around the base of his statue. But he would have liked the weeds and wild grasses at his feet, would have preferred them, she knew, to clipped borders and domesticated flowers.

An old woman on the bench next to her was staring straight ahead, the rims of her eyes inflamed and crusty, the lined face wrapped in a soiled babushka. She hardly seemed to breathe. What images faded or fresh moved through her mind? Unlikely they had anything to do with her countryman whose statue was casting a shadow toward her shoes of thin leather. She who had survived a revolution, famine, wars, epidemics, purges, and sorrow, was hardly thinking of those characters created by Gogol, not the little clerk and his overcoat or Assessor Kovalyov looking for his nose, hardly Chichikov buying souls already dead. Did she come to the bench each day when it was not too cold or raining to escape the tiny apartment, her nagging daughter, an indifferent son-in-law, the two noisy grandchildren? Were there any tender memories left in her ancient brain? Did she who sat so still, did she hear only weeping, see only burning villages, the bodies hanging? Remember only hunger, the small portions of bread and potatoes, the occasional spoonful of cabbage? Did she any longer even remember what she was doing when the word finally reached her months late? Her husband and sons killed or starved. Taken away? Vanished?

She walked back to the hotel. Taxis and cars rushed by her down wide avenues. She walked among the people crowding the sidewalks, spilling up from the subways. She passed fat women with peasant faces and poorly dyed hair and she caught the eyes of girls not many years younger than herself, strolling arm in arm, coiffured with old-fashioned bows. She looked at the Russians hurrying home with their frayed pocketbooks and worn briefcases and bunches of flowers and she knew she could not hate them.

That night after dinner she wrote several postcards, one to Thatcher, and she packed. She packed the little wooden man beating the drum for his dancing bear, a present she had bought for Abraham. Presenting it she would tease him, say she had performed once but would not dance again. And she packed the small black lacquered box with the painting of St. Basil on its lid, a present she bought for herself, because she knew whenever she looked at it she would see something that was not there, Patrick and the motorcycle floating around the cathedral's fairy domes.

No, she did not fail and she made those last steps to the barrier at Le Bourget where Abraham was waiting and she made them without tears by blurting out that he had been right, that the Russkies had not looked into anyone's pocketbook, had not opened anyone's luggage.

Later that evening to celebrate her return, her brief sin of commitment as she called it, she and Abraham went out for a drink. They crossed the rue de l'Abbaye, walked slowly past the church, stopping for a moment to look up at its tower, silent above the traffic, the shifting waves of people, its simple beauty veiled in light against the black sky. They crossed to the Deux Magots, saw no free tables there or at the Flore. The September *rentrée* of Parisians was complete and the Swedes and Germans and Japanese and Americans were still hanging on for a few days longer before returning home. Abraham, stooped but tall, a thin scarecrow on stilts, looked and saw across the boulevard an empty table at Brasserie Lipp. When they reached the other side of St.-Germain, she slipped her arm from his, told him to go ahead, what to order for her. She needed to buy shampoo to wash the Russian dust, the scent of cabbage from her hair and she left him, disappeared through the crowd at the entrance, went down the steps into the store.

And Abraham, a few minutes later, seeing the waiter come toward him, was about to give the order when he heard the blast and then the screaming and saw the push of people. He rushed against the wall of panic, but he was stopped. His thin legs moved up and down as though he were treading water. He saw the jagged hole, the shattered glass and twisted metal, and he heard the sirens. Then he felt around him an emptiness. He had felt the same emptiness once before, when he was a small child and had been pulled from someone's arms. Since then, he had moved in a circle of silence he had never expected could or would be broken. But it had begun to be, and by her, she whom he had known for only a few weeks. But now she was gone. He knew it. And he was sure he knew, too, why the store had been bombed. And like Job he cried out in his heart to his God and to the God of his fathers: "When will it be over for me? When will it be over for us?"

Yes, he had been right about her. And he might be proven right about the reason for the bombing. The next day and the days following the radio and television newscasts would carry appeals by the Paris police, appeals to people who had been on the scene, persons who might have information to come forward. And speculation of the authorities on the motive of the violence? The store was owned by a rich businessman. A Jew.

Yes, Abraham was right. She was gone. She who did not believe in commitment, who had simply wanted to be a person, who had not wanted to be a part of anything, or if you prefer, part of everything, she was gone. Her face and watch, vanished; her corduroy jacket in shreds and her boots spattered with someone else's blood.

IV

La Humanidad

THE PALMS along the Malecón lean away from the sea. Their fronds move neither up nor down but hang horizontal and always pointing toward the Field of Cinders. The steady, unchanging wind which holds them there never touches us or the Bay. Not a hair on our heads is lifted, not a ripple appears on the water. At least that is what everyone in the Territory believes, everyone except José. Now José is dead. No one listened to him, his voice weak, his body undistinguished. But when I watched the eyes in his dull face burn I knew he saw beyond the Bay, beyond the Field of Cinders. He dared to speak of other possibilities, other ways. He taught me what to listen for, and he showed me things the villagers refused to see. And it was José who begged me to nourish the colt. By law our dead must be interred with ceremony. But I was not allowed to speak. I am not of age and I am female. José's grave remains unmarked.

Yes, it was he who spoke of the colt. It struggles in the flowerless meadow beyond the village border near the edge of the Forbidden Frontier. I go each day to observe its progress. Yes, near the end when I was fanning José's burns, when I was trying to make them less painful, it was then he revealed the place where blades of grass still grow and begged me to care for the colt.

Little changes in the village. The women wait beyond the

hill, always in sight of the shack. Only now José as well as Maria is gone. For a long time the men complained about Maria, wrinkled, whiskers embracing her chin. When she lost her last tooth, when it became embedded in the rotten and half-eaten ear of corn thrown by one of the villagers, they found their justification. She was forced across the road into the Field of Cinders. José tried to stop them. The men shoved him aside. But he was able to slip the stones into her ancient hand. He managed to do this before that giant of a man, his left arm withered, Hernández, flung him back toward the Plaza. Yes, they sent Maria away with only one thin and soiled blanket and a rusty pot for boiling water. Now she is invisible, a speck, sometimes moving, but almost imperceptibly, on the Horizon.

It was a rat. I too saw its tail in the rubble of the collapsed bridge. I even glimpsed one furry leg. The few villagers who bothered to come did not notice me, a child. They laughed at José. "Dreamer." They touched their heads. "Idiot." Only a stick, they said, trapped between concrete slabs and left there years before by the last tide.

Later it was the shadow sweeping across the ground bringing the cool freshness. José pulled my head back gently and I saw the bird, a gull, its huge wings spread. I watched as it climbed higher and higher and then descended in widening circles until its shadow had touched the whole Territory. When José called, the villagers dozing on the dilapidated benches around the Zócalo awoke. "Where?" they demanded. "There! There!" José pointed, following with his finger the flight of the bird. Angry, they yelled: "Fraud! Impostor!" and Hernández, his withered arm curled back on itself, leaned down and slapped José's cheek.

That morning before dawn, when José and I sat huddled together listening, and he did not awaken the others, I wondered if he had lost his courage. The donkey brayed until the first rim of the sun showed above the Bay. And one evening, the moon high above us and full, when José failed to arouse the villagers or alert the women or shake the fishermen from their hopeless dreams, I was sure he had become afraid, that he no longer dared. The sound was faint but unmistakable. The dog howled past midnight.

But when the waves came crashing, José, his voice grown even weaker now, lost no time in finding me. A child's voice does not carry far. And yet they all came running, even the fishermen who gave up hope long ago, who for years have spent their days and nights on the beach, slumped against decaying boats, their eyes closed. Sun and moonlight blind them. They visit the women only at dusk or before dawn or when the moon has waned. Not that the women are idle. In addition to the service there are the roots to boil, the frayed sacks to mend. But if by chance one of the fishermen is unfortunate, if desire makes demands when the sun is in midsky, then he is forced to squint through coarse fingers as he stumbles up the hill and can let his hands fall to his sides only when he is in the windowless shack with the female he has chosen. Yes, everyone came running. Even the women dared to defy the rules and rushed halfway down the hill. The waves kept coming and coming, crashing, and all over the Bay fish leaped, silver. Our feet were bathed in foam and the spray flying cooled our faces. Salty drops ran down our cheeks. But they denied it, the villagers, even the fishermen who wanted to believe. The women squatting halfway down the hill were silent, but the reflection in their eyes was skeptical. When someone spat and snarled, "Betrayer! Criminal!" Hernández, the only one I fear, for the others have not noticed me, my breasts still small, Hernández, the humiliating arm twitching, seized José and hurled him upward out of sight. When José finally fell back, his crumpled body sank into the stony earth. The villagers turned away, and the fishermen, squinting, stumbled to seek their silent boats. And the women fled to their places beyond the Hill.

Hernández, his withered arm flapping, dragged me to the Plaza. He forced me up the ruined steps of the roofless and sunken bandstand, its paint peeling, its carved railing gone. I could no longer hear the waves. If I left the circle of rotting timber I would be dispatched. If I continued to believe in José's lies, if I insisted on sharing his illusions, I would be sent beyond the Hill. I would be sent to take Maria's place before my time.

But at siesta when Hernández began to snore, his withered arm restless, I crept back to the beach. There was a thin line of blood across José's forehead. At the edge of the Bay I found an unbroken shell, left, I knew, by the waves. I dipped it into the mute water and when I had washed away the blood, I touched José's right hand and a finger moved. I leaned over his shrunken ear. "I saw the rat's tail," I whispered, "and I watched the gull curve its wings upward. I heard the donkey and I listened to the howling dog and I felt the spray on my face, the salt on my cheeks. I did!" José's lids quivered and between the narrow slits I saw the eyes burning.

Yes, each day at siesta when Hernández began to snore, I left the deserted bandstand. I moved backward down the treacherous steps, always careful to place my feet where I had first put them. Hernández still appears in the early morning, his useless arm subdued, and throws me a torn root. He never fails to bend his strong body. He inspects to be sure there are no fresh footprints. He acts on his own. The villagers know nothing of my confinement. They would not be interested. Nor do the fishermen know. They would not care. The women? They learned long ago to mind their own business.

Yes, each afternoon I went to measure José's strength. It was the time the siesta lasted all day, the yearly celebration the reason for which no one remembered, the special day when even the women were allowed to close their eyes, to ignore the tasteless roots, to forget the torn sacks. When the fishermen could dream and redream their tragic histories through long hours, and Hernández could deny his shameful arm, could thrust it from him under the straw. The hours when the ceaseless snores rolled back and forth across the sleeping villagers — it was then I found José gone. I knelt by the outline of his abused body left in the earth.

But he had not forgotten me. An arrow made of pebbles pointed westward toward the failed pyramid, and it was there, where twisted metal was piled on shards of rubber and melted glass, where broken nails and headless screws lay unwanted by tools bereft of sharpness, where the shell of ancient machine, its wheelless chassis ignored by time, leaned against the circle of orange dust. . . It was there I came upon José. His hands were raw, bleeding, his mouth toothless, and his body shrunk to half its lean size. But the machine was upright, cleansed of the crusted sand, the steering wheel faint but visible; the unoiled instruments glowing.

Yes, I found José there. I came upon him pouring in the dark liquid, and I saw the floating motes of orange dust. "They will ignite!" I cried. "You must wait," I begged. José shook his head. There was no time left for draining the tank, searching for impurities. But he was mistaken. It was not yet the moment for the bell in the forgotten tower to ring.

I watched José climb the swaying ladder with its rungs missing. I saw him sink into the hole where once a seat had been. I heard the creaky belt pulled from the dangling roller and I listened to the rusty key turn. The last hope, I thought. I did not know about the colt.

The explosion settled on what was left of the pyramid. But José would not let me come near him until the cloud of flame had drifted across the road to the Field of Cinders. I could not take a step until the cyclone of smoke had disappeared underground. No, I was not allowed to lift him from the wreckage until the ashes had ceased to murmur.

I laid José in the shadow of the undisturbed circle of dust. It was then, when I was fanning the burns, that he made with his charred finger the feeble signs in the air. It was then that I learned where the few blades of grass still grow and that he begged me to nourish the colt. And it was the moment, too, when the bell in the forgotten tower began to ring, its ancestral sound ending the fiesta of extended sleep.

Yes, Maria has been banished to the horizon and José laid in an unmarked grave and I am detained in this diseased and depraved bandstand. But I do not despair. Before the villagers remark, before some fisherman through squinting eyes notices my enlarging breasts, before the women whisper, "Soon she will be here, among us," I will have fled this round of sinking wood, and I will have left the flowerless meadow. For the colt gathers strength, too. It has turned on its side, its legs no longer point stiffly upward. The mane is beginning to grow thick and glossy, and each afternoon when I put a blade of grass in its mouth, the tongue becomes warmer.

No, it will not be long before we escape, before we cross the Forbidden Frontier.